THE GRACE OF GOD

by
William Staub

Coastal Winds Publishing House
Port Arthur TX 77640
publisher@coastalwindspublishinghouse.co

Coastal Winds Publishing House
3167 63rd Street
Port Arthur, Texas 77640

Copyright © 2022 by William Staub

All rights reserved. No part of this book shall be reproduced, stored in a retrieval system, or transmitted by any means, electronic, mechanical, photocopied, recorded, or otherwise, without explicit written permission by the publisher. No liability is assumed for any damaged resulting from the contents or use of information contained within.

For information contact: Coastal Winds Publishing House
Email: publisher@coastalwindspublishinghouse.co

ISBN: 978-0-578-88750-0

Library of Congress Control No. 2022908638

Publisher: Pamela Joy Licatino, Port Arthur, Texas

Author: William Staub
Editor: Pamela Joy Licatino
Cover design and layout: Pamela Joy Licatino
Printing/Distribution: Lightning Source /Ingram

DEDICATION

To All Military Personnel
fighting to defeat their nation's enemy
without losing their souls,
know this,

You can do it.

~Chapter One~

Army Sergeant First Class Orson Kincaid felt the insects taking their pound of flesh and he let them have their fill without flinching. After several years of working as a special operations sniper, he knew how to concentrate on the job without moving a muscle for hours before each kill. He ignored the uncomfortable but familiar feeling of their bites as he placed his rifle scope's crosshairs over his first victim of the night. *Victim* was not actually the most correct description of his targets. These two high-value targets—HVTs—had been the primary executioners of most Americans taken hostage in Syria over the past two years. That was why Kincaid and his team had taken this rescue mission: to end that reign of terror.

Hours after sundown, his sweat still soaked the warm sand beneath him. Another drop of perspiration made rivulets down his face. Sand fleas continued to claim their pound of flesh, but he didn't begrudge them their meal. A cool breeze brought the aroma of food cooking on a hearth. He watched as the women scurried around the village, cleaning up, after the evening meal.

Kincaid had more kills than most snipers in the Special Operations Command, in the past eighteen months. After four years, he finally started to enjoy his job—like the other operators. He felt a bit uneasy about killing on his first two missions four years ago, and his fellow operators had been merciless in their joking about it for weeks afterward. He had failed to see the humor in it and tried to overlook the jokes, telling himself it was the professional thing to do.

He reached into his pack and took the rifle's bipod from its sheath. Snapping it under the upper handguard of his Smith and Wesson M&P 10 .308 caliber rifle, he laid it in place, pointing it at the subject compound. As the sun dipped below the horizon, he slid the Leupold Mark 4 multi-mode scope onto the track. He then flipped on the power and switched it to night vision. Pulling out two magazines, he checked again to make sure they were both fully loaded, and slowly snapped the first one into the rifle's magazine well. As soon as his partner was ready, he would chamber the first round.

Kincaid heard his partner, Ted Pineda, brushing the sand away so his spotter's scope would sit on level ground. Pineda's job was to measure and relay the current readings for wind direction and speed, precise distance to target, humidity, and ambient temperature. Kincaid would adjust his settings to make the first shot count, based on those readings. They constantly debated which job was more important: sniper or spotter. Although they never agreed on the best answer, they did agree that it took both working together to hit the target.

Having such an experienced, competent spotter and a good friend on this mission was Kincaid's ideal assignment. They had worked together for the past eighteen months, had known each other for about twenty years, and they trusted each other.

The five hostages in the compound consisted of one news correspondent, two U.S. soldiers, and two civilian contractors. They had all been deployed to Syria for several months, and they had all become lax in their personal security practices around their FOBs—Forward Operating Bases. The enemy had abducted them at roadblocks or when the men were feeling the effects of too many drinks, after a grueling day of work behind battle lines.

The capturing rebels had appeared at the roadblock as if they had been watching for hours or even days. They had *abducted* their targets when they were least protected and least prepared to resist. The Syrian soldiers who manned the roadblocks stood back and allowed the rebels to do what they wanted. These rebels had threatened the families of the soldiers, should they interfere for any reason.

Kincaid and Pineda were one component of the rescue team in Syria to liberate the hostages and save them from public execution. The rebel leaders planned to transmit the executions via live feed over the internet. The rescue team's operations order called for Kincaid to open the assault by shooting one of the two executioners in the forehead. The other operators of the team, the door kickers, were to set off their explosive device to breach the mud wall directly behind the HVTs. Then they would rush in, kill as many terrorists—Tangos—as possible, take control of the hostages, and return on foot to their extraction helicopters.

Major Will Harris, the team commander, had informed them a source of theirs on the inside, had secreted several microphones around the compound so the team would hear what was happening while they moved into position. Their source also had taken video cameras, but he balked at placing them around the compound, claiming he was too nervous about getting caught. Human sources were like that. If the team paid him more money, it might have solved that problem. But, then again, it might have gotten them and all the hostages killed.

"This is our final rehearsal. Let's do it right, this time," said a booming voice, from the compound, in Arabic, into their earbuds.

Both Kincaid and Pineda jumped at the sudden noise in their ears, instantly returning to their scopes to see what action was taking place.

The Tango video director motioned for illumination, flood lights snapped on bathing the compound in bright lights. He then made another gesture as he called for the cameraman to start recording.

The entire team of operators had seen videos from past executions when the director had used that *final rehearsal* ruse to keep the hostages from panicking. It made for less mess and better video if the hostages were not aware of the moment when their actual demise had arrived.

Two men wearing all-black clothing and a black ski mask stepped to center stage. A handgun holster clung to the right hip of the tallest one. The shorter man had a knife sheath on his left hip, strapped on for a cross draw with the right hand. The taller man jerked the sack off the head of each infidel as he turned and swaggered behind them. Pulling a well-used, long-blade knife from the sheath at his hip, the shorter man scrutinized the blade with dramatic appreciation, for his viewers.

When the two executioners pulled the masks from their own faces, they looked straight into the camera. The shorter man had long, straight black hair that cascaded over his shoulders. On the right side of his head, a shock of white hair blazed in the sea of black. His face was clean-shaven, with high cheekbones that could have been Asian, Native American, or any number of ethnic groups from around the world. His sunken, dark eyes glared into the camera, making his work more personal. He was trying to please Allah and his nearly one million internet viewers.

The taller man had a full dark beard and medium-length black hair on his head. His glare gave him a brutal look as bad as they came.

"Now is the day when Allah will show his great power," the shorter executioner yelled in a garish voice. "Allah will exercise his judgment over the infidels of the Earth who refuse to bend their knees and witness *he* is the one and *only* great god of the universe."

Major Will Harris spoke into his radio, with his scraping voice. "Sierra Five. This is Sierra One. Take good photos of this yahoo, for HQ to identify him. Later."

Click...

The camera in the spotter scope took several photos from straight forward and both profiles as the man moved. "Roger, Sierra One," returned Pineda into his radio mike. Thirty seconds later, he added, "It's done."

"We, the servants of Allah, have pleaded with the infidels..." continued the executioner.

"Sierra One, this is Three. Okay if we mute this Tango, now?" inquired Rodriguez.

"Negative, Three. Wait until Five takes his first shot," said One.

"Roger," answered a deflated Three.

"So, he turned his back on them and cast them out of his presence," the executioner continued.

"Five, this is One. We're ready to breach the wall as soon as you take your first shot. Make it count."

Will Harris had assembled this team and trained these operators himself. He expected them to be professional, and he knew they each understood his standards and goals for this mission. In the case of Kincaid and Pineda, he had hoped to break their religious streak while training them. Faith in God was the one thing he considered to be a detriment on the battlefield—and Mormons were some of the worst when it came to having a loud conscience.

"Roger, One."

"These infidels before me will become an example to the world of what will happen to all who refuse to fall down before Allah and confess that *he* is the one God."

Without another word from his partner, the taller executioner grasped the knife with his right hand. He thrust his long blade upward, from its scabbard. Snatching a hunk of the first hostage's hair with his left hand, he pulled it backward. Holding the knife high above his head, he paused for effect. This gave Kincaid the opportunity he needed. The sounds of bloodlust echoed in his earbud.

Kincaid methodically placed his crosshairs on the taller executioner's chin, then slowly moved it up toward his forehead. The rancid bile began to rise up in his throat. He wanted this killer dead but looking him in the face for the kill shot was quickly becoming too difficult for him.

This kill was somehow different from his previous missions. Now, he suddenly realized he didn't want to do this job anymore. The emotional scars it was etching on his psyche were becoming much too long and too deep. He had fretted over this issue within himself for weeks. He finally decided he wanted out—out of the unit and out of the business. He didn't want to kill any more HVTs. He closed his eyes and quickly took the shot.

Pfft!

"Shot!"

"Shot! You put a hole under his left eye. Take shot two," Pineda reported the suppressed shot over the radio.

Kincaid quickly shifted fire to where the shorter executioner had stood moments earlier. He saw a look of shock on the dark figure as his partner dropped into the same dirt. Furtively glancing left and right, he shifted his weight indecisively, to run or fight. Kincaid quickly put three rounds at the moving figure, before all hell broke loose in the compound.

"Shot two. Dang, partner. You caught his hand. We gotta *get* this guy," Pineda reported.

Boom!

The ten-foot mud wall behind the shorter executioner instantly disintegrated with dust and debris, blasting everyone standing nearby, including the blindfolded and kneeling hostages who fell to their faces.

The American operators swarmed through the three-man wide hole in the wall and deployed in all directions throughout the modest compound. They shot out the stage lighting, then searched for and eliminated all visible Tangos, sighting through their night optical devices—NODs.

Kincaid reacquired and killed two more Tangos who tried to squirt out of the compound, in the darkness. Although he frantically searched, he could not locate the shorter executioner. Whenever he could shoot without looking at their faces, Kincaid had no problem with his assignment, but looking them in the eye made it more difficult to end them.

"Where's the shorter executioner?" Kincaid demanded with a definite note of urgency in his voice as the fog of uncertainty lifted from his mind.

"I can't see through the dust cloud. Give me a minute," Pineda returned.

"We don't *have* a minute," Kincaid insisted. He was sure he had hit what he had aimed for, but he now needed to kill the monster, while it was less personal. They had to find him in the next twenty seconds, or Kincaid would catch it for his unconfirmed kill.

Both men saw the black-clad figure crawling through the dust at the same time.

"There he is!"

Pfft!

"You wounded him. Shoot again!"

Pfft! Pfft!

"You missed! You shot off a couple of his fingers, but now he's gone!!"

The team's hugest operator raced toward the video camera. It was still broadcasting from its position on the ground, but the camera operator was face down in the dirt. The last scene the internet viewers around the world observed was the masked face of the American operator as he snatched the camera off its stand and sneered into the lens. The transmission blacked out as he ripped it from the tripod and jammed it in his pouch.

Still taking fire, the team commander spoke into his microphone. "All Sierra Elements, move out," he ordered. The operators grabbed and cut free the hands and feet of all five hostages. They quickly exited through the hole they had breached in the wall and raced to their rally point as the last of the dust glided to the ground. The extremist group compound was still and void of life. The Executioner had escaped them. Before long, the armed villagers from down the road would arrive to assist.

Kincaid and Pineda folded up their weapons, scopes, and equipment. They hustled to the rally point to meet up with their team. Clicking their radios through a two-man intercom, and keeping communication open along the way, they jogged to the helicopter landing zone.

After sprinting the first quarter mile, Kincaid stopped along the trail and brushed off some of the last hangers-on of the carnivorous bugs who were still chewing on him.

Pineda took up an advantageous security position during the unscheduled break. "What happened back there? You had your laser right on that second guy's forehead," Pineda demanded as they continued racing toward their LZ.

"I took his gun hand away from him." Kincaid boasted, referring to the Tango's fingers he had blown away. "That should be enough for now."

"You were supposed to *kill* him!!" Pineda stopped, turned around, and pushed one hand up against his partner's chest. He stared into his partner's eyes searching for an answer. "Wait. You *didn't* miss, did you?" It was more of an accusation than a question.

"Yeah, well, I hit exactly what I aimed for. And at five-hundred meters, that's good shooting." Kincaid stepped over several large rocks in the middle of the goat trail to pass around his partner.

"Orson, you've *got* to get over your issues. It's ancient history, partner. Talk it over with your father and let it go, so we can get back to work!"

Kincaid gritted his teeth, but he said nothing. His partner knew him too well. The problem had everything to do with the ongoing feud between his father and him. Kincaid had just recently begun to understand how much his history affected his work. Although he didn't want to admit it, that feud had played a large part in his decision to *leave* this job. Every time he put a human face in his crosshairs, he trembled and had nightmares for at least a week after each mission. He realized it would be the same thing tonight. But he wasn't sure what else he could do, professionally. He was also unsure how to break it to his partner of two years—and friend of almost twenty years.

"You know, it wouldn't hurt if you attended church with me," Pineda offered as they rounded a bend in a dry riverbed, two hundred meters from the rally point. "You could find forgiveness within yourself and peace with your father. Then you could get *on* with your life."

"Ted, we've been through this before. I'm *not* a religious guy. That's *your* game. You do well enough for the both of us."

"Yeah, about that, salvation isn't a team sport."

"We're a *good* team," Kincaid quipped, knowing that was not the answer Pineda wanted to hear.

"We're a *great* team. But you'd be able to forgive yourself and move on if you understood how atonement works. Then, you could ask for your father's forgiveness."

Kincaid, having heard enough, stopped, and spun, glaring his partner in the face. "Tell me, Ted, how *does* that work?" He hoped Pineda realized it was time to back down—that Kincaid was finished listening.

"I've told you more than a dozen times, Orson. You already *know* how it works. You just don't *want* to know."

"Forgiveness is what Jesus does," Kincaid jested, as he turned around to continue their trek to the helicopters. "I don't *have* to forgive myself. He can forgive me and make it all better, right?"

"Forget it. You're hopeless," Pineda exclaimed with a loving smirk. He reached forward and slapped Kincaid on the shoulder.

"Now Ted, Jesus wouldn't like it if you gave up on me, would he?" Kincaid mock-scolded his friend in a sing-songy voice. He played his part in this familiar game they always played whenever Pineda brought up the subject of the LDS Church. But it wasn't a game to Pineda. It was a matter of eternal destiny.

Ted shook his head in the darkness and reminded himself he had to *lead* his friend to the Gospel. He could not drag him kicking and screaming into the waters of baptism.

They arrived at the LZ, clicking the red-light signal on their flashlights, so the others would not shoot them. Two others had already arrived. The operators bringing in the hostages would be along soon. Kincaid and Pineda took up security positions and watched through their NODs for friend or foe.

The Blackhawk helicopter pilot started up his engines.

As soon as Kincaid settled himself into position, with his rifle aimed away from the chopper, he reflected on his shots, earlier tonight. As much as he had wanted to kill his Tango, he just couldn't do it.

He would never forget the arrogant sneer of the shorter executioner and the unique white stripe in his jet-black hair. Despite his issues with killing, Kincaid already craved another chance to end that egotistical killer, another day.

~Chapter Two~

"That's not what I said," Pineda laughed as they argued while cruising down Morganton Road. They were in Kincaid's old truck, driving into Fayetteville, North Carolina.

"But that's what I heard," Kincaid countered. "You said the Navy SEALS were better than the Army Spec Ops people, and I disagreed. If you take a SEAL away from the water, they're just like us, no better, no worse." Kincaid looked down at his gas gauge. It was gently nudging the empty post. Seeing a gas station up ahead, he took his foot off the accelerator and flicked on his blinker.

"What about their training? Do you think it's more difficult than the training we got at Camp McCall?"

"Definitely *not*. It's just more water oriented. But their snipers are no better than ours. Their door kickers are no better than ours. Ahh!" With his finger pointed into the air, "Our linguists are better than theirs. They don't focus as much attention on getting along with the indiges," Kincaid said, referring to the indigenous or local people of any country where they've fought. "They just go in and kill them."

"Okay, I'll give you that. Their job is to go in and kill, not to win the hearts and minds of the common people," Pineda replied.

"Yeah. If I thought the SEALs were better, I would have joined *them*," Kincaid said as he stopped in front of the pump and jumped out of his truck. He liked debating military topics with Pineda. It made life easier when he could predict and respond to his friend's arguments about joining the Church of Jesus Christ of Latter-day Saints. That was one argument Kincaid had no intention of ever losing.

"Do you want anything from inside?" Kincaid asked his partner as he jumped out of the truck and headed toward the cashier.

"No. I'm good."

Kincaid went inside the gas station and laid down a twenty-dollar bill on the counter. "Give me twenty on pump three."

Walking back to his truck, Kincaid saw Pineda waving his arm out the window, holding a smartphone. "Orson, it's Major Harris."

"What? I thought he got out of the military! What's he calling *me* for?"

"Answer it," Pineda said, throwing the smartphone out the window, to his partner.

"You take the pump," Kincaid said, lurching to catch the phone.

"Yeah, sure." Pineda jumped out of the truck and started pumping gas into the truck Kincaid had driven since high school. Pineda chuckled to himself, thinking about how he had clocked more time in the shotgun seat of *that* truck than any other vehicle. They had both used it driving in the Dragoon Mountains of Southeast Arizona, during high school outside their hometown of Saint David.

Kincaid tapped the green button and put the phone to his ear. "Sir? Aren't you a civilian, now?"

"That doesn't mean I've changed occupations. Just offices," the naturally gruff voice said. "You got your partner anywhere near you?"

"Yes, sir. He's here, now. Why?"

"I want to talk to the two of you about a career change. It's something you and Pineda might be interested in."

Pineda finished putting fuel into the truck's tank, returned the hose to the pump and walked over to hear what Kincaid was saying.

"Sir, that's very kind of you, but I don't think …"

"Don't give me an answer now. Just come to my new office and let me give you my pitch. Afterward, if you still aren't interested, then at least I can tell my boss I tried."

"Okay, sir," Kincaid said, shaking his head at his partner. "When and where?"

"How about now?"

"What does he want?" Pineda impatiently whispered.

Kincaid put up a finger to silence his partner. "Okay, give me the address," he said as he stuck his head into the truck and scrambled for the pencil he always kept on the dash. He wrote an address on a scrap of paper he found on the bench seat. "Yes, I know where that is. We'll be there in about twenty minutes." He tapped the red button on the phone and tossed it onto his seat. "Major Harris has a job offer for us."

"Really?" Cautious curiosity dripped from the single word. "Where at?"

They both shut their doors and put on their seat belts.

Kincaid started the engine and handed the piece of paper to Pineda. "He wants us to go to this address."

"Then let's go listen to the man," Pineda said with his mischievous half grin.

* * * * *

Kincaid pulled into the parking lot in front of a large, cinderblock building and looked for the address his former commander had given him. The unadorned building was two-hundred meters long, forty meters wide, and ten meters high. There was very little activity anywhere, although the signs over the few doors indicated several local businesses-maintained offices inside. Kincaid looked up and saw video cameras perched atop the structure at regular intervals.

"Pull around back," Pineda urged, searching for the right numbers while Kincaid drove at parking lot speed. "Maybe his door is back there."

Kincaid slowly drove around the building. The same kind of video cameras sat up on the top of the back side of the building. Four loading docks with roll-up doors gave them more hope of finding their objective. In between the doors, was a small staircase with the numbers from the paper in six-inch metal, screwed into the cinder block, above each door.

Kincaid shook his head. "I guess this is it," he said. He combat-parked the truck, with the tailgate against the building, and turned off the engine.

As soon as they slammed the truck doors closed, Major Harris, now *Mister* Harris, opened the single door to the building. "Welcome to my new home," Harris said spreading his arms to indicate the entire structure. His face suddenly changed, with a tighter smile and hollow eyes. Kincaid didn't know what to make of it.

Kincaid immediately noticed their former team commander was wearing civilian clothing. He didn't think Harris looked quite comfortable in the outfit, but he looked like he was trying hard to play the part of CEO.

Pineda looked up at the roof and saw two cameras had swiveled and were focusing on the door from different angles. "You saw us coming, didn't you?" he asked.

"Yes, I did. Come on inside." He held the door open for them, then closed and locked it from the inside. Leading them down a short hallway, he opened a heavy steel door and took them into his unadorned office.

Before going inside, Kincaid and Pineda both noticed the large and dark warehouse setting with bulky shadows lightly cast from covered pallets of equipment. Pallets of covered supplies, without any clear shape or definition, sat against one wall. Close by, they saw power tools and hand tools, construction materials, and sawdust—lots of sawdust—lying on the floor. But all was quiet and still, at the moment.

The modest office was gaunt and still under construction. It had one simple desk with a laptop computer on it and an expensive-looking office chair. The only other furniture was two steel folding chairs, placed in front of and facing the desk.

Harris sat in his plush chair and gestured for both young men to take those seats. "I guess I could start by catching up on old times and asking how you and your families are doing. But somehow, I don't think you'd do well with that approach. Am I right?"

Harris considered this his last chance to totally break their faith in an invisible god. He knew if he could get them to see the real world outside the protections of the military, they would see the horrors of the real world and begin to question their faith. That would be how he would start. If *he* didn't have faith in a god, neither should anyone else.

Kincaid and Pineda nodded. Kincaid hoped his partner and he were both of the same mind: Listen to the pitch, then go home without making any commitments.

Harris smiled. "Just like I wanted, I've started my own business. I contracted with the US Military to go into other countries with my teams, to ensure Americans and American interests are safe. I'm putting my first team together right now, and I want the both of you to join me."

He told them how the mission was righteous. The need was definite. The other former soldiers he had hired were truly skilled and experienced, but Harris determined to give both Kincaid and Pineda assignments that would revolt them. When they saw the kind of blood and carnage the cartel fighters were willing to generate on the battlefield, they would begin to question the reality of *any* god who would allow humans to do that against each other.

~Chapter Three~

Mr. Will Harris, US Army Retired, leaned forward at his desk. "I have already found my door kickers and knuckle draggers. I need two solo snipers for this first mission. Then, if you work out well, I'll get you another mission. That way, I can keep you working two weeks each month and you get two weeks of vacation every month. I can pay you three times what the Army gives you now, with a full benefits package and guaranteed raises after each successful mission. How's that sound?"

Kincaid looked at his partner with a question in his eye. *Ready to leave?*

Pineda smiled at Harris, refusing to look at Kincaid, for the moment. "How can you use *military* personnel in your missions?"

Harris shook his head. "I can't. All my guys are civilians—with spec ops experience. If you want out of the Army, I can make that happen. I know you two. You're tired of the red tape bureaucracy and waiting for nothing to happen. You enjoy your work, the travel, and the *mystique* of making things happen around the world. I was the same way when I was your age."

Pineda finally turned and looked at Kincaid. "No red tape?"

Kincaid wasn't sold on the idea, but now he was curious. "We still have a couple of years before our enlistments are up. How can you get around that?"

"Good question! If you leave the service now, you will have to pay part of your re-enlistment bonus back to the Army. If you come with me, I'll pay back the Army what you still owe them, and I'll give you an extra month's pay as an enlistment bonus. You can't beat that."

"I don't know…" Kincaid said. Harris sounded far too cocky for his liking. This wasn't the same man he had followed into combat on more missions than he could count. This man was somehow different—more like a sketchy salesman than a military commander.

"Come on, Orson," Pineda chided. "I won't do it without you, but this sounds like a good deal."

Kincaid looked down at his boots, taking time to think of an excuse. "When is our first mission?"

Harris leaned forward and focused his stare on Kincaid's face. "We have to leave in the next forty-eight hours, on a time-sensitive mission."

"It would take at least that many *days* to process out of the Army."

"Is that a *yes*? If I can get you out of the Army in the next twelve hours, you'll sign with me?"

Kincaid looked at Pineda, whose head was bobbing up and down. "Yeah. We'll join if you can *do* that," he said, calling his bluff.

Harris reached into his desk and pulled out two sheets of paper. He laid them on his desk in front of each of his former soldiers and new employees. "These are your DD 214 forms, plus proof of your service, training, and promotions. I even got you an additional sixty days in the service to cover that much time of administrative leave. That way, if anything bad happens on this first mission, you are *still* officially in the Army. But you are ADCON—administrative control—and OPCON—operational control—to *me* during the next sixty days."

Both young men picked up their forms and inspected them. They looked official enough. Kincaid silently grinned. "How did you get these?"

"I figured you were both the kind of warriors who would

enjoy this kind of assignment, so I coaxed the Army into helping me prep you for your ETS."

Pineda looked at Harris. "Sir, I guess *we're* your huckleberries," he said, quoting Doc Holiday, from the movie, *Tombstone*.

They spent the next two hours going over the pay and benefits package, insurance policies, and scribbling their signatures in all the right places.

Smiling, Harris pulled out two envelopes from the same desk drawer and handed them to Kincaid and Pineda. "Take these forms back to your unit. Don't tell them anything about your new jobs. They just need to know you are working for another unit, so they don't turn you in as AWOL." He man-hugged each man and welcomed them to the company. "Come back here at seventeen hundred hours with all your field gear—minus weapons. I'll provide all the hardware you'll need for each mission. I'll introduce you to the rest of the team and give everyone the operations order at that time. We'll start prepping for the mission right afterward, and get a few hours sleep before we're wheels up at zero-four-hundred hours."

*****

Harris watched his operators through the window in his office as they met, rekindled old alliances, made new associates, and discovered what each member brought to the team. He also needed to understand the skills and talents of all his people, and which sub-groups quickly bonded better, to make up the smaller partnerships within the entire team.

The files of all his people sat inside his locked desk drawer. He had read them all dozens of times and knew them well. Orson Kincaid had been in the Army almost ten years and had a lot of natural talent with weapons. But he could be stubborn. Pineda was more prone to be happy-go-lucky, which could irritate some of the more somber team members. Harris wondered if he might have to keep his sniper team under a tight rein. He planned to speak with them after the mission briefing.

Harris walked into the large warehouse bay and to the lectern at the front of the room. He stood up front and waited for them to find seats. It didn't take long since they were as eager to hear their mission briefing as Harris was to give it.

"Our mission is to rescue five American hostages—in Mexico."

A low buzz started among the operators. Harris had expected as much.

Harris studied his operators, again. They all had been good soldiers, well-trained and combat tested. Now, he needed to tap into their soldiering skills to do the same dedicated work as civilian contractors. He had hand-chosen each one of them for this particular mission and believed each of them would do their part in the operation to successfully bring the five hostages—a family of three and two reporters—home.

Harris searched for two godless snipers, but on short notice, Kincaid and Pineda were the best he could find. He hoped they wouldn't cause any problems because he expected this mission to get filthier than most military missions.

"Two days ago, at the Mexican resort town of Puerto Lobos, the Sinaloa Drug Cartel took as hostage a family of three American tourists, consisting of the husband, Michael Hampstead, his wife, Joy Hampstead, and their seven-year-old daughter, Melissa." A photo of the family appeared on the screen behind him. "Earlier today, the same cartel group officially claims responsibility for the kidnapping of this family. They said they will execute these *infidels* forty-five hours from… now," he said, checking his watch. "The two other hostages are freelance reporters who have contacts with the Washington Post and New York Times. They have been hostages for more than a month."

"Sir, that makes little sense," said one operator.

"Yeah, that's a Muslim threat, calling them *infidels*," said another.

"That's right," replied Harris, taking back the floor to continue his briefing. "Our intelligence sources indicate about three weeks ago, an unknown faction of Muslim extremists entered Mexico, with at least twenty fighters, intending to join forces with the Sinaloa Cartel. Another indicator that Muslim extremists are involved is that they have made *unreasonable* ransom demands." He read from his papers: 'Unless the United States closes the detention facility at Guantanamo and frees all the Muslim prisoners within the next forty-five hours, they will execute their hostages,' simply for *not* being Muslim."

"What has the Mexican government said about this?" asked another operator.

"Both the Sonoran State government and the Mexican federal government have called the bluff of the Sinaloa Cartel. They said they will *not* get involved diplomatically or militarily."

"That's a crock of..."

"However," Harris broke in, "without admitting it in public, the Mexican Federales have spoken with Washington on back channels. Both nations agreed they will secretly authorize a one-time only, limited use of US Military troops to free the American hostages in a covert-action rescue mission, as long as we play by *their* rules."

"What, do we have to take Mexican soldiers in with us?"

"Maybe they want us to use their choppers and their weapons."

"No, they don't want us to take in *any* close air support. Only the aircraft we fly in on that bring us back home with the hostages," Harris said. "They also won't authorize more than *ten* operators, plus the helicopter crews."

The room was silent.

Harris continued. "Our government is unwilling to commit US Military personnel, aircraft, or equipment to fight in a neighboring country at this time. That's why they have hired *us* to do the job. If *we* get caught in Mexico, we are civilians and will be arrested and jailed like any other Americans caught battling in *their* country."

"The Mexican government is in a bind. They recognize standing by while anyone who executes Americans in Mexico could lead to an American invasion if it continued. They also know their military is not prepared to intervene in such an incident involving the major drug cartel *and* a terrorist organization. No one wants word to get out we are American contractors being used in a combat role, within the Mexican borders. So, we will be wearing slicks—no markings on our uniforms. We have to get in, get the hostages and get out *without* getting caught on You-Tube, Facebook, or the evening news—in either country."

"Sir, what kind of resistance do you think we might come up against?" asked one team member.

"Good question," Harris confessed. "First, we can't assume the cartel or the Muslim extremists are an inferior fighting force with old weapons and minimal ammunition. The cartels always arm their men with the best. We know they have small arms, rifles, machine guns, *and* RPGs. There have been reports of at least one anti-aircraft and anti-tank weapon that might actually be some kind of modern chain gun. We will need to hit first, go in fast, hit hardest, and get out with the hostages. Now, listen up to my operations order."

For the next two hours, Harris briefed his team on every aspect of the raid necessary from air insertion to air extraction. He divided the team into two sub-teams and stated he would lead the first group, the first assault team. Kincaid and Pineda were the only ones who would not assault the hacienda where the hostages were located. They would provide surgical supporting fire with their sniper rifles, from two separate locations, as two individual snipers. Harris knew that was not the usual way to position a s niper team, but he considered it the best tactical deployment in this situation.

~Chapter Four~

At 1835 hours, Will Harris finished answering all their questions. He then dismissed his team to take care of their personal business, with instructions to return no later than 0200 hours, local.

"Kincaid! Pineda!" Harris called over his shoulder as he walked toward his Spartan office.

Kincaid grabbed his partner and they both double-timed the few steps to catch up with their team commander. "Yes, sir?"

They stepped aside to let Harris into his office first and then shut the door behind them. Harris sat in his chair at the desk and said, "Take a seat," gesturing his subordinates to the only other chairs in the office.

This was peculiar, and Kincaid's internal warning lights flashed, trying to remember what he could have said or done wrong and what Harris might have in store for them, next.

Harris had never engaged in small talk; he got right to business. "We believe this guy holding the hostages is the same one we were after a month ago, in Syria."

"Wait. What?" Kincaid's attention snapped one-hundred percent on his new boss.

"Remember we couldn't account for his body without taking too long on the X?"

"Yeah, all that dust was in the air from the wall breach explosion," recalled Pineda.

"Well, we picked him up on satellite photos, entering Mexico last week. We think he's tied into this cartel activity near Imuris."

"Outstanding! Are we gonna get another crack at the Executioner? Who is he, really? What's his name?" the subordinates asked, moving to the edge of their seats.

Harris nodded his head. "He calls himself Mohammad, and yes, you will. This time, you don't have a spotter. Remember, both of you will operate independent of each other, but in coordination with each other."

"Mohammad, huh? Sir, as long as we get him, that's all we could ask."

"This time, you need to take him out," Harris said.

"Sir?" Kincaid asked, his mouth suddenly dry, his voice raspy.

Pineda squirmed in his seat but said nothing.

"I know what happened in Syria. I know what you did. I don't know what your problem is, but you can't let it affect this mission. Am I understood?"

"Yes, sir," Kincaid said. What else could he say? Kincaid knew he couldn't afford to let Harris down, again.

Harris surveyed his own hands, clasped together on his desk. "I understand you two boys are both Mormons?" It was a question asking for confirmation.

"No, sir," Pineda said. "Kincaid isn't Mormon. He just grew up in a town where most people were LDS. So, he doesn't mind hanging around Mormons."

"Isn't Orson a Mormon name?" Harris asked.

"Yes, sir," Kincaid confirmed. "My parents didn't want me to have the same problem they had, growing up in a small Mormon town in southeast Arizona, so they gave me and my brother and sister names that came from Mormon Pioneer days, … so we would fit in better."

Harris considered this new information. "Are you boys both from Saint David, Arizona?"

"Yes, sir. How did you know?"

"I went to some training at Fort Huachuca and drove through

Saint David several times on the way to Benson. It's just a wide spot in the road, isn't it? Do the people still go to that old chapel on Highway 80?"

Pineda found his voice. "No, sir. That old building was torn down. One of the church members donated some land for a new chapel, just half a mile from the old building."

"Tore it down, huh? I bet they got some grief from some of the old people living there."

Pineda laughed. "Yes, sir. They did. But the new chapel is very nice."

Harris looked at his hands again, then sighed. "Do either of you boys have any issues with this mission?"

Kincaid and Pineda looked at each other for some clue, then shook their heads. "No, sir. Why?" Kincaid finally said.

"I don't claim to know much about you Mormons, but I thought this kind of assignment might give you a problem."

"Problem, sir?"

"I mean, this is not a military organization. You were hired to rescue innocent hostages, but you will have to kill people in the process. Does your church have anything to say about mercenary work?"

"Mercenaries? We're mercs?" Kincaid nearly shouted.

"Yes, but for your own country."

Pineda furrowed his eyebrows and withdrew into himself to ponder the question. "Sir, I don't know how to answer your question. I've been a Mormon all my life and I have no idea where they would stand on this situation."

"I have no concerns with it," answered Kincaid.

"I'll look into it, sir. But I'm not worried about it, either," Pineda said.

"Good. You have your orders and that bit of extra information. Now, I have your word you'll do your job. Right?"

Kincaid and Pineda both nodded their heads.

"Then you're dismissed."

As they walked out to the truck, Kincaid turned to Pineda and said, "Does the Church have any problems with mercenary work?"

Pineda slowly shook his head. "I don't think so, but I'm not sure." Then he perked up. "Let's go somewhere fancy for dinner."

Kincaid smirked. "What do you have in mind?"

"I don't know. Sizzler? Or Golden Corral? Let's make it the works!"

*****

The tourist trade in Mexico made a lucrative business in flying small helicopters around the coastal and tourist regions. Most small groups either wanted to see the coast and its beaches, or they wanted to see the ancient Toltec Ruins north of Mexico City or the Mayan temples in the thick jungles of the Yucatan. By tradition, those helicopters flew solo, at one-thousand feet above the ground level and never at night. That was what made this small armada of helicopters different and remarkable.

The 2/13th Aviation Regiment at Fort Huachuca, Arizona managed and operated four hangars and three runways at nearby Libby Army Airfield. When informed of the need for extra space, they had no problem giving it to the venerable 160th Special Operations Aviation, the Nightstalker Regiment. Their mission required space for four small helicopters, for one week, and two Blackhawks. Everyone in the 2/13th knew not to speak to any of the visiting personnel unless they spoke first, and to stay far away from their six aircrafts.

After dark, and well after normal duty hours for the resident workers, four unmarked SUVs pulled up to Hangar Number Two and unloaded ten personnel, their weapons, and gear. These men were dressed all in black with no designating patches, tapes, or tabs on their uniforms. They put their gear down beside the birds, then went into the hangar's office, without a sound.

Shortly afterward, their two Blackhawks flew into Libby Army Airfield and parked in the back of the secure hangar. Then, two AC-130 aircraft flew in and taxied to the same hangar. The crew chief on each bird lowered its rear ramp and off-loaded two Little Birds, with their rotors folded up. Their personnel wheeled them into the hangar and parked them. The hangar doors started closing before the fourth and final Little Bird was fully inside the hangar.

*****

Four unmarked Little Bird helicopters entered Mexican airspace from the north, under an order of radio silence. They flew south-southwest for twenty minutes at an elevation of 100 meters AGL—above ground level. They then dispersed on their individual trajectories according to their flight plans and operations orders.

Harris' team had departed from Libby Army Airfield and was in the air, en route to their target in Mexico. Ted Pineda leaned toward Kincaid and yelled in his ear, over the noise of the overhead rotors. "Do you remember when we first became friends?"

Kincaid looked at him in astonishment, wondering why he would approach this topic now. He shook his head, not able to remember when they had met. They had always been friends, in Kincaid's mind.

"It was in fourth grade. We were both ten years old. My parents had sent me to the post office on my bike to mail bills for them. Another heathen kid saw me coming and tried to stop me from putting anything in the outgoing mailbox."

"Hey, I was one of those heathen kids," Kincaid cried back.

"Yeah, but you weren't this kid. He had been the butt of jokes from the Mormon kids for a long time and he was tired of it."

Kincaid nodded his head. "Yeah, I remember the kid. Chubby. Bad teeth."

Pineda laughed. "That's him. Anyway, he grabbed the envelopes from my hand and was ready to tear them up when you came around the corner of the post office. The kid didn't see you until you were almost on top of him. When he finally saw you, he panicked and dropped my envelopes to the ground."

Kincaid gave his partner a confused look and shook his head. "Sorry, Ted. I don't remember. It sounds like a small incident, anyway."

"No, it wasn't. I was on the bad side of my parents at the time. This was their test to see if I would follow their instructions." He paused and watched the passing terrain below their feet. He recognized Mesquite trees, patches of Prickly Pear Cactus, and a lot of arid Sonoran Desert dirt. Then he looked back at Kincaid. "After that, I knew I could count on you. And you've never let me down." He put a fist up near Kincaid's shoulder.

Kincaid bumped his friend's fist. "True to the end," he said.

"To the end and beyond," Pineda expanded.

In the dark of night, under a monsoon-cloudy sky, the four Little Birds flared for a landing and dropped off their five operators three kilometers away from their target. The four Little Birds then returned to Libby Airfield. Their job was complete for the night. They would pass the two Blackhawk helicopters at the border that would bring the team and the freed hostages home, after the operation. The Blackhawks would wait for them at the assigned LZ.

As hesitant as the operators were to act on the word of one HUMINT source, they had also received backup intelligence from satellite videos and thermal images, giving them confirmation that five prisoners, one smaller than the other four, were being held. With that supporting intelligence, the team had locked their plans in place, knowing the lives of the hostages were suddenly on a time clock.

Each operator carried one liter of water and no food. The door kickers carried at least four hundred rounds of ammunition. Pineda and Kincaid carried two-hundred rounds of their 7.62 mm rounds, along with their Smith and Wesson AR-10 sniper rifles. Their rounds were heavier and could knock down a target at three hundred meters.

Ted Pineda and Orson Kincaid were the closest to their sites when they hit the ground from their Little Bird. After the bird took off again, they flipped down their NODs and took off running over the uneven terrain and through the dark. After racing the first two-hundred meters on the opposite side of the ridgeline from the hacienda, they dashed uphill toward the crest. Before reaching the peak, they stopped, took up a low crawl, and peered cautiously over the top, at the hacienda compound.

A short line of rocks protruded from the ridge at the military crest, about twenty meters north of their current position. "I'll take this spot," Kincaid whispered to his partner, pointing to those rocks.

Pineda canvased the ridgeline more to the south. "I'll take that one, about twenty meters south and lower on the ridge."

Kincaid didn't like it. but could not see a better position. "Your position's a little close to the hacienda. Make sure you don't let them see your flash," Kincaid admonished his partner, referring to the flash from the muzzle of his rifle when it shot.

"Roger that," Pineda admitted, in a cheery whisper.

With that, they each low-crawled over the top of the ridge and downhill to their chosen positions.

"Easy, peasy," Pineda said to himself.

~Chapter Five~

"Sierra team, this is Sierra Lead. Status," Harris whispered into his radio.

"Sierra One, all elements in position. The hacienda looks empty from this angle," reported the warrant officer in charge of Assault Team One.

"Sierra Two will be in position in thirty secs," estimated the lead for Assault Team Two.

"Sierra Three Alpha in position. No visual activity from this angle," Kincaid reported.

"Sierra Three Bravo setting up. Will be ready in two mikes—two minutes," said Ted Pineda.

"All Sierra elements keep your eyes on the target. Wait for my command," Harris said.

"Sierra Two elements are now in position."

"Both Sierra Three units, ready. Negative report." No changes.

"Roger, out," Harris said, after hearing his entire team was in position and ready.

Suddenly, several people came out of the buildings.

"I've got movement inside the compound," Kincaid called over the radio.

"I've got nothing yet," Harris replied. "No, wait. Now, I see them. They're moving to the center of the courtyard."

"Roger," Kincaid replied.

A guard marched the five hostages into position. Drivers

of a few trucks and various other vehicles started their engines. Other people lingered around the hacienda, walking like in a dream. *Something was not right*, Kincaid thought.

Kincaid worried about the seemingly sudden choreographed activities in the hacienda. He watched through his scope, hoping to catch site of Mohammad. Suddenly, he observed a familiar figure moving in and out of his view, almost as if he was aware Kincaid was waiting. But the sniper couldn't see him long enough to positively identify him. After a brief pause, he recognized the same executioner he had wounded in Syria. The man stepped behind a line where five kneeling hostages had been placed. He stopped, looked up, right into Kincaid's scope—and smiled, without a speck of humor on his face.

He knows we're here, Kincaid realized.

Without the normal fanfare, Mohammad brought his knife from behind his back and dragged it across the throat of the first hostage—the younger of the two male correspondents. Kincaid shifted left to get a clear shot, but could not keep his target in sight, due to the slow movement of vehicles and people in and around the area. This would have been a lot easier with his spotter. Kincaid decided Pineda must be experiencing similar problems from his angle.

"Sierra One, go."

Boom!

A wall breach announced the beginning of the assault. The familiar sound of suppressed M4 assault rifles firing in controlled bursts pierced the night air and lit the area, as they rushed inside. The attacking operators yelled into their radios, giving warnings, and shouting orders. Kincaid knew the entire situation felt wrong. He might have lost the Executioner, again. He gnashed his teeth at the thought. Because of parked vehicles blocking his view and the smoke and flying dust, he couldn't see anything around the hacienda buildings.

Kincaid could taste the bile rising in his throat. "Not again," he fiercely growled to himself. "Not *this* time." With sudden rage, he searched through his scope for Mohammad inside the courtyard. He *had* to find and kill that man.

A vehicle sped out of the way, and Mohammad stepped into the crosshairs of Kincaid's rifle scope. Despite the nausea, Kincaid pulled the trigger.

Mohammad unexpectedly side-stepped to grab his next hostage. The 7.62mm round tore through his shoulder, spinning him backward and to the ground. He scrambled away where Kincaid could not see him. The sniper saw a single boot, from behind a pickup truck. He shot again, then watched as the dirt near Mohammad's foot kicked into the air. He'd missed the chance to kill this maniac, *again*! This time, it was not because he didn't try. But the thought didn't make Kincaid feel any better. He felt the need to kill this guy. His anger at having missed filled his breast and rose to his face.

While Kincaid searched his scope for another target, he noticed Pineda was firing more rounds than normal. His field of fire must be full of targets. "Ted, take your time. Don't let them zero in on your muzzle flash," he warned his partner over the radio. They were only forty meters away from each other and four-hundred meters from the nearest part of the hacienda. But he knew how the enemy could watch for his shot, see the spit of fire, and return effective suppressing fire at him.

"Roger that. Have you seen the number of Tangos down there? Our guys are severely outnumbered and outgunned. We *have* to help them, somehow."

"Sierra Three, take a break. Pick your shots and keep them on target when you fire," ordered Harris.

Both Kincaid and Pineda confirmed their orders and kept watching for high-threat targets.

In a flash of insight, Kincaid realized the problem. There were no lights, no camera to send the performance over the internet.

"Sierra Lead, this is Sierra Three-Alpha. It's a set-up," Kincaid cried into his microphone. "There're no lights or camera. This guy glories in the Hollywood nature of his work."

"Three-Alpha, it's too late, now. Let's get the job done and get out of here."

"Roger, Sierra Lead," Kincaid answered, as he returned to shooting as many enemy fighters as possible.

Four seconds after Pineda fired his next round, there was the larger flash of an RPG—rocket-propelled grenade—coming right at him. It was capable of taking out a tank or knocking a hole in a building.

Kincaid watched his partner grab his gear and scramble out of his makeshift nest. But the grenade hit before he could get to safety. The explosion struck low, but hurled shrapnel and pieces of rock right at Pineda, launching his body at least twenty feet downhill before he fell, limp, on the jagged rocks of the ridge.

"Ted!" Kincaid screamed. He grabbed his gear and raced the forty meters downhill using his NODs toward his partner in mere seconds.

When he reached Pineda, Kincaid knelt and assessed the damage. Despite his body armor, several pieces of metal shrapnel had pinwheeled into Ted's lower gut. Who knew how many pieces of rock had struck him even before he slammed down on the rocky mountainside? Kincaid sat down and put his hand under his partner's head, feeling for a broken neck. Slowly, he lifted Ted's upper torso onto his own legs.

The assault continued at full force. Both sides used their ammunition with total abandon, struggling to totally eliminate the enemy. The Sierra team radio traffic was feverish and near-constant, one transmission walking over the next.

Pineda opened his eyes. "Whew! That was close. I guess you were right," he said to his partner with his trademark boyish grin.

"Don't worry about it," Kincaid responded. "Can you feel

your legs?"

Pineda's eyes closed. "Yeah, but they're like a bulldozer rolled over them."

The sounds of gunfire in and around the hacienda tapered to short bursts. First one side and then the other.

Suddenly, it got quiet.

"This is Sierra Lead. We have three of the hostages and the others are dead. All Sierra elements get to the LZ, now," Harris called over the radio.

All members of the Sierra team reported in and rogered their understanding.

"That means they're all still alive," Kincaid said to himself. Then he looked down at his partner. "Think you can walk?"

"Let's try. We gotta get to the LZ, to go home," said Pineda through gritted teeth. Kincaid recognized that tone of voice. Whenever his friend was hurt, he refused to admit it to anyone else.

"Let's take it slow. We have almost a mile to run until we get to the Blackhawks," Kincaid said, lifting his partner's broken body. He grabbed his rifle in one hand and put his other arm around his partner's back. Pineda did the same so he could return fire with his own rifle if they ran into any hostiles along the way. Kincaid clambered downhill watching for anyone, holding his partner on his feet, and keeping his weapon ready—just in case.

Gradually, the rugged downhill scramble turned into a rocky animal path which changed to a sandy wash at the bottom. Kincaid felt his partner's strength ebbing as they continued their movement.

"Hey, was that your sandwich I took from the fridge before we left?" Kincaid asked in a low tone.

"What? That was you?"

"Yeah, but I'll get you another one when we get back. What kind do you want?"

"What are you tryin' to do?"

Kincaid knew he had to keep his partner's mind off his wounds. "What kind?" he insisted.

"It was a *tuna* sandwich, wasn't it?"

"Yeah. It was *good*, too."

"Then you *better* get me another tuna sandwich as soon as we get back."

Kincaid suddenly sensed a change in the tempo of the gunshots on the target. They had picked up again, and they were on the move—getting closer to the Blackhawks. The remaining elements from the hacienda were following the team through the desert brush, trying to kill all of them as a lesson to the United States.

"We're almost there, Ted. Think you can make it a few more steps?"

"I'm trying," Pineda answered, as he winced.

Kincaid shook his head. He knew they were both fighting a losing battle. Neither of them wanted to give up while the other was still alive. Kincaid pulled up under an exposed tree root at one side of the wash. He reached into his partner's pocket and pulled out the single shot of morphine each of them carried and pumped it into Pineda's thigh. He knew his friend didn't like using the narcotic, but it might be his only chance at survival, this time.

"Whoa! What was that?" Pineda jumped, feeling the unfamiliar effects of the morphine.

"That was the morphine you've been so stubborn about never taking," Kincaid answered. "C'mon, let's go." He lifted Pineda back to his feet. Then he felt and saw a large puddle of blood coming from his partner's lower back. "We gotta go, now!" Kincaid felt a lump growing in his throat, and it wasn't bile.

"Let's do it. I'm strong enough. I'm okay," the drugged Pineda declared, with boldness. As he tried to stand, he dropped his rifle.

Kincaid was near panic. Ted needed immediate medical

help. He had to carry his friend and partner to the Blackhawks. After about twenty meters in the loose, deep sand of the dry wash, he stumbled and fell. Ted Pineda fell on top of him. How would he ever get him back to the helicopter in time for medical help? Kincaid anguished to himself.

"Hey, get off me," said a confused Pineda in a slurred voice from atop Kincaid.

Kincaid rolled his friend over and propped up his head to make sure he could still breathe.

"Don't leave me," Pineda whispered.

"I won't go anywhere without you, amigo," Kincaid assured him, forcing back his own tears. "I promise."

"Don't worry," Pineda whispered.

Kincaid could see the blood—all the blood, coming out. "What do you mean?" Kincaid said, choking on the question. *Couldn't his friend see all the blood coming out of his body?*

"It's all good," Pineda said, in a dream-like state. "I'll wait for you on the other side."

"What? We've *gotta* get you to that helicopter." Kincaid decided Pineda was hallucinating and didn't realize what he was saying.

"No, really. You'll find peace in this life and I'll wait for you."

"Yeah... you will." Kincaid smiled, suddenly knowing it was useless. He could almost see the life force leaving his friend's body as a cloud swept a shadow between them and the full moon.

Pineda reached up and patted his friend's cheek, smearing blood on him. His smile faded, his eyes glazed over and his hand dropped limp to his side.

Kincaid was stunned. Speechless. He wanted to scream. He wanted to run back to the hacienda and kill all the cartel people and terrorists he could find; he wanted to rant and rave at an unfeeling God who would take from him his only real friend.

Ultimately, he wanted the chance to mourn. But he knew he

had no time for any of that. He gritted his teeth and set his face like stone. Reaching down, he picked up his friend and carried him over his shoulder. In less than two minutes, his legs had no strength to allow him to carry his partner any farther.

Kincaid saw the two Blackhawks up ahead, sitting on the sand with their rotors running as if they would take off at the first order to do so. Several of the operators hobbled toward the birds, helping each other climb aboard as others returned fire to an approaching enemy that seemed relentless in their pursuit. Kincaid had no more strength to carry his friend. He determined to remain behind with Pineda if he couldn't get him onboard their ride back home. Hearing shots fired two hundred meters away, he knew they were getting closer. He saw puffs of desert sand erupt around him, as enemy bullets errantly slammed into the loose powdery sand before he realized they were shooting at him.

He stumbled to his feet in the deep sand of the dry wash, dropped Pineda, and took another moment to catch his breath. While bending down to get his wounded partner, one more time, several more shots rang out. The bullets again splashed in the surrounding sand. One round slammed into Kincaid's back, below the right side of his ribcage. He spun with the force of the lead, raised his rifle behind him, and landed on top of Pineda's dead body. Firing continuous three-round bursts from the hip at the unseen enemy, Kincaid hoped to give his team members time to get aboard the Blackhawks.

Harris saw Kincaid's plight in the dry wash. He instantly slapped the chest of the man beside him to get his attention. When the man turned, Harris pointed at Kincaid and Pineda. The man instantly nodded, slammed a full magazine of rounds into his rifle, and sprinted down the dry wash toward the pair of operators. He shot bursts of rounds at the cartel men he saw approaching their position.

When Kincaid saw the man racing toward them, he rolled

off Pineda. His teammate knelt and hoisted Pineda's limp body onto one shoulder.

"Can you walk? Are you wounded?" He shot the questions at Kincaid.

"I can make it, if you'll take him," he said, feeling numb as he scrambled to his feet.

"I've got him. Don't worry," the teammate said. He picked up Pineda's rifle in his free hand and returned fire as they all sprinted down the dry wash. Both men raced toward the Blackhawks as shots rang out from behind them. Bursts of sand kicked up and ricocheted off nearby rocks all around him.

They kept running. Twice, the operator spun around and returned fire at the hostiles pursuing them. He stopped beside the nearest chopper and dropped Pineda's body onto the skid to get a better grip. "Is everyone accounted for?" he yelled to his second-in-command.

Kincaid roared at his warrant officer. "Get him on the bird. I'll hold them off. They've got RPGs. We can't let them use 'em against us in the air."

The Blackhawk's crew chief jumped onto the ground and took hold of the dead body.

Kincaid turned Pineda's body over to the crew chief with terse gestures. Harris didn't like the idea of Kincaid remaining behind, but the RPGs had to be stopped before they locked onto either of the birds, or they were all dead.

Automatic rifle bursts rang out from multiple weapons, all aiming at the helicopters. Harris' team returned fire, blanketing the foliage at the edge of the wash with hot lead. The door gunner swung the .50 caliber door gun at the source of the enemy fire and held down the trigger. The constant stream of .50 caliber rounds cut down the foliage on the edge of the wash and killed four cartel men trying to hide behind it.

"I'll stay behind so the birds can get to safety," Kincaid yelled.

Harris focused his gaze on the young man. *Only a Christian would do such a lunatic thing*, he thought to himself. He gave him a thumbs-up signal, then grabbed the handheld radio from his kit and hurled it at Kincaid. He gestured to the crew chief to lift off. The door gunner jabbed his finger in Kincaid's direction, asking for his status. Harris shook his head and told the crew chief to get the bird off the ground.

The enemy was stronger and more numerous than Harris had thought—more numerous than intelligence had forecasted. They were lucky to have freed any of the hostages. Unfortunately, Harris' plan to get Kincaid and Pineda into the hacienda did not come about. They were forced to take the hostages they had and retreat for their lives. Now, Pineda was dead, and Kincaid was still on the ground.

The crew chief held his microphone to his mouth and spoke to the pilot. Both Blackhawks lifted into the air. They spun away from the gunfire and soared away from the area.

Two RPG gunners raced out into the open and leveled their launchers at the fleeing Blackhawks. With four shots, Kincaid took both of them out before they could fire their heat-seeking rockets.

Kincaid listened for any further enemy gunfire.

Nothing.

He cautiously crept into the clearing and picked up the radio.

"I saw them setting up a roadblock about one mile north of here," Harris yelled above the rotary engines. "When you can, go northwest. Turn on your GPS and cross the border near Nogales, Arizona. I'll have someone meet you there."

Kincaid pushed the PTT button on the radio. "Yes, sir," he replied.

With the diminishing sounds of the Blackhawk rotors, no sounds of gunfire, voices, or footsteps were heard in the desert sand, so Kincaid took off running north. He avoided the roads and sped across the Sonoran Desert, around the prickly pear cactus, and over the hot desert sand. From the briefing Harris had given them, he remembered a small village between his current position and Nogales. He hoped to get there before dark, but even more, he hoped all the cartel men had given up on them, so no one would pursue any farther.

As he ran, Kincaid kept checking his wound. It hurt like someone had placed hot coals inside him. He slowed down and looked for a place to hide out so he could tend to his wound before he bled out.

*****

In the lead Blackhawk, Harris' eyes darted from the ground below to the dead body of Ted Pineda in the cabin, to the other members of his team. Right after take-off, he started coming up with another plan to save Kincaid.

What a fiasco! One killed, several others wounded, only some of the hostages rescued, and now, Kincaid remained behind to make sure they could get away safely. His eyes instantly focused on one of his men—the one who had rushed out and brought Pineda to the chopper while Kincaid returned fire from the ground. His shirt was covered with blood and was ripped in places by the vicious desert underbrush.

He pointed to the man and leaned toward him in his seat. "Take off your shirt!"

The man had not thought he'd heard his commander correctly. He could see no reason in the command. "What?"

"Take it off! Give me your shirt."

The man took off his kit without question. As he unbuttoned his torn and bloodied shirt, Harris leaned toward the crew chief. "Take the bird down!" he roared over the engine sounds.

The crew chief shook his head in disbelief.

"Have the pilot take it down to fifty feet AGL, for one

moment."

The crew chief shook his head again but adjusted his mike and spoke to the pilot. After a pause, he pursed his lips and nodded his head.

The Blackhawk started its descent. Harris grabbed the bloodied shirt from his team member. As soon as the bird leveled off at twenty feet AGL, he threw the shirt out, hoping it would land near the trail he observed, with what looked like fresh tire tracks.

Harris bit his lip. Christian or not, he admired Kincaid. Throwing the bloodied shirt to the ground in a different direction than Kincaid was taking, would be all he could do to help the man. He hoped it would make a difference. *Good luck, Kincaid. I hope to see you again in this life.*

~Chapter Six~

Elder Sebastiano Ramirez came from a home in Mexico City where he and his older sister lived together. Their parents had been killed several years earlier during a gang struggle for dominion of their neighborhood. As a schoolboy, Sebastiano had been beaten up by neighborhood toughs. When the weaker boy fell to the ground, the older boys took his shoes and ran away with them.

Minutes later, a pair of missionaries showed up and carried Sebastiano home, to his sister. They introduced themselves and helped get the boy cleaned up and bandaged before they left. The next day, they returned with a pair of replacement shoes for Sebastiano, and his sister invited them to stay to teach their first discussion.

Elder Ramirez had been on his mission for almost one year now and had found it to be the most rewarding year of his life. He had served as a junior companion to three Mexican missionaries in that first year and had learned to preach the Gospel with fluency and confidence in his own language. Next, he wanted to learn to preach the Gospel in English. But he needed a companion from the United States to teach him. Now, the mission president had sent him to preach in a new area in the small village of Imuris. His new companion was a greenie—from the United States.

Rival drug cartels fighting a turf war plagued the small village of Imuris. Elder Ramirez remembered all too well his problems with drugs and gangs which had made his early life as difficult as it had been.

Although he had never been to Imuris before, he had heard about it from other missionaries who had served in nearby villages and towns. There were still no church members living in the village. For the first time, two missionaries had been assigned to Imuris to preach the Gospel, convert as many people as God had prepared to receive their message, organize a small branch of the church, and teach them how to apply gospel principles to their lives.

Although the Prophet knew full well of the cartel activities in and around Imuris, he had decided the time was right for the missionaries to preach full-time in that small community. Elder Ramirez waited at the bus station in Hermosillo for his new companion to arrive. This would be his first opportunity to be a *senior* companion. He wanted to make a good impression on his new junior from the start.

*****

Elder Daniel MacKay was a fifth-generation Mormon from a well-to-do family in Salt Lake City, Utah. He had been raised in the LDS Church and had always looked forward to serving in a Spanish-speaking mission—he didn't care which one. From a young age, his parents had both taught him gospel principles and the survival skills he would need during his mission. Coming to Mexico, he was equipped with sewing needles, a small bicycle tool kit, electric hair trimmers, and a meager set of kitchenware. He also had a tube of Goop to put on the bottom of his shoes when his socks winked through holes in their soles. Wanting to continue serving, he considered hunger, thirst, and other necessary discomforts as mere distractions.

Elder MacKay was a new missionary—a greenie—and his first posting was to be in a village called Imuris, in northern Sonora, Mexico. Elder Ramirez, his senior companion, had never been to the United States and did not understand or speak English. At first, the two young elders did not seem to have much in common. But they shared the same enthusiasm for the Gospel of Jesus Christ and enjoyed singing the more popular church hymns together each evening.

"I want to learn to preach the Gospel in English," Elder Ramirez told his partner in Spanish, after their first night together. "After my mission, I want to go to the United States and get a job, and take my sister with me, get married to a fine woman, and raise my children there."

"Of course," Elder MacKay said in Spanish. "I would love to teach you. That can be part of our study program in the evenings." Elder MacKay had also brought an English translation of the *Preach My Gospel Manual*. The Book of Mormon in English was also brought along to check his translations as he needed. He knew that would be a good place to start with Elder Ramirez.

The mission president had given them enough money to stay in a modest hotel for only three nights. They had to find their own apartment within that time. There were no five-star hotels in Imuris and no vacation resorts. They located the only hotel in the village and rented a room there. The toilet was down the hall, and the only shower was a short hose with a bucket of water beside the toilet.

While searching for an apartment, they preached the Gospel. Elder Ramirez taught Elder MacKay how to approach people on the street and at bus stops to encourage people to listen to their message. Elder Ramirez was pleased that his companion's Spanish was so good because his own English was limited to isolated words like *cowboy, saloon,* and *shoot*. Those were words he had remembered from the movie *Tombstone*, which he had seen several times in a television store in Mexico City.

The two Elders packed their bags and left the hotel after three nights, still not having found an apartment, but believing the Lord would provide one for them. They prayed for people to listen to their message and for the Lord to lead them to find the apartment He had prepared for them.

As the sun struck the horizon at the end of that fourth day, they knocked on one more door. It was a humble place they had almost missed, tucked away north of Avenida Limón, in the nearby village of La Estación.

"We are missionaries of The Church of Jesus Christ of Latter-day Saints, and we are looking for an apartment to rent. Can you help us?" Elder MacKay announced their need, in Spanish, to the middle-aged lady who answered the door.

The lady hastily crossed herself. Her eyes bulged as she stared at them. She seemed relieved by their appearance at her door. "O, Dios, Mio," she exclaimed. "The timing of your arrival must be a sign from God. Earlier today, I cleaned up the apartment after an elderly gentleman passed away in his sleep, two days ago," she responded in Spanish.

She introduced herself as Señora Nuñez. "You must be messengers of God," she said. She reached beside her door and brought out a keyring that hung on the wall. She then stepped outside as the last of the day's sunbeams faded and waddled to the door at the back of her small house.

While showing the two polite young men the apartment, she gave them a tour of the small place. "It only has one room with three fold-out beds. But it has a small kitchen, toilet, and a shower. I don't want you to make the place smell of feet—or worse."

Elder Ramirez looked around the small apartment and nodded his head. It had bare wood floors, toilet, and a shower without a door or curtain. A bare wire wrapped around the pipe at the shower, would provide their only hot water. A small kitchen counter with a short refrigerator, an electric hot plate on the counter, and two cupboards completed the tour.

Elder MacKay looked around the small two-room apartment. He

choked down the urge to retch as he saw several large cockroaches trying to retreat with a large crumb of bread between them.

"This is great, Señora Nuñez. It reminds me of the first apartment my sister and I lived in together. This will do fine," Elder Ramirez said with a confident smile. As the senior companion, he accepted the place. He then looked at Elder MacKay for confirmation of his decision.

Elder MacKay's eyes bulged, and his lip seemed to curl inward. What was it? Disgust? Then he seemed to relax. With a weak smile, Elder MacKay said, "Yes, it is a nice apartment, Señora. We won't need the third bed though. There is only the two of us."

Their new landlady waved off the problem with a chuckle. "Then just leave it in the corner," she said.

She walked over to the only door. "You should use this latch when you sleep," she warned, showing them the eye bolt and hook that was screwed into the door and its frame. "You'll be safe as long as you don't forget. This is a quiet village."

She looked over her shoulder with a twisted smirk, walked to the corner of the room, and pulled the small wooden bookshelf away from the wall. She called them closer with a gesture, then stooped down and lifted a floorboard from its place. "There is no lock on the door. So, when you leave during the day, put your valuables in here. No one will find them."

Elder MacKay bent down to look into the small hidey-hole. He stopped to brush away the dirt on the bare wood floor and tried to look into the hole without letting his trousers touch the floor. The hole seemed about four feet long, eighteen inches wide and about a foot deep, even though the board that covered it was only about six inches by two feet.

"My dear departed husband, may God rest his soul, built that security box for our first tenant, many years ago," Señora Nuñez said, as she crossed herself. "The man who lived here thought I didn't know about it. He would try to hide his Tequila in there. But I knew what he had done. It has also come in handy several times since my husband's death." She laughed out loud at her own joke.

Elder MacKay nodded his tentative approval and put the board back in place. It fit well. He had to hook his little finger in a small knot hole to lift it upward. "That should work well," he said, trying to smile as he spoke. "We have no money or valuables, so security won't be a problem."

"All the same," their new landlady said, "Use it as you like."

Elder Ramirez spoke with Señora Nuñez about the rental fee. They agreed on the amount after a couple more questions. Then, he handed her an envelope with the money inside.

"Muchas gracias," she said, taking the envelope and securing it in her apron pocket. She turned to leave and then turned back to them. "This is the *middle* of the month. Your rent will be due this same day every month. Okay?"

Both Elders silently nodded.

"We have electricity, but when the storms come, *our* power is the first to go wrong. Don't play any music loud at night and no computers. They trip the switch, and all of *my* electricity goes out, too."

Again, the young Elders nodded their understanding.

With that, Señora Nuñez turned and walked out, shutting the door behind her. "Don't forget to latch the door at night," she yelled through the closed door.

Only then did Elder MacKay turn to his companion and exclaim in Spanish, "Elder, this place is not safe. The floor is dirty and not even the window locks. If I swept the floor, the boards would fall apart. How can we *live* here?"

"Now, now, Elder MacKay, this is a wonderful place to live while we serve the Lord. Is this not as good as your family has at home?"

Elder MacKay's mouth fell open. Then he quickly closed it and shook his head. He composed himself and selected one bed from the three and pulled it away from the wall. As he unfolded it, he quietly sang a hymn that came to mind. "I'll go where you ask me to go, dear Lord." Then he improvised. "I'll live where you want me to live."

Elder Ramirez's smile showed his teeth. "Yes, yes, I also know that hymn. Will you teach it to me in English?" he asked.

*****

Weeks later, Elders Ramirez and MacKay finished their evening scripture study and English lesson. They then sang a few hymns before ending their day. In the time they had been in their apartment, they had discovered Señora Nuñez enjoyed their singing. Several times, when they finished singing, she pounded on the wall and yelled for them to "Sing it again! Sing it again!"

The English lessons went well. Elder Ramirez learned how to read from the *Preach My Gospel* book and Book of Mormon, as Elder MacKay had planned. Practicing was a little more difficult because no one in Imuris spoke English, except Elder MacKay.

"How does this place compare to your apartment in Mexico City?" Elder MacKay asked his companion in English. His face was drawn tight as if he feared the answer to his own question.

Elder Ramirez looked around him with a wistful smile. "This is *much* better," he said. "My sister's apartment is on the sixth floor of an old concrete building that has no elevator. The elevator has never worked as long as we have lived there. Roaches are the size of mice and mice the size of a javelina. The entire building is run by the drug dealers who intimidate the other occupants into buying or selling their drugs for them."

He stopped for a few seconds and took a deep breath. After letting out the air, he said, "Her rent is cheap, but if she had another place to go, I'm sure my sister would leave. The Spirit of God is not in that place. Then again, my sister says, if she were ever to leave, there might be no righteous person left in the building to protect the drug dealers until they repent."

"Your sister thinks she can *convert* the druggies?" Elder MacKay was aghast at the thought.

"No, I don't think she's like that. She never preaches to them. She tries to give them an example of the *joy* that comes to a person while living a righteous life," Elder Ramirez said.

"I'm sure they see her example every time they look at her," Elder MacKay said, with American sarcasm.

Elder Ramirez had become accustomed to that idiosyncrasy from his companion, and he smiled. "Yes, I'm sure, too. Let's have prayer and go to sleep."

*****

By the time Orson Kincaid stumbled into La Estación, searching for a place to hide, the overcast sky was dark without a moon. Even though he couldn't see much, he left his NODs in their pouch to avoid drawing the attention of anyone else he might run into—as if his manner of dress, his weapons, and his skulking around their fair village would not have been enough already for anyone to be suspicious of him. He knew the cartel killers had not given up searching for him. He also knew he had to find a place to hold up until morning.

Kincaid stopped behind an abandoned garage and checked his wound. The bullet had entered in the backside, under his lowest rib on the right, and exited out the front side. The steel jacketed projectile had done enough damage in the split second it had been inside him to make him bleed, extensively. He had been shot once before, but the medics had been nearby, then. They had given him first aid and taken him to a field hospital within minutes. This situation gave him serious questions about his future. He needed a hiding place, not just to avoid the drug cartel soldiers, but also to take care of his wound.

The sound of several old SUVs driving along the rutted dirt

road into the village alerted him. He saw the bouncing headlights of at least five vehicles speeding along the pressed sand road and ducked behind a nearby patch of prickly pear cactus against the garage. After the lights had passed, he got up and checked the doors of nearby homes that might be open, hoping the owners or occupants might not shoot at him if he blundered into their unlocked residence.

Coming to a single-level, humble adobe house, he saw a light on the inside. There was a back door to a separate apartment that looked unused. He cautiously tested the door and found it unlocked.

The sounds of several more vehicles, and men running alongside, drove nearby his present position. He kicked the apartment door open and prepared to hold the occupants at bay with his weapons, if necessary.

As he stumbled into the small apartment, he saw two young men on their knees with their arms crossed. They were staring at him with bulging eyes and open mouths. Their heads seemed to have been bowed as if they had been uttering a prayer. Kincaid got the distinct impression the darker of the two young men seemed to be smiling at him.

*****

Coronel Guillermo Rondo of the Sonoran State Police stepped out of the front seat of his pickup truck as soon as it stopped. His crisp brown uniform and highly glossed black leather boots spoke to his pride and attention to detail. "Surround this village so the American clown-of-a-soldier cannot escape," he ordered in Spanish. "He missed his chance to escape and I don't want to give him another. Find him so I can kill him myself." Earlier in the day, Rondo had *deputized* the cartel fighters with him for this search-and-destroy operation.

Sergeant Jorge Molina Esteban, the local constabulary

representative, brought his 1980s Chrysler K-Car Sedan to a stop nearby Rondo. He struggled to get his bulk out of his vehicle. As the only police officer in the quiet village of Imuris, he didn't like it when outsiders came bustling in and giving orders. He was determined to find out what was going on. Half-heartedly adjusting his holster around his ample girth, he walked over to the one who looked to be in charge. "What's going on here?" he said with a smile and in an easy tone, trying not to alienate the stranger from the start.

Rondo looked at the fat man with amusement as he waddled closer. "Excuse me," Rondo said to the officer. "Are you the only police officer in this town?"

Esteban puffed out his chest. "Yes, sir. My name is Constable Jorge Molina Esteban. What is...?"

Before he could finish his query, Rondo took out his Glock .40 caliber handgun and put two rounds in the constable's chest. When Esteban hit the ground, Rondo sauntered over and put one more round in his forehead. Then he looked around at his deputies. "There should be no additional problems with law enforcement agencies in this town before we finish our business. Now, *find* that gringo!"

*****

Orson Kincaid, with his SIG Sauer in hand, turned to look out the window again, in time to see the cartel leader gun down the uniformed cop. "Snap!" he hissed to himself. With a scuffling of feet behind him, he spun around, aiming his SIG at the sound. He found the two young men crouching behind him, peering through the window with him. He still didn't know who they were.

"I need to hide here," he said in Spanish. Kincaid realized that both young men had probably just witnessed the horror that awaited anyone outside. They may never want to go outside for any reason, again. Neither of them had probably ever expected or wanted this kind of excitement, in their life.

"Bueno," said Elder Ramirez, the darker of the two. "How can we help?"

"The men out there work for a drug cartel, and they want to kill me," Kincaid said in a strained whisper, in accented Spanish. "I need a place to hide."

For the first time, Kincaid scrutinized both of them. They wore short-sleeved white shirts with name tags on their shirt pockets, and neckties loosely tied around their necks. The tags said their names were: Elder MacKay and Elder Ramirez.

Kincaid shook his head. "For crying out loud!" he growled. "You're *Mormon* missionaries, aren't you?" His mind raced back to the deathbed promise he had made to his partner. He wondered how Pineda had arranged for this to happen from the Mormon spirit world, or wherever he was, right now.

The missionaries both nodded their heads in expectation of more questions, waiting for something else.

They were probably scared out of their wits, Kincaid realized. He gritted his teeth and snarled at his ironically bad luck. He looked back out the window searching for any other place he could hide from the cartel.

Nothing.

Before long, the fighters would see this small apartment and they would break down the door in search of their quarry.

Kincaid examined the room for heavy furniture to barricade the door and block the windows, in anticipation of a gunfight, if it should come to it. He resolved not to be taken alive.

Again, nothing.

He winced, checking his wound. It had broken open again and slowly oozed a dark, mushy fluid. The blood-soaked half of his right pant leg was sticky in his own blood. If he waited any longer, he might bleed to death. If he tried to run for it, they would catch him within minutes. He estimated it was still at least twenty miles to the American border and realized he would not be able to make it, right now.

Even though they were Mormons, Kincaid didn't want to involve these missionaries in a gunfight, if he could avoid it.

Now, he had to figure out the best course of action—for the three of them.

~*Chapter Seven*~

Kincaid's great-grandfather had been a silver miner in Tombstone. Unlike most miners, when he struck it rich, he purchased land in the Curtis Flats area, outside St. David, and there he'd stayed for the rest of his life. He bought and raised cattle and sheep, planted, and harvested the meager crops his family needed to eat. The region had been blessed with artesian wells after the earthquake of 1887. That helped all the ranchers water their cattle and crops.

Only after he had staked his land claim in the Cochise County Office in Tombstone, did he discover his new neighbors were Mormons. He just shook his head and said to his wife, "There goes the value of our land!" But the family had never left.

Three generations later, Kincaid's family still owned and cultivated his great-grandfather's land. Orson had attended St. David High School as a teenager. Most of the Mormon students shunned him because he was not a member of their church. Since his family attended none of the religious meetings, just about everyone else in town avoided his family. The people called them *heathens*.

Yes, Kincaid knew a little about the Mormon Church through the examples from his youth. Those memories were not fond ones. His parents had even given him a traditional Mormon name in hopes he would fit in better than either of them had fit into the community.

It hadn't worked.

What Orson knew about the Mormon religion, he had overheard in conversations between other students at school, on the bus, or anywhere he went that Mormon teenagers also frequented.

"Is it against your religion to hide me? To help me? Give me sanctuary?" Kincaid inquired in Spanish.

The missionaries looked at each other and shrugged.

Elder Ramirez pursed his lips in determination. "Elder, I think we should help this good brother," he declared to his companion, in Spanish.

"Hey, get this straight," Kincaid said, interrupting their moment of decision. "I ain't your *brother*. I need help for a few hours, and I'll be on my way."

The two missionaries spoke in Spanish for about two minutes while Kincaid peered out the window again. He watched the movements of the cartel gunners, as they went door to door, searching the houses and sheds in the village. He also assessed his chances of finding anywhere else to hide—anywhere away from this apartment. At the same time, he divided his attention to listening in on the conversation of the missionaries behind him. Most of it was too fast for him, but he caught the main points.

The lighter of the two missionaries stepped closer to their unexpected guest and crouched a few feet away. "My name is Elder MacKay," he said in unaccented English.

Kincaid looked at him with suspicion. "You're *American*?"

"That's right," Elder MacKay said with a weak smile. "I just arrived here a few weeks ago."

"Does your partner speak English, too?" Kincaid asked, jerking his head in the direction of the other missionary.

"A little. He's from Mexico City, but I'm teaching him English. He's learning." Elder MacKay crept closer to the wounded American. "What's your name?" he inquired.

"Orson."

"Good. Brother Orson..." he started.

"I already said, I *ain't* your brother. Call me Orson, but not brother. I'll call you Ramirez and MacKay," Kincaid added, glancing at their name tags one more time.

"None of this was included in the classes at the MTC,"— the Missionary Training Center, Elder MacKay informed his companion.

Kincaid winced at the sudden sharp pain in his side. Shifting his rifle to his left hand, he put more pressure on his injured side with his right hand. "Do you have a first aid kit here?"

The missionaries suddenly noticed for the first time that their unforeseen visitor was bleeding. His shirt and pants were both covered in dark blood.

"Yes," Ramirez said, jumping to his feet and rushing into the bathroom.

MacKay moved closer to Kincaid and examined the wound closer. "We will need to wash and bandage this and hope the bleeding stops. You need a doctor." He used great care as he helped Kincaid lay on the floor, on his left side so they could take care of his wound. The wounded American hesitated from leaving a position where he could see out the window.

"That's a shame, because unless either of you went to medical school, what's waiting for me out there," he jerked his thumb toward the window, "is a slow and painful death at the hands of those killers."

"Okay, then we will do the best we can." MacKay jumped up and ran to the bathroom just as Ramirez came back out with their small First Aid Kit.

In just seconds, MacKay returned with a wet towel he had wrung out. He gently wiped the dried blood from off the skin surrounding the wound, noticing it was large enough to stick one finger inside it. When blood oozed from the bullet hole near his stomach area, MacKay turned green, dropped the blood-soaked towel onto the wound, and ran to the bathroom.

Kincaid heard the reverberated sounds of puking into the

toilet and snickered. "I guess your partner is not used to seeing blood."

Ramirez jumped in to care for the wound. "No, he is not. But I used to help my wounded friends before I left home." With great caution, he rolled Kincaid forward and saw a smaller bullet hole in his back. "Do you know you have another hole in your back?"

"Yeah. Same bullet. Two holes. What a deal! The one in front is bleeding more." Kincaid reached into his kit and pulled out a bag of powder. "Here, pour this on both wounds. It's a clotting agent that will help the bleeding stop." It didn't translate well into Spanish, but Kincaid did the best he could.

Ramirez looked puzzled, at first. But he took the pouch and noticed it was a powder. Ripping open the package, he poured it onto both wounds, like he was born to be a doctor, one day.

When MacKay returned, he wiped his mouth on his white shirt sleeve and walked toward the others with a wobbly gait. Ramirez had just finished bandaging both bullet holes.

"I have an idea," Kincaid announced in Spanish. "First, I need scissors and a razor."

"Scissors? Why?"

"I need to cut my hair and shave. Do you have any clothes that might fit me?"

"Why?"

"I need to look like another missionary so when they come in here, they will think I'm one of you." His longer hair usually let Kincaid blend into the populace when he needed to do so. But in this case, it would backfire on him if the cartel fighters saw him. So, he needed to look almost military, which meant—like a Mormon Missionary.

The two missionaries looked at Kincaid with vacant eyes.

Kincaid simplified his plan for them. "Don't you think they will eventually search inside every house in this village?" he asked, using basic reasoning. "When they come inside *here*, they won't worry about me if they think I am also a missionary."

"We will have to start now, in case they come, soon," MacKay urged. He opened a drawer and pulled out a small bag. "We have scissors, but I could cut your hair faster and better with these hair clippers."

"You also must shower," Ramirez said. "You're about my size, so you can wear my other white shirt, necktie, and dress trousers."

MacKay looked at his companion. "We need another name tag," he said in Spanish. "What should we do?"

Ramirez thought for a moment. "I have an extra one from my last companion, who forgot it when he went home at the end of his mission. I was going to mail it to him, someday. We can use that."

"Good. Go get it," MacKay said as he pulled out a chair from their small kitchen table. He motioned for Kincaid to sit. "I will give you a missionary haircut that would even convince your mother you've been converted," he said with pride.

Kincaid hesitated as he sat down in the chair. "Don't go crazy, now," Kincaid said. He worried about what MacKay's description might mean.

MacKay put the towel around Kincaid's neck and combed the tangles out of his hair. He cringed at seeing all the blood on Kincaid's clothing, staining the bottom of his shirt and the top of his trousers. He fought to keep his stomach from erupting again. "After you shower, we will need to check your bandage again. It looks like it might need stitches."

MacKay cut Kincaid's hair in short order, and sent him into the bathroom to shave, bathe and dress in his new missionary clothing. Kincaid took his Kit, NODs, AR-10 sniper rifle, SIG Sauer P226 handgun, and body armor into the bathroom with him. Not that he didn't trust these two missionaries, but he wanted to be ready to shoot his way out of there if the cartel killers burst in while he was showering. He recognized that would be his most vulnerable moment, so he showered with haste.

Six minutes later, a clean-cut, smooth-shaven Kincaid came out, tucking the tails of a too-small, white shirt into dress pants that were too big on him. Without the four days' growth of facial hair, he looked ten years younger. Perfect for a new missionary.

Ramirez looked him over once and smiled. "Elder Gomez," he declared with a grin, handing Kincaid a name tag and necktie to put on.

"What? Who's Elder Gomez?" Kincaid asked.

"You are," replied MacKay, with a chuckle. "Your name tag says your name is Elder Gomez, so don't forget that, when you're talking to the drug cartel."

Seeing their guest was struggling with the name tag, Ramirez stepped in and helped him secure it to the breast pocket of his white shirt.

Kincaid returned to the bathroom and got his gear. He held up his dirty, bloody uniform and weapons. "Where can we hide these?" he said.

"I'll take those," MacKay said, with a smile. He pulled the bookshelf away from the wall, reached down, and pulled up the floorboard their landlady had shown them for anything they needed to secure—or, in this case, *hide*. "The hole should be big enough for your weapons, uniform, and gear," he said to an anxious Elder Gomez.

When MacKay had reached for the weapons, Kincaid instinctively pulled back.

"Okay, *you* put them in," MacKay offered, stepping out of the way.

Kincaid stuck his hand inside the hole to find out how big it was and to make sure his gear wouldn't simply fall under the house. Only then did he place his NODs, rifle, uniform, and body armor inside. He replaced the board, briefly admiring the work and convenience of having such a hidey-hole. He kept his SIG and stuck it in his waistband at the small of his back.

Kincaid lowered himself into the nearest of two chairs and took a deep breath, looking out the two windows for any activity. Ramirez pulled out the third roll-away bed and made it up for Elder Gomez.

MacKay sat down with their new third companion and pulled out his scriptures.

Kincaid looked at the book as if it contained the coronavirus. "What are you *doing*?" he asked, with growing suspicion. "I won't read from your Mormon Bible as part of this deal."

MacKay remained undaunted. "If the cartel men ask you questions about the LDS Church, you should have the right answers. If not, they might not buy your story about *being* a missionary."

Kincaid hesitated but gave in with a huff. "All right. But give me the down-and-dirty version, so I can fool them without having to listen to your *whole* spiel. Okay?"

At that moment, Ramirez finished making the third bed and brought out his companion's English translation of the *Preach My Gospel*. He gladly sat on the floor beside his companion to teach and learn more English at the same time.

"Joseph Smith was a fourteen-year-old boy, living in upstate New York in the early 1800s when he read in the New Testament, the Epistle of James, chapter one, verse five, that says, 'If any of you lack wisdom, let him ask of God, that giveth to all men liberally and upbraideth not; and it shall be given him.'"

Elder Ramirez picked up the story in his limited English. "So, Joseph went into a grove of trees one morning to pray and ask the Heavenly Father for help, because he didn't know which church to join."

Both Elders related the story of the first vision and how it led to the restoration of the complete gospel of Jesus Christ along with the authority to act in the name of God in matters pertaining to the Kingdom of God on Earth. They also testified of the Book of Mormon, which served as another witness of Jesus Christ, supporting the Bible—not superseding it or changing it.

At several points in the story, Kincaid almost stopped them, because it all sounded too fantastic to be true. As they spoke, Kincaid looked up from his book suddenly startled. For just a moment, he thought he saw his partner, Ted Pineda, sitting between the two missionaries. Ted seemed to gaze at Kincaid with an easy smile. After just a moment, the image was gone. But it left a warm feeling inside Kincaid that made him want to hear more of their message.

As the two young missionaries finished their recital, Kincaid asked almost flippantly, "What makes it so important to believe in Jesus Christ, Joseph Smith, the Book of Mormon, and this restored church of yours?"

MacKay looked at his companion with a big smile and gave him a slight nod. This was the part that Ramirez could teach in English as well as MacKay.

"Before we came to Earth in our mortal bodies," began Ramirez, "we lived with Heavenly Father, who *is* our Father—the father of our spirits. He knows and loves us, and he taught us everything we could learn as spirits. The next step was to take mortal bodies, come to this Earth to learn and experience more, and to prove ourselves worthy of returning to his presence after our death."

Both Elders took part in teaching Kincaid about the Plan of Salvation, the Atonement, the Resurrection, Judgment Day, and how little children do not need to be baptised.

"Wait. Go back," Kincaid snapped. The missionary's words had struck him like a bolt of lightning. "Why don't little children need baptism?"

"Baptism is an ordinance performed to cleanse a person from their *own* sins," MacKay expounded. "Little children can't sin, so they have no need to be baptized."

Kincaid held up one finger and looked down at the floor, trying to think. "How old do you need to be to qualify as a little child?" he finally asked.

"Eight years old."

"What happens if a child is younger than eight and commits a grave sin?"

"Nothing. The child did not understand he or she was doing anything wrong, so the wrong is not accounted to them," MacKay explained.

That was the missing piece of the puzzle that now lifted a great weight from Kincaid's shoulders. It was a weight he had carried for most of his life. The best part was it made *perfect sense*.

A thunderous knock at the door jolted the three of them to their feet. By reflex, Kincaid put his right hand behind his back, prepared to pull out his SIG Sauer.

"Open up!" a deep voice commanded in Spanish.

~Chapter Eight~

Ramirez went to open the door and welcome their unannounced guests, still carrying *Preach My Gospel* in his hand.

"When they come in, call us *Elder* MacKay and *Elder* Ramirez," Elder MacKay cautioned Kincaid.

Kincaid nodded. He reached over and placed his SIG Sauer under the pillow on his bed. "What'll I do when they ask me questions?"

"The same as *any* foreigner new to any country would do. Try your best, and I will help you when you need it."

When the door opened, three of the cartel killers shoved Elder Ramirez out of their way, aiming their rifles at each of the three younger men in white shirts. They thoroughly searched the small apartment for anyone else and found nothing suspicious.

"Who are you?" asked the one in charge, as he strode through the open door with no weapons in hand and without introducing himself. He was a middle-aged man who wore the tan uniform of the Sonora Police with high black boots and black leather gloves. He also wore a hip holster with an automatic pistol cradled in it.

Elder Ramirez answered in Spanish. "We are missionaries of The Church of Jesus Christ of Latter-day Saints." His smile wavered with concern for the unknown.

"Coronel Rondo, these are religious fanatics," the dirtiest deputized cartel fighter proclaimed. "They are stupid, but harmless."

Rondo ignored the remark and looked at the name tag on the shirt of one young man, then sauntered over to the other young men and scrutinized their name tags. He spotted Elder Gomez and looked into the face of the man. "Gomez is a Mexican name," he said in Spanish.

Elder Gomez swallowed. "Si, my father came from Monterrey, Mexico with his parents." He started, in Spanish, but did not have the vocabulary to continue. He looked at Elder MacKay for help.

"My companion has a Mexican *name*, but he was born in the United States," Elder MacKay explained. "He arrived in Mexico three weeks ago and is still learning to speak Spanish."

Rondo looked the young man up and down with disdain. "American?"

"Yes, I am also American," Elder MacKay said. "We came here to preach the gospel of Jesus Christ for two years. What do *you* know about your Savior?" he asked the Coronel with boldness, deflecting his interest away from Elder Gomez.

Rondo first sneered at Elder MacKay, then turned back to Elder Gomez. He did not think any of them looked like American Special Forces soldiers. But it perturbed him to no end that they would presume to come to his country to preach to him and his people about religion when they already had the Catholic Church.

He faced the young Gomez and sneered again at him. Both men were about the same height but there was at least twenty-five years difference between Rondo and them. Rondo saw a different look in this young man's eye—was it a look of aggression? Defiance? He could not tell for sure. But he looked somehow different from the other two. "I speak a little English," Rondo announced while standing close enough for his tobacco breath to flutter the clean hair of Elder Gomez. "Are you so much better than we Mexicans that you come here to preach to us about God?"

Kincaid did not know what to say. He tried to remain calm,

to slow his breathing and control his pulse. After two deep breaths, he smiled at Coronel Rondo. "No, sir. I am no better than you. I want to share our special message with you and your people," Kincaid said, amazed at himself. "So, you can find inner peace and happiness." He did not avert his eyes from Rondo and kept smiling—he hoped it was a humble smile.

Rondo thumped his own chest and moved a few inches closer to this Gomez. "My priest baptized me a few days after my birth," he said in a proud voice. "My family has been Catholic for generations." He glared at this American, Gomez, trying to make the impertinent youth look away, first.

Silence.

"That's wonderful, sir," Kincaid finally said without averting his eyes. "The Catholic church does a lot of good in this world. I hope you will stay close to the church all your life. In fact, we have a lot in common with the Catholic Church." As soon as he had closed his mouth, he shuddered, wondering where those words had come from. He had never had anything good to say about any religion in his life, let alone the Mother of Christianity. Kincaid hoped what he had said about the Catholic Church would be impossible for Rondo to find fault with.

"Why do you not insult my religion, like other preachers do?"

"I only arrived in Mexico a few weeks ago," Elder Gomez said with a smile. "I got assigned to Elder Ramirez and Elder MacKay and came here to meet them as soon as possible. Why would we want to insult our hosts when we are merely guests in your country?"

"What does your church preach that makes it so special?" Rondo asked. He picked up a Book of Mormon from Elder Gomez's bed and quickly thumbed through it. He slowly turned his head to Gomez, demanding an answer with his glare.

Gomez flinched, hoping Rondo would not move his pillow on the bed, and uncover his SIG.

"We preach of a God who loves all his children, equally. He wants us to be worthy to return home to him after we finish our work here on Earth," Gomez replied, without hesitation.

"And why do you not wear the collar or the robes of the clergy? You look..."

Kincaid glanced over at both missionaries. They blanched and looked like they might pass out. He realized now, *he* had to take charge. "We look like clean-cut young men, trying to do good in this world, right?" He said with a smile. He wanted to get away from that bit about the robes because he didn't know the answer. "We have been ordained to preach the Gospel, but we are no better and no different than you or anyone else in this village," Elder Gomez said, pointing to the three-armed thugs Rondo had brought in with him. "We are all God's children."

Elder MacKay stood behind Elder Gomez as he spoke with Coronel Rondo. MacKay looked down at the white shirt Gomez wore and saw a small red blossom of blood seeping through the bandage. It was wet and was staining the white shirt. He moved closer to Kincaid's side, to help mask the blood and bullet wounds, hoping their visitors would not notice.

Rondo started to ask another question. But before he could say anything, the door flew open, and another armed thug rushed inside. He jostled two of the men already inside the small apartment.

"Jefe, we have found a shirt with blood on it, east of Imuris," he said in Spanish.

Rondo looked at the messenger, turned back to Elder Gomez, and grabbed him by his necktie. "Do not come knocking on *my* door to preach your religion, or I will give you a Colombian Necktie you will *never* take off."

Rondo turned to glare at Elders MacKay and Ramirez—who had been deathly quiet during the interrogation—before he and his men stormed out of their apartment. "Take me to the evidence," he ordered his men in Spanish. He slammed the door behind him, knocking the eyebolt of its latch to the floor. The door swung free in the slight evening breeze.

All three young missionaries stood quietly, staring at each other for several poignant moments as they caught their breath.

Elder MacKay fell to his knees and sobbed. When he raised his head, he asked, "What is a Colombian necktie?" He and Elder Ramirez both looked to Elder Gomez for an answer.

"It's when they cut your throat open, reach inside and pull your tongue out, so it hangs from your throat like a necktie," Kincaid explained.

Elder Ramirez solemnly nodded his understanding. Elder MacKay turned green and ran for the toilet, once again.

Kincaid paced to the door and back to the side of his bed, chewing on his upper lip. He was worried about the shirt and blood they had found in the desert. He was the only one who had remained behind. The rest had flown away to Fort Huachuca. He hoped the shirt was a false clue Harris had left behind to help him. Silently thanking God for the wisdom of his mission leader, he reached down and put the eyebolt back in place.

As Kincaid looked out the door, the armed cartel guards still stalked the streets and drove through the village, hoping to find the wounded gringo. Maybe after midnight, he could make his getaway. "I can't leave, yet" Kincaid announced as he turned away from the window.

"You're welcome to spend the night," Elder MacKay said with a weak smile, not wanting their guest to leave just yet. "You're still bleeding, and you could use the rest to let it heal at least for a few hours."

Kincaid thought about it for a moment. He stopped his pacing, went back to the bed, and withdrew his SIG Sauer. He nervously pulled the slide halfway open and looked inside to make sure he had a round in the chamber; letting it go, the slide closed on the chambered round with a metallic *thunk*. The magazine was also full. Returning the gun and holster to the small of his back, he thought about his plight, trying to plan his foot journey back home.

Elders MacKay and Ramirez both sat on the floor. Kincaid thought about taking a chair, but he joined them. It felt right to be at the same level they were on.

"How did you think of those answers to the man's questions so *fast*?" Elder MacKay asked.

"Yes, how *did* you do that?" echoed the senior companion. "Have you ever been in our church before?"

Kincaid smiled, then shook his head. "No, I've never been a Mormon. But I was raised in a small Mormon town in Arizona, so I've heard parts of your story since I was young."

"So, you already knew what we taught you?" Elder Ramirez asked, in his halting English.

Kincaid chuckled. "No, and that confused me too. I just seemed to *know* how to answer his questions without having to *think* about it." He slowly lifted the *Book of Mormon* they had offered him earlier, then returned it to the bed. "Give me a few minutes to change my bandage. Then, can we read more about Nephi, Mormon, and Moroni?" he said.

With all three of them working together, it only took a few minutes to clean the wounds, spread more coagulant powder on the holes, and put new bandages over the wounds. Then they returned to their studies.

For the next four hours—until well after the time their lights were supposed to be turned out—Elder MacKay and Elder Ramirez bore pure testimony to Kincaid of the truthfulness of the Gospel of Jesus Christ. They told him Joseph Smith was a prophet of God; that Jesus Christ and Heavenly Father both wanted all their children to return home to them.

"Have you *killed* people?" Elder MacKay asked, in a gentle voice, not wanting to offend or anger their guest. He thought he already knew the answer, but he felt the need to ask. Someone who handled his weapons with such familiarity must have used them in combat, Elder MacKay thought.

"Yes, I have," Kincaid admitted. For the first time, he felt shame as he confessed. "My *job* is to kill our enemies." He looked into their eyes and was surprised he didn't see blame or judgment there. He saw—what was it—compassion? Love? He didn't know what he saw in their eyes. "Earlier today, my team saved a family the cartel was going to execute just because they were American."

"There were no patches or pins on your uniform shirt, to identify your unit. You are in the Army, aren't you?" Elder MacKay asked.

"No, I work for a contract company. We were hired by the US Government to rescue that family."

"You're a mercenary?" Elder MacKay asked.

Kincaid shook his head. "I *hate* that term… but I guess you're right."

"Then that changes everything." Elder MacKay said.

Elder Ramirez sat looking from one man to the other as they spoke. He understood they were speaking about the sin of killing, but he could not understand their exact conversation. His ability in English was not sufficient to follow, and he quickly fell behind.

"If I was interested right now, could I be baptized?" Kincaid placed his open palm against his chest, looking from one missionary to the other.

Elder Ramirez was first to speak up. "Anyone can be baptized and forgiven for their sins. But there are those who have committed mortal sins, like murder, who must first speak with one of the general authorities. Then, *they* will decide whether you are eligible. Or they will tell you how you must prepare yourself to be forgiven."

Again, Kincaid heard Elder Ramirez speak as if his native language was English. He was almost eloquent in his simple statement, even though he had not contributed much to the overall conversation.

His simple statement made Kincaid want to listen to more of these missionaries' message. With his heart thumping in his chest, he stopped and tried to listen or feel for the Holy Spirit. He bowed his head and prayed a simple prayer for greater sensitivity to the urgings of the spirit so he could hear, understand, and know the truth of the missionaries' words. But he admitted to himself he still had more from his past to work out before he would be ready for baptism.

"Yes, but that does not apply to soldiers. When a soldier kills in battle, the sin will be upon the political leaders who sent him to war," Elder MacKay added. "But I think a mercenary soldier would have a wounded spirit from so much killing."

Kincaid thought about his occupation and all the death he had caused. He did not understand what the Spirit of God would tell him about his childhood mistakes—the murder he had committed as a child. He needed time on his own to repent and petition God for that forgiveness.

Was this feeling of love and desire for forgiveness what Ted Pineda had wanted to share with him? If so, Kincaid considered himself a true fool for ignoring and even making fun of his friend for trying to share it with him for so many years.

Elder Ramirez stood and stretched. "I think it is time to sleep. We have much to do tomorrow and you must get back across the border."

Elder MacKay prayed as all three of them knelt, before getting into bed. Kincaid rinsed out his uniform so most of the blood was gone, but he put it back on and slept on the floor, in one corner of the room, with his back up against the wall. The hidey-hole that still concealed his kit and vest was right at his feet. His SIG was holstered, and his rifle laid across his lap.

Kincaid hoped to get a few hours of sleep, but his soul was restless, and he remained awake almost all that night.

In the few minutes he slept, he saw a handgun and was jarred by a single gunshot, then a young boy fell to the floor. He heard enough screaming to make the mountains fall. The darkness gathered around him in the dream and he felt a dreadful cold snuggle against him. He saw his father and reached out to him, but his father turned and walked away. Then his father returned carrying another gun. He gave it to his son, but Kincaid didn't want to take it. He got a coppery taste in his mouth and he felt like he would puke. Then he reluctantly took the weapon from his father with tears in his eyes.

Kincaid awoke with a knot in his stomach and, for an unknown reason, he held himself responsible for his father's renunciation of him. He had tried to awaken several times, knowing it was only a dream, but he could not stop the dream until he finally screamed and jolted himself out of bed. At first, he felt the sweat streaming down his face, his back, and his chest. Next, he looked down at his rifle and realized he was lucky he had not had his finger on the trigger, during the nightmare.

After several tries to slow his heartbeat, he finally got control of his breathing, which helped slow his pulse. He opened his eyes to the sun peaking in the window over his bed, as it slowly scaled the horizon.

Elder Ramirez was cheerfully singing a church hymn in the shower.

Elder MacKay stood at the hot plate, making rice and beans for three when he saw Kincaid stand from his corner and stretch. "Good morning, Orson. I'm sorry you had such a fitful night." He went to the refrigerator, took out their last hotdog, cut it into pieces, and threw it in with the rice. "We were afraid to try to wake you while you slept with your finger on the trigger of your gun."

Kincaid yawned and stretched. "You did right." He moved so he could stay away from the windows as much as possible. Looking down at his uniform, he noticed it was dry, knowing he would not pick up as much dust on his trek that would have weighed him down.

"Have you heard any vehicles or men anywhere in the village?" he asked Elder MacKay. Then, not waiting for an answer, he bent down and inventoried all his gear to make sure he had left nothing behind. He did a cursory dust off of his weapons, then checked each chamber, and both magazines to make sure each one had a full load.

"No. It's been quiet. They must have given up looking for you."

The shower water stopped in the other room, and so did the singing.

"Will you stay for breakfast?" Elder MacKay asked.

Kincaid pulled up the floorboard, picked up his body armor, and slid into it. "I should only stay a few minutes. I have to get across the border before it gets too hot outside."

Elder Ramirez came out dressed in his short-sleeve white shirt, trousers, and tie. His short, black hair was still wet and stood on end. "Good morning, everyone," he said, as he took his place at the table.

After only a couple of hours sleep, they all shared the chores of preparing for breakfast. Kincaid didn't know anything about cooking, but he helped where he could, setting their small table for three. He watched the two missionaries as they worked and joked together, admiring their positive attitudes and uplifting spirits.

When they all sat to eat, Kincaid stopped and said, "I want to feel the way… you look like you feel." He looked at both of the missionaries. "I want to be… forgiven for my sins, but I have a lot of blood on my hands. What do I have to do to *be* forgiven?"

Kincaid was conflicted. He needed to hurry and leave, but he wanted to continue feeling the spirit these two missionaries carried with them. And he didn't want to stay long enough that word might get out an American was hiding here. That would not end well for any of them. No, he decided, he had to leave right after breakfast.

Elder MacKay looked around the table. "Let's bless the meal so we can eat. I'm sure Heavenly Father will help us know what he wants us to do."

The others nodded without speaking.

"It's your turn," said Elder Ramirez, smiling at his companion.

Elder MacKay bowed his head and folded his arms across his chest. "Dear Father in Heaven. We thank thee for providing us this food and for bringing this good brother to our humble apartment. We ask thee to bless this food to nourish our bodies and give us the health and strength we seek by eating it, so we may do thy work. We also ask thee to bless Orson so he will know thy will—what thou wouldst have him do with his life—so he can enter thy good graces and be forgiven from his sins. In the name of Jesus Christ, our Savior, Amen."

Kincaid kept his head bowed for a moment longer after the amen. His lips moved, but he put no audible voice to the words he spoke. When Kincaid raised his head, he reached for the bowl of rice, hot dog pieces, and beans without explanation. The missionaries both looked at him with knowing smiles. He felt more at peace at that moment than he had in several years. "I want you to give my name to your commander," he said. "Have him pass it to the prophet, and I will go to Salt Lake City to speak with him about baptism in a few months."

"Why a few months?" Elder Ramirez asked.

"It's gonna take me that long to get away from my job."

Kincaid was ravenous. He had wanted to eat a lot of the hotdog pieces, cut up and cooked in rice with black beans until he saw this was all they had. Then he took only a moderate portion.

As the missionaries continued preparing for the new day, Kincaid opened the door, and looked back one more time with a radiant smile. He ran down the empty street, keeping to the protective shadows of dawn. He wanted to thank them but knew he would end up crying like a baby. So, no goodbyes. Not this time.

*****

Once he was north of Imuris, Kincaid jogged through the desert, paralleling the highway heading north, toward the border. A chill went up his spine as he thought he was being followed. He knew he didn't have the strength to run all the way to the border, so he kept walking until he came to a large rock lying along his current path. Rounding the rock, he hid on the far side. He pulled his SIG, flicked off the safety, and waited.

Within minutes, Kincaid heard uneven footsteps in the sand, coming from the same direction he had just walked. He hugged the rock and aimed his weapon at a height where he thought a person's head might be. While waiting, he looked at the sun, the terrain, and the highway to his right. He estimated he was about five miles away from the safety of the border.

A single man walked past the rock, looking down as if following footprints in the desert sand.

Kincaid took solid aim at his head, then quickly lowered his weapon.

Will Harris walked past the rock, then stopped and stared at Kincaid. A wash of relief spread across his face when he saw his subordinate.

"What are you doing out here, just five miles from the US border?" Kincaid asked his commander.

"I thought you might run into trouble, so I told the pilot to drop me off. Then I jumped from the helicopter when it was close to the ground, and waited to give you backup, just in case. Is everything all right?" Harris said with a cockeyed smile.

"Yes," Kincaid said. "I had a run-in with a cartel leader, but I talked my way out," he said, allowing the mystery to settle between them.

"Yeah, and you also cut your own *hair*? Or did you stop at the local hair salon for a shave and a haircut?"

Kincaid laughed. "It's a long story, sir. For now, let's just get out of here."

Harris nodded and they both took up an airborne shuffle toward home.

As they hustled the home stretch toward the border, Kincaid realized he had been smiling—almost grinning. He caught Harris staring at him several times with a quizzical look on his face.

"What's the matter?" Kincaid finally asked.

"I don't know. You look different—not meaning your haircut. You're injured, but you're smiling. What gives?"

Kincaid grinned. He knew what was different, but he didn't think Harris would understand or appreciate what had happened to him, last night. He sloughed it off. "It's nothing. I'm just glad to be less than a mile from the border. Do you think we'll run into U.S. Border Patrol officers, who'll give us a ride?"

"If we do, they won't believe whatever we tell them until they have official confirmation. So, expect them to confiscate our weapons and body armor until later."

Letting a chuckle slip out, Kincaid said, "Good! I'm worn out from carrying all this gear, anyway."

At the border, they saw a few people hiding in the shadows of the flowering oleander bushes, near the simple barbwire fence. They were waiting for the sun to set, so they could sneak across the border, unnoticed. The people seemed surprised when two Americans in uniform and body armor, carrying weapons, walked right past them. The two men stepped through the hole in the fence and confidently strolled across the border, into the United States, as if it was that easy.

Within minutes, two official SUVs, white with a green diagonal stripe, sped toward them from different directions. With calm assurance, Harris and Kincaid placed their weapons on the ground and clasped their fingers behind their heads, smiling.

Harris looked at his fellow operator. "I guess we get a ride, after all. You've really earned it."

~Chapter Nine~

Orson Kincaid sat on the edge of his hospital bed with his feet dangling toward the floor. He was bored. His injuries had come from one bullet that had entered beneath his ribs—where his body armor didn't protect him—and became septic because he had used Mexican water to wash the blood off in the shower. He had been a patient at Canyon Vista Hospital, in Sierra Vista, Arizona for two months because of that pernicious infection. The doctors and therapists had worked miracles on him during that time.

Now, with the infection on the run, Kincaid was getting edgy. It was time to return home. He needed to find out his official status with the Army and with Harris' contract company. Now that he'd had time to make a decision about joining the contract company, he did not feel comfortable with it. He had joined because Ted Pineda had wanted it. Now, with Ted dead, he didn't want any part of it. He wanted to take his DD-214 paperwork and leave the military and paramilitary work behind him.

Two months in the hospital had given him time to think about his brief hours with the missionaries in Mexico, and how much it meant to his future—to his eternal destiny. He had not waned in his blossoming faith in what they had taught him. Nor had he weakened in his desire to learn more, to get baptized, and live a better life.

Kincaid didn't want to discuss his experience with anyone else just yet—not until he was ready. He also wanted to read the

Book of Mormon on his own, but he didn't yet have his own copy.

He didn't know what profession he might move into as a civilian besides conducting special operations warfare. He was a soldier—a sniper. That was all he had done his whole adult life. So, he didn't know what he should do after healing, other than to find a Mormon chapel in Fayetteville and attend meetings as soon as possible.

His doctor walked into the room wearing a smile. "Mister Kincaid, it's time to release you," he said without preface or context.

The announcement put a grin on Kincaid's face. "Give me my papers and I'll be on my way doc."

The doctor ignored the request and lifted Kincaid's shirt to admire his surgical work, one last time. The scar on the right side of his abdomen was the shape of a nine-inch figure eight from both the entry and exit wounds and including the surgical work to repair the damage and cleanse the infection. "I'm discharging you and giving you a scrip for one month of limited duty. Then you can go do whatever it is you do for the Army, to your heart's content."

Kincaid smiled. He knew the doctors and nurses had not been told how or where he had been wounded. All they saw were the bullet wounds. They also heard what Harris had told them about leaving his story alone.

One month of limited duty was still better than being in the hospital. "I can do a month standing on my head," he said. "Just let me go back home; I'll be fine."

"The nurse will be with you shortly, to explain how to process out of the hospital. He will also give you the record of your stay with us. Good luck." The physician smiled and nodded at his patient, turned, and left the room.

The nurse entered mere minutes, later. He spent time explaining what Kincaid had to do to get out of the hospital. Leaving behind a stack of signed papers, he wished Kincaid well and left the room.

Next, a young orderly materialized in the doorway with a wheelchair. The man appeared to have worked in hospitals for many years, judging by the way he carried himself and maneuvered the wheelchair.

Kincaid scowled at the chair.

"Now, don't give me any trouble about riding to the door," the orderly warned, waggling a finger in the air at his patient. "Hospital policy requires you to ride this chair to the hospital's front door. After that, you can ride a *skateboard*, if you want."

Kincaid swallowed his pride. He posted his best Prozac smile on his face, stood, and moved, delicately, toward the chair. Although the doctor had proclaimed his patient healed, Kincaid still felt a little uneasy about moving with regard to the injury.

*****

When Kincaid returned to the contract company warehouse building in Fayetteville, North Carolina, he got the regular "wounded hero's" welcome from the other operators.

"Welcome home, hero," said one operator, in passing.

"Good to have you back, Kincaid," said another.

But after a few days sitting at his desk, it seemed like either he or the unit had changed. He couldn't quite identify what had transformed, and worse yet, he didn't know if it was them or he who had changed. He suspected he was the one who had changed, but he was suspicious and careful.

After the first two days, the greetings became epithets, which dwindled to normalcy within a week.

"Kincaid!" called Harris, from his office. The construction contractors had now finished putting in the final touches on his office, along with several other rooms in the building. But it still looked sterile, without anything to tell about the man who used the room to conduct his business.

"Sir!" Kincaid bellowed from down the hall.

"Get over here. We need to talk."

Harris was amazed at this young operator, but he had also noticed the man was smiling more constantly since their last op. He didn't like it. Snipers weren't supposed to smile, at least not on *his* teams.

Kincaid put down the box he had been returning to storage and walked to Harris' office with a sense of urgency.

"Sit," Harris commanded when Kincaid entered the small office.

Kincaid sat in the same metal folding chair that faced Harris' desk as he had, several months ago, with Ted Pineda beside him. He remained silent, waiting for the boss to speak. His work, his punctuality, and his attitude had been exemplary—especially since returning from the mission in Mexico. He had no reason to expect anything adverse to come.

Harris drummed on his desk with the eraser end of a mechanical pencil for several beats. He then stopped and looked up at Kincaid. "You haven't discussed anything about your time in Mexico after the Blackhawk flew away, leaving you to cover our six. Whatever happened, has changed the way you perform your duties. You seem more… distracted. Can you tell me what *that* is all about, and how we can get you *back*—mind and body?"

"What do you mean, sir?"

"Well, for starters, you *smile* far too much for a government-trained assassin. You also seem to enjoy the administrative part of this job far too much."

That was a frequent joke among operators, that said, *Government-trained assassins did not smile because their work was somber. So, they should be serious all the time.*

"Uh, sir?" Kincaid had not expected that question. He didn't have an answer prepared to give the boss. "I mean, I know what happened, and it was extraordinary. But I'm not sure how to explain it."

"So, you think I'm too *stupid* to understand. Right?"

"*No*, sir. I don't think I understand well enough to put it into words."

Harris drummed the pencil on his desk again. He did it for an entire minute before he stopped, sighed, and looked up at Kincaid. "If you want out," Harris said, "Say so. No one's forcing you to work with us. But don't expect me to make it easy for you." Harris's tone of voice had changed. He now sounded angry, instead of how he normally yelled at his people for show.

Kincaid pursed his lips. "Yes, sir," he whispered. "I'll submit my resignation this week. I just don't think I can *do* this work anymore."

Harris put down his pencil but kept the same tone in his voice. "Orson, you have an incredible amount of talent, and I'm not simply referring to your hand-eye coordination. Make sure this is what you want because there's no returning to this organization after running out on us."

Kincaid's heart sank. He furrowed his brow. "Thank you, sir… I'll let you know."

Harris picked up his pencil again and drummed once with it. "I'll give you your out-processing paperwork as soon as you give me your resignation. Do you have anything else for me?"

Kincaid stood and thought about it for a moment. "No, sir."

"You're dismissed," Harris said, harshly, almost as if Kincaid had betrayed him and the unit.

Kincaid hustled to the door and back to the cardboard box he had abandoned, earlier. He was elated and depressed at the same time. *Elated* because he was already planning his trip to Utah to talk with one of the LDS Church leaders, so he could get baptized. *Depressed* because he felt like he was leaving his entire adult life behind him—ten years, with nothing to show for it.

He had forgotten how perceptive Harris could be. Kincaid only now realized he must have telegraphed his soul-searching, soul-changing experience without even meaning to do so. He wondered if any of the others in the organization had noticed. He hoped not. Betrayal was not something he wanted them to remember him for.

Two days later, Kincaid submitted his resignation. He did not know what he would do on the outside, but he realized his time with Special Operations was over. He didn't want to experience another pucker-factor incident like he had survived in Mexico. So, it was time to go. His resignation papers from the contract company gave him ten working days to process out and be on his way.

*****

One week later, Kincaid received a letter from the post office, posted from Salt Lake City, Utah. The return address showed it had come from "The Office of the President of The Church of Jesus Christ of Latter-day Saints."

Before opening the envelope, at least a thousand questions flooded his mind: What was this all about? How did the LDS Church find him? Would they tell him not to bother trying to get baptized?

After gawking at the front of the envelope for several minutes, he finally opened it. The letter began: *"The President of The Church of Jesus Christ of Latter-day Saints requests the honor of your presence for a private discussion concerning the extraordinary circumstances surrounding your desire to become a member of the above-mentioned church."* The Prophet even signed his name to the letter. It didn't have any of the markings of a form letter. It seemed individually crafted.

Kincaid sat back in his chair with his mouth open. The letter in one hand dropped to his lap. The only thought he had now was that the missionaries in Mexico must have reported to their chain of command about their encounter with him. But he didn't think he had given them enough identifying information to find him.

He shook his head, guessing he had been wrong.

Returning to the letter, Kincaid saw it gave him a telephone number to arrange a specific appointment whenever he arrived in the Salt Lake City area.

This was turning out to be an exciting adventure. He decided to stay in his apartment for the rest of the month, give his landlord two weeks' notice, and leave at the beginning of the next month. That would give him enough time to plan his trip, arrange his finances, and make sure his truck was in good running condition for the twenty-one-hundred-mile journey. The only remaining problem was that he also had no one with whom he could talk to about the letter and its ramifications.

Then he realized, "There must be LDS Church members living in this area; after all, it's a worldwide religion. Maybe I could learn more about the Church by going to their worship service my last two Sundays in North Carolina."

~*Chapter Ten*~

Temple Square in Salt Lake City, Utah, was the equivalent of four city blocks in the middle of town. The square sat about four feet lower than the streets around it and included two office buildings of the LDS Church leadership and many of its administrative employees.

The buildings around the square ranged from the one-hundred-fifty-year-old Tabernacle to the more modern Church Office Building. The Square also had an abundance of trees, shrubs, and flowering plants and several reflection pools. Main Street ran north to south, but cut off at Temple Square, to keep traffic from running through the middle of the Square. Kincaid decided the entire Square was gorgeous, and wagered to himself that it would be gorgeous any time of the year.

Before former Army Sergeant First Class Orson Kincaid showed up for his appointment with the Prophet, he took a self-guided tour of Temple Square and the two Visitor Centers—North and South. His military and intelligence training still filled his mind and his heart, so he subconsciously sought for hiding places, surveillance cameras, dead zones, and escape routes. But he was also enjoying the uplifting spirit of the area. He grinned at the dichotomy of it all.

Kincaid walked inside the North Visitor Center for a moment and found himself transfixed, gazing at the Christus Statue in all its majesty.

"May I help you?" a young woman asked, as he stared at

the Statue.

"Uh, no, thank you. I'm just trying to take it all in." Kincaid snapped out of the warm reverie. Staring at the statue had suddenly made him aware of the other people around him.

"This statue brings out the deepest feelings in most people who stand in that very spot," she said, gesturing to Kincaid's feet.

"Yes, I'm *sure* it does," Kincaid mused.

"Are you a member of The Church of Jesus Christ of Latter-day Saints?" Two more sister missionaries had approached the visitor and one of them had asked the question.

Kincaid smiled. "Not yet, but I hope to be one, soon," he said. "Thank you for your kindness." He eyed them, for a moment, and realized they emanated the same spirit the missionaries in Mexico had about them.

"Have a wonderful day," the other sister said as Kincaid turned away from them. The three sister missionaries smiled as Kincaid turned and walked toward the exit.

While approaching the LDS Church Office Building, Kincaid remembered his visits to the Fayetteville First Ward in North Carolina, after his repatriation, and while he was waiting out his final weeks in that state. The first time he had entered the chapel for a worship service—Sacrament Meeting—he had been greeted like a lifetime member. That had been both good and bad. It felt good because it was like he was already a member of a grander family. That was what he needed because it made him feel like he was in the right place.

But it was also bad. Kincaid discovered right away that Mormons generally wanted to become his best friend within the first five minutes of meeting him. Their questions were innocent but penetrating and he always felt a little uncomfortable while speaking with them. He knew he couldn't tell them anything about his work with the Army while at Fort Bragg. In fact, he didn't *want* to tell them anything about his work because, he guessed, it would probably disgust them and make them shy away from him.

Kincaid started telling people he was not a member of the church but planned to rectify that error as soon as he returned home and could be baptized by his father. It was kind of a lie, but it was also kind of the truth. Kincaid felt like Salt Lake City would be his new home before he had even arrived. Although his real father would disown him even more for joining the LDS Church, his Father in Heaven was going to allow him to be baptized. So, in a way, he told the truth.

He consulted his smartphone as he approached the Church Office Building. He was going to be right on time if all went well. The building was a high-rise structure and, without stopping to count, Kincaid estimated it had between twenty-five and thirty floors. His military training had taught him to be a few minutes early or on time, but never late.

He stopped inside the doors and looked around. Everyone else in the building seemed to wear a coat and tie for the men and a dress or skirt and blouse for the women. In his navy-blue polo shirt and khaki cargo pants, he suddenly felt underdressed.

Two men in dark blazers, white shirts, and neckties approached him. The bulges at their waists told him they were discreet in the way they carried their concealed weapons. They came from the security checkpoint between the door and the elevators.

The checkpoint included a high-powered metal-detection gate, a state-of-the-art x-ray machine, and a single unadorned door nearby. That was probably where they took potential threats for a little friendly interrogation. Kincaid smiled to himself. The Church had gone to a lot of expense, making their high-tech equipment appear non-threatening.

"Good morning, sir," said an approaching guard, with a smile. "May I help you?" He held an electronic tablet in one hand at his side—the opposite side from his bulge.

As Kincaid walked toward the security station, the other

guard fell into step beside him. Kincaid took out a piece of paper from his cargo pants pocket. "I was told to come here to meet with the Prophet," he said, trying to sound casual while handing the paper to the guard with the tablet.

The checkpoint became quiet. Several of the guards scrutinized Kincaid before returning to their job of checking people entering the building.

The guard with the tablet scanned its top page, with care. "May I see your ID, sir?" the guard said.

Kincaid already had his North Carolina driver's license out and extended it toward the man.

The guard took the driver's license and matched it against the names on his paper until he found the right one. "Here we are, Brother Kincaid," the guard said.

"Oh, I'm not a *brother*, yet... until after I speak to him," Kincaid avowed with a smile, as he took back his driver's license and returned it to his wallet.

"Yes, sir," the supervisor said, as he waved toward another guard. "You're actually in the wrong building. Brother Everett, here, will show you the way to the Prophet's Office."

A third guard stepped forward. His slight build and ill-fitting suit made him appear younger, and less experienced. But his smile radiated that same good spirit that was so common among Mormons. Kincaid wondered how much security training members of the Church's security force received. Whatever it was, he thought it probably was more than enough, since assassins, saboteurs, and fanatics rarely attack churches.

"Good morning, sir. I'm Brother Everett," the new guard said as he extended his hand in greeting.

"Good morning, Brother Everett. How far do we have to go?" Kincaid asked.

"Oh, not far. Would you like to take the scenic route or the quickest route?"

Kincaid checked the time on his phone. He winced. "Well, I

will be late if we take the scenic route, so maybe I can come back another day for the tour."

"That's fine, sir. We'll take the underground route, and I'll try to get you there on time."

With that, Kincaid went through the metal detector and picked up a Visitor's Badge. Both men took the stairs down one floor and walked the halls of the underground garage beneath Temple Square.

Kincaid scrutinized the directional signs as they passed by them. "I guess this passage between buildings makes it easier in the winter months."

"You bet. It's also easier whenever it rains."

Kincaid looked over at Everett and decided he would go out on a limb. "If I may ask, how much security training do you guys get for this job?"

"Well, I'm an intern. But I'm studying Law Enforcement in college and hope to go to law school in a few years."

"Any marksmanship training?"

By reflex, the intern nudged the weapon on his hip. "Yes sir, but most of it is self-taught. How about you?"

Kincaid was surprised at the question. "I got out of the Army after ten years, so I've fired a few rounds downrange in my day. Do they give you any martial arts training?"

"No, but I hold black belts in Tae Kwan Do and Ju Jitsu from before I started working here."

"Do you *like* working here?" Kincaid asked.

"You bet. I have never felt the Spirit stronger in any of the other places I've worked."

The two men came to a set of stairs. They went up one floor and found themselves inside another building.

"What building is this?" Kincaid asked.

"This is the Church Administration Building. We call it the CAB. It's the older and smaller of the two buildings. The other building is the Church Office Building..."

" ... And you call it the COB?" Kincaid completed the explanation.

"Yes. We do," Brother Everett said with a big smile.

They came to a bank of elevators, pushed the up button, and waited. When the doors opened, they stepped inside, and Brother Everett pushed a button for the floor they wanted. They were alone in the elevator and faced the front, watching the numbers as they changed. The music piped into the elevator sounded like choir music.

When the doors opened again, Brother Everett led the way down a quiet hallway with a tiled floor. Outside one office door sat a man at a small desk who, oddly enough, seemed out of place. The man made a professional assessment of the visitor by looking at Kincaid up and down. In those few seconds, Kincaid felt like he had been assessed and judged not to be a security threat. He noticed a bulge under the man's left arm, which told him he was also a security guard. Could he be the Prophet's bodyguard? This man was large, muscular, and reeked of expert training and combat experience.

When the man nodded to the guard escorting Kincaid, they entered a modest carpeted office with one sofa and a coffee-type table with a few church magazines on it. One large picture on the wall was of Jesus standing in the sky; the other was of three elderly men. Kincaid recognized none of them but figured the one in the middle must be the Prophet.

The entire waiting room gave Kincaid a sense of unworthiness to enter. He started to panic, and his eyes filled with tears, but he couldn't understand why. He was confused, but he also had a feeling he wanted to return, often. Maybe that was what other church members meant when they bore their testimonies of faith, truth, and love.

One large desk rested in the middle of the room and a middle-aged male secretary sat behind it. He looked up with a stern face as they entered. Kincaid thought of leaving, under the man's glare, but realized if he ran, they would stop him, thinking he had committed a crime that made him run.

"Elder Hollister, this is Brother Kincaid," announced Brother Everett. "I believe he has an appointment to see the Prophet."

"Yes. Welcome, Brother Kincaid." The secretary stood and greeted him with an easy smile and a warm handshake. "We've been expecting you, although you are a few minutes late. Please have a seat, and the Prophet will be with you, momentarily." He motioned toward the sofa.

Brother Everett nodded at Kincaid and backed out of the office, looking around at everything as if it was the first time he had ever been there.

"I'm not a *brother*, yet," Kincaid said to Elder Hollister, trying hard not to give people any wrong impressions.

"Well, we can help you feel like family while you're here," Elder Hollister said with a voice that reflected more sincerity than his wrinkled face showed.

An aide rolled another elderly man into the office in his wheelchair and around to where he could leave a stack of papers for Elder Hollister. The man in the chair must have been in his late eighties or early nineties, thought Kincaid, judging by his wispy white hair, cavernous eyes, and myriads of wrinkles on his hands and face. The aide was a younger old man, maybe in his sixties. Kincaid smiled as the man in the wheelchair gazed in his direction. Then Kincaid snapped his head back to the wall with the picture of the three men and did a double take. This man in the wheelchair was a member of the First Presidency, so he *must* work with the Prophet every day.

The man placed a short stack of papers on Elder Hollister's desk. "These are the names of the brethren who will attend the new temple dedication in New Jersey," he said in a hoarse, but soft voice.

"Why thank you, President," Elder Hollister said in a soft

tone.

The elderly man again fixed his eyes on Kincaid. Without saying a word, the aide rolled the wheelchair over to him. Kincaid considered standing, but he didn't want to look down at the man who could not stand. So, he sat forward on the edge of the sofa.

The wrinkled old man extended his hand toward Kincaid, who met the hand and carefully shook it. The proffered hand was cold and weak, but there was another kind of strength in it and his piercing eyes that Kincaid couldn't pinpoint. Yet, he felt a friendly warmth from the cold hand which filled him with a self-confidence with which he was not familiar.

The elderly man held onto Kincaid's hand longer than most handshakes. He opened his mouth and spoke in almost a whisper. Not as if he wanted to share a secret, but as if he could only speak that loud. "You are a good man," he said without introduction. "You can be forgiven of *everything* in your past if you will forsake it and embrace your Savior."

Kincaid reflected on how uncomfortable such an occurrence would have made him feel two years ago. But he felt nothing except love and gratitude for this man—whose name he didn't even know.

"Thank you," Kincaid said. "That's why I came here."

"I know," the elderly man affirmed as he released Kincaid's hand from his grip. He waggled one gnarled finger at Kincaid as his aide moved his wheelchair backward. "You will be the means of saving many lives and even more souls before the Lord is finished with you." He chuckled and winked as the aide turned the chair and rolled it out into the hallway.

As if on cue, the Prophet's office door opened, and a large man filled the doorway. He wore a dark gray dress suit which looked impeccable on him. The twinkle in his eye, when he saw Kincaid, warmed him starting from the inside and working its way down his limbs. Any fears or reluctance Kincaid might have had before now were gone, the instant he saw the Prophet.

He walked over to Kincaid, who jumped to his feet and immediately extended his hand. The large man stepped past the extended hand and embraced the younger man with both arms. Kincaid was not the hugging type and usually kept his greetings to simple handshakes. But he did not feel awkward in this man's embrace. He went to return the hug and found he could not put his arms around the man—there was too much of him.

The Prophet pulled back and left one arm around Kincaid's shoulder as he ushered him into his office. "I understand you met two of our missionaries in Mexico a few months ago, Brother Kincaid. Is that right?"

"Yes, sir," Kincaid replied. "That's why I'm here. But I'm not a brother yet… "

"Nonsense," the Prophet interrupted. "We're all children of God, so we are officially and automatically brothers and sisters, even though we may not know each other well. So, let's see about fixing that lack of familiarity, now." He motioned Kincaid to sit in a rich leather easy chair and sat on the forward edge of a matching easy chair facing the younger man. "In all my years, I have never heard a conversion story quite as lively as yours. But I haven't yet heard all the details. Tell me what led you to your meeting with the missionaries in Mexico, and what happened that made you believe their testimonies."

Elder Hollister closed the office door from the outside, leaving the two men alone. Kincaid heard the hum of the air circulation system and marveled at how quiet the room was, almost as if the rest of the world was far, far away.

He swallowed a lump in his throat, trying to consider what to tell the Prophet and what to leave out as classified information.

Taking a deep breath, Kincaid let it out, slowly. He told the Prophet about growing up in St. David, Arizona; how his partner and friend had been killed during an operation; how the operation had gone wrong, and how he had to run for his life, into the missionaries' apartment.

When Kincaid got to the part about barging into the missionaries' apartment, the Prophet slapped his knee and roared in laughter. "I wish I could have seen their faces," he said. "They wrote and told me they had been praying for a person or family to teach when you stormed through their door."

"I didn't know *that* part," Kincaid said, smiling as he was infected by the Prophet's contagious laughter.

The part Kincaid found so fascinating was that the Prophet listened to everything he said. Sitting on the edge of his seat, the man listened, as if for the first time, to a prodigal son upon his return, where the prodigal had failed on his own and returned to his family, instead of starving. He seemed to want to understand how to love this young man, effectively.

In the silence, the Church President relaxed his smile. "You have led the kind of life that damages and destroys weaker people. I am glad you survived it. I'm also glad you came to see me today." He took a deep breath, all the while staring at Kincaid as if pondering a vital point. "How many people have you *killed* in combat who were not trying to kill you?"

The question had come out of nowhere. Kincaid gripped the arms of his chair as a sudden wave of vertigo washed over him. That question had always haunted him when anyone outside of the unit asked it because it was always based on morbid curiosity. He had always shied away from a true answer, but he sensed the Prophet had not asked out of any sense of morbidity or idle curiosity.

Kincaid stared into the Prophet's eyes. They were glistening. Was it tears? "Thirty-one," Kincaid said, dipping his head, unable to look the Prophet in the eyes when he said it. "Why did you ask that question?" he asked, in a weak voice, with his eyes still on the carpeted floor in front of him.

The Prophet reached forward with one hand and placed it on Kincaid's shoulder. "Although you lowered your head in humility and shame at your answer, I also sensed a degree of pride," the Prophet explained. "Am I right?"

Kincaid nodded. "We always keep track of our confirmed kills. The higher the number, the more assignments we got and the faster the numbers would grow. So, yes, I guess there is a little pride there," he conceded. He didn't want to keep anything from the man of God in front of him.

"That is all behind you now, and the numbers will return to zero once you are baptized and forgiven of your sins. Have you forgiven yourself, yet?"

"I....don't know how to do that, sir," Kincaid said as if his salvation depended upon knowing how to forgive himself. "I need to know that Christ has forgiven me, so I can forgive myself and wash it away."

The Prophet looked down at his own hands, seeming to ponder the answer. "That is a common issue of those who feel their sins are too gross or too many to be forgiven. Believe me, when I say, it is possible—*after* you have forgiven yourself, been baptized, forego your pride and that business behind you."

The Prophet stood, walked behind Kincaid, and placed his large hands on the younger man's shoulders, pulling him back into the easy chair. "I believe there have been several times in your life when you have been protected and saved by the grace of God, Brother Kincaid. The Lord has a work for you to do," he said, patting Kincaid's shoulder once. "What is your complete name?"

"Orson Hunter Kincaid." He wondered why the Prophet had asked.

Without another word, the Prophet placed both hands on Kincaid's head, pronounced his name, stated his authority, and gave the young penitent sinner an extensive and personal blessing—a blessing through a prophet of God, from his Heavenly Father.

Kincaid had never received a priesthood blessing before— let alone a blessing from the Prophet himself. He listened intently and tried to memorize the words. But when the Prophet said 'Amen,' all he could remember was the full and rich feeling in his heart. He felt like only the Prophet's hands kept him from floating away, or as if a heavy burden had been lifted from his shoulders, allowing him to move more easily and freely.

They spoke for several more minutes and Kincaid told the Prophet the burden he had carried since childhood and how it had affected and harmed his relationship with his father.

The Prophet gave Kincaid more guidance. "I think you would be more comfortable waiting, before we conduct your baptism, until you have taken care of your business with your parents, and learned how to forgive yourself," he said, softly. "What do you think?"

Kincaid thought about what the Prophet had just said. Somehow, he already knew it to be true and best for him. "I don't understand how to go about doing *that* either," Kincaid said.

"You already know God knows you. He has protected and preserved you for a purpose. But he hasn't told me what that purpose is. Now you need to learn as much as you can about the doctrines of the Gospel of Jesus Christ and tie up those loose ends from your past. When you are ready, come back to see me. I will tell Elder Hollister you have a standing appointment whenever you come by. You just have to catch me when I'm in my office. The Lord's work does not allow me to remain here for long."

Kincaid nodded his head. He had come expecting to get a piece of paper authorizing his baptism. But he left with an intangible gift considerably more valuable—a determination to *earn* that piece of paper, and the understanding of what he had to do to earn it.

*****

A few minutes later, Kincaid and the Prophet both came out of the office, with big smiles on their faces. They embraced again, and Kincaid decided if that was how happy he would feel if the Savior ever embraced him, he would do whatever it took to be worthy of that.

"Brother Kincaid, I'm sure your contribution to the kingdom will be substantial," the Prophet said. "Get with your new bishop this week and let him know what you are working on."

"As soon as I find a job, I'll get an apartment and I'll know where my new ward is."

"You need work?" the Prophet inquired with sudden interest.

"The Lord will provide," Kincaid replied, meaning it with all his heart.

"Yes, He will. In fact, with your background and experience, I'm sure we could find a spot for you in our Personal Services Department. Interested?"

Kincaid had no other plans, but a job in an office called "Personal Services" sounded boring. He wanted to turn it down, but the Prophet had just made salvation possible for him by lighting the path. Kincaid didn't know how to turn down such an offer—especially when he *needed* a job. "Yes, sir. I'd appreciate it."

"Elder Hollister," the Prophet said, turning and looking at his secretary. "Call Brother Tanner and tell him an applicant is coming over—with me as a personal and professional reference."

Elder Hollister smiled. "Yes, President. I'll make that call, then print out an application for Brother Kincaid, give it to you for signature, and show him the way to Personal Services." He rattled off each point as if this kind of administrative leap happens every day.

Elder Hollister immediately turned toward his keyboard and started typing.

The Prophet waved one more time, then returned to his office.

"Excuse me," Kincaid addressed Elder Hollister. "I heard you call the Prophet 'President,' didn't I?"

"Yes, he's the President of the Church of Jesus Christ of Latter-day Saints. Although he is a prophet, seer, and revelator, we address him and his two counselors as 'Presidents.'"

"Thank you." Kincaid nodded, thoughtfully. He sat in the Prophet's waiting room while he waited for the application to be signed and returned to him. When he left the office with Elder Hollister, Kincaid held the signed application as if it were a sacred document.

"I am sure there are going to be quite a few new pieces of information about the Church you will learn in the next several weeks," Elder Hollister said, with a wink.

~Chapter Eleven~

Elder Hollister took Kincaid to the elevator and they rode it down to the first basement. He then pointed the direction toward the elevator up to the COB. "Take that elevator up to level…"

Just then, another young security guard dressed in khaki slacks, white shirt, and a navy-blue blazer, walked by. "Excuse me, Brother, would you please take Brother Kincaid to see Director Tanner?"

The guard looked from Elder Hollister to the unfamiliar face and smiled. "Yes, of course, sir."

The Prophet's Secretary bid Kincaid farewell. He then turned to walk back to his office.

The guard shook Kincaid's hand and walked with him to the Office of Personal Services. This time, Kincaid did not ask the guard any questions, and the guard opened no conversation between them. They traced the same route back to the COB and took the elevator up to what felt like a long ride before getting out. They walked a short way down a long corridor; the guard turned and invited Kincaid to enter the small waiting room with a silent wave of his arm.

"If you'll wait here, Sister Christian will assist you." The guard then gestured to a woman sitting at her desk and left, to return to his duties. "Good luck, Brother Kincaid."

Kincaid nodded to the departing guard and handed his referral to the Director's secretary. "Hello, Sister Christian. I'm looking for Brother Tanner," Kincaid said, trying to sound like a regular church member.

Sister Christian took the paper and glanced at it. She caught her breath, placed the form on a clipboard, and handed it back to Kincaid. The form was blank except for the Prophet's signature where it asked for personal references and again for professional references. "Please fill in the rest of the form, and I will inform Director Tanner you're here for an interview," she said, pointing to a nearby padded chair.

Kincaid used a pen lying on the table in front of him. As he filled in the blanks on the form, he knew he could not include the facts of his entire ten-year military career. Where the form asked for his training, he included his Special Forces training, intelligence, counterterrorism, and sniper training. For his experience, he wrote he had four years of experience deployed as a sniper. That would be all he could tell them. He hoped they wouldn't ask for more information, knowing it would sound lame for him to reply, *"I'm sorry, that is classified."*

Kincaid had just finished filling out the application form when the Director's office door opened. A man on the high-end of middle age with short, dark, graying hair stepped through the door and handed some papers to his secretary. He was dressed like an executive and walked with the confidence only law enforcement or combat experience could have given him—he seemed to have a tired edge about him. His coat was unbuttoned, exposing the beginnings of an ample belly. A bulge at his right hip told Kincaid this man was armed. He judged the Director could probably handle himself in a fight. But why put such a man in a position to direct a no-action service? And why did *he* carry a weapon inside church headquarters?

The Director eyed Kincaid, perhaps trying to see what the Prophet had seen in him that would qualify him for a job with the Service. With just a hint of a smile, he stopped in front of Kincaid and extended his right hand in greeting. "Hi, I'm

Jedediah Tanner," the Director said with a broadening, over-used smile.

Kincaid stood, reached out, and took the extended hand. "I'm Orson Kincaid."

"Orson is a good Mormon name," Tanner said. "Has your family been in the church for long?"

Kincaid chuckled to himself. "No sir. No one in my family is in the church, but I will be baptized sometime within the next year. I interviewed with the Prophet a few minutes ago."

"You don't have a temple recommend?"

"No, sir."

"Employees are usually current temple recommend holders."

"I'm sorry, sir. I'll get one as soon as I can."

Tanner scowled and gestured for Kincaid to come with him. He then walked toward his private office.

Kincaid followed him through the door and surveyed the conservative office. The windows looked out onto Temple Square. Everything in the office was neat and orderly. The desk was almost bare except for an electronic tablet off to one side and a land-line telephone on the other. A small stack of papers loomed in the middle of the desk as if he had been working on them.

Director Tanner's '*I-love-me'wall* had a certificate from the Utah Police Academy, a photograph of himself in a grip-and-grin with a member of the Quorum of Twelve—Kincaid didn't know which one, but he knew he was an apostle—and another photograph of him standing beside the younger President George Bush. A small bust of a Green Beret sat on the shelf along the same wall with a pair of dog tags lying in front.

Tanner walked around his desk and turned the papers upside down. He sat and gestured for Kincaid to sit in the only other chair in the office. He reached out his hand for Kincaid's application.

Although not bid to do so, Kincaid surrendered it to him and took a seat, himself.

Director Tanner looked over the application. At one point, he drew in a slow, deep breath, and let it out with a sigh. He eyed Kincaid and tried to give him the same penetrating look-into-your-soul glance the Prophet had used. On Tanner, it didn't quite have the same effect, but Kincaid could tell the attempt was not new to him.

"I see no law enforcement experience on your resumé," Tanner said, matter-of-factly.

"No, sir." Kincaid didn't elaborate. "Why would I need law enforcement experience to work a desk job for the Church?"

Tanner disregarded the remark and continued with his questions. "One of the most basic requirements for a job anywhere in this building is a temple recommend. You said you aren't even baptized, yet. Did the Prophet say why he thought you were qualified to work for the Service?"

Kincaid had heard that twice now and guessed *The Service* was the nickname for the Church Personal Services Department. "No, sir," he reiterated, again without elaboration. The Prophet had told him he would not have to mention his work in the Army ever again.

It was the temple recommend issue that worried him. If he had to have one of those, he wouldn't qualify for the job until sometime *after* he was baptized. He wasn't sure how he would get around that point unless the Prophet's reference *trumped* the recommend.

Tanner put out both hands in front of him with his palms up. "You've got to give me more to go on, Brother Kincaid," he said, almost sounding like he was begging.

"I just got out of the Army," Kincaid said.

The Director leaned forward in his seat. "Good. What was your MOS?" he asked, referring to the military occupational specialties all soldiers have.

"I was an 18-series, guy," Kincaid said, hoping Tanner would recognize the Special Forces MOS and drop it there.

"Yeah?" Tanner said, keeping his voice even. "I also have special forces experience." What group were you in?"

Here's where it would get sticky, if Kincaid didn't shut it down, soon. "I worked for Special Operations Command," he said, glancing again at the small bust on the shelf. "Which group were you in, sir?" he inquired.

Tanner sat back in his chair. "I was with the First of the First, in Okinawa," he said, putting one hand up to his chin.

"So, you worked in Southeast Asia?"

"Yes," Tanner confessed. "The Philippines and Malaysia."

"First Group is a good group. I jumped into Mindanao twice for asymmetrical warfare operations—Operation Balikatan."

"Yes, I've heard of it, but I never took part. You said asymmetrical operations?"

"Yes, sir. I believe in your day it was called unconventional warfare."

Tanner let the reference to his age slide. "Oh, yes. Well, after six years, I got out of the Army and went to work with another government agency," Tanner added.

The phrase Other Government Agency—or OGA—was spook-speak for CIA. That told Kincaid all he needed to know about the Chief of the Church's Personal Services. He was the *real deal*. Kincaid suddenly wanted this job more than anything, even if it was just pushing papers. But why would Tanner work in a boring, service-oriented job?

Tanner smiled, took a deep breath, and stared down at the completed job application still sitting in front of him. "We have one opening, but I'm afraid it may prove too boring, compared to your military training and experience. You might have *too* much combat experience for this kind of position.

Kincaid shook his head once. "I'm not looking for excitement, sir," he said. "I'm trying to leave all that behind me."

"Okay, you're hired," Tanner said, pursing his lips. He stood and picked up the application. "I'll show you to your new desk and take you to the Personnel Office to start your in-processing. That should take you two full days, but don't worry. No one will steal your seat in the meantime." He finished with a smile.

As they stepped into the main foyer, Kincaid saw a young lady coming out of a small office down the hall. She was in her late twenties, with honey brown hair pulled back into a tight ponytail. She turned and walked about twenty feet ahead of Director Tanner and Kincaid.

"Oh, Special Agent Parker?" Tanner called to the woman.

She stopped and turned toward them, giving Kincaid a cursory glance. She glanced back at Director Tanner with a smile of recognition. Kincaid also noticed her puppy-dog eyes that looked like they could turn into the eyes of a military working dog whenever she needed them.

Tanner gestured toward his neophyte. "I'd like you to meet Orson...uh," he turned to look at his new-hire with suddenly vacant eyes.

"Kincaid."

"Yes, of course. Orson Kincaid. This is FBI Special Agent Haley Parker. She's our liaison officer from the FBI office in Salt Lake City."

Both Parker and Kincaid smiled and shook hands in greeting.

"Pleased to meet you," Parker said.

"Same here." Kincaid noted her handshake was firm, but not like she had to prove she was as strong as he was. He liked that. A medium-strength handshake meant the woman was confident in her abilities and didn't feel threatened by the men working around her.

"Brother Kincaid will fill the void at that empty desk in your office," Tanner said. "So, meet your new partner."

Parker tensed. Her smile became colder, and more passed on. "Oh, good. I'll take the few boxes of books and office supplies off the desk, so you can move in as soon as you're ready."

Kincaid didn't believe she was happy about the sudden partnership. "Don't hurry. I understand it will take me two days to in-process." Once again, Kincaid had more questions than answers. Why would a paper-pushing department need an FBI Special Agent for a liaison officer? And why would Kincaid and she be teamed up to do *desk work* together? Neither of those questions made a lick of sense to Kincaid. So far, it did not add up to a boring desk job, but he couldn't put his finger on precisely what kind of work it was going to be.

"All the same, I'll clear it off, so you can move in when you're ready."

Tanner pointed to the small office out of which Parker had just come. "This will be your new office," he said to Kincaid. He turned toward the elevator. "You two can get to know each other, later. Right now, I have to get him to Personnel," he told Parker.

"Nice meeting you," Parker said to Kincaid, nodding, curtly.

"Same here." Kincaid sensed this handshake was softer and less caring.

*****

Even before he checked in and picked up the keys to his new apartment, Kincaid drove to Sugar House Park and jogged around the loop. He had conducted a Google Maps recon of the Salt Lake Valley and determined he would prefer to live in this community. His jog confirmed the decision. The nearby park had been an attraction for him, to avoid driving miles for his exercise. He had studied the park's trail map beforehand to avoid getting lost.

Once he started running, Kincaid realized he would not have to worry about losing his way. The white lines on the road for vehicles also showed where the runners' and cyclists' lanes were, so he couldn't go astray. What he hadn't counted on was the change of elevation from Fort Bragg to the Wasatch Front. Before he had run his first mile, he started sucking wind, like an amateur, and was forced to slow down to catch his breath.

By force of habit, he always ran through his new neighborhoods to familiarize himself with his new stomping grounds. Where were the picnic areas? The restrooms and parking lots? Those were the areas of interest to him. Where were the neighborhoods most likely to be used by drug dealers and other shady characters? Those were the areas he wanted to stay away from.

He chuckled to himself as he thought about shady characters in Salt Lake City. *Heck! This is Zion!* Then he remembered the radio newscast he had listened to on the drive to the park. Zion seemed to have the same kind of crime and lowlifes that plagued the rest of the world. *Maybe there weren't as many bad guys here*, he thought, with a wince. He could only hope.

*****

Kincaid called the moving and storage company on the same day he moved into Hidden Hollow Apartments, in Sugar House, Utah, to have his belongings delivered. They said it would take two weeks for the shipment to arrive. He had the money to get settled in his new job and apartment, but until then, he would have to do without all of his creature comforts pending the arrival of his belongings.

Kincaid used the key to open his first apartment in the civilian world. He walked into a bare, two-bedroom, fourth-floor apartment with tile floors and bare windows. He shut the door, dropped his duffel bag, and toured his new digs. Shaking his head, he confessed to himself, it had looked better when he toured the model apartment the manager kept open. It was much like the unmarried, senior enlisted barracks on the military bases he had inhabited. At least this time, he didn't have to share it with any other people, so he was content.

His new dwelling appeared clean and in good repair. The apartment came with a full-sized refrigerator, a four-burner gas stove, and a full-sized oven with a space on the counter for a microwave. A map to the laundry room in the basement where everyone used the same quarter-eating washers and dryers, completed his map recon of the place. He smirked. A good many customs were the same in both worlds, it seemed—military and civilian.

He slid open the double glass doors to the patio, off the small dining room, and looked out over his new kingdom. Once again, he cased the place for likely escape routes and hiding places for his weapons. The fourth floor was too high to jump from, but the balconies all had rails he could use to get down, in an emergency. The ledge of the kitchen counter was wide enough for him to hide one of his handguns—not that he would ever need anything like that while working for the *Service*. But he had lived a dangerous life for too long to put it all behind him, in a single day.

Since his talk with the Prophet, Kincaid realized he would have to plan a trip back home, to southeast Arizona, in the near future. His sister would probably give him her famous flying hug that could choke a bear. His mother would probably fret that he was too thin and needed to eat more home cooking.

It would probably surprise his father to see he still drove the same pickup truck he'd had in high school. But, if the past was any sign of the future, his father would not spend much time talking with his only son.

So far, Kincaid had seen a lot of other pickup trucks on the Utah roads, but not so much in the Church Office Building parking lots. He held his jaw firm, refusing to sell the truck. He realized if he was to ever reconcile with his father, retaining the truck would be one factor in his favor. After all, his father had given him the truck for his seventeenth birthday.

It was Saturday and all his clothes were dirty. Kincaid ran out to his truck to get a handful of quarters, took his duffle bag down to the laundry room, and loaded two of the ten machines—whites and darks. "Well, well, well," said a sultry voice near the door. Kincaid turned and saw a lady— in her late 30s and wearing heavy makeup—standing in the doorway, carrying a basketfull of dirty underclothes. She was conducting a different kind of visual assessment of him than the Prophet, Director, or even Special Agent Parker had conducted. "Hi," he said with a Prozac smile, as he closed both lids and pushed the start buttons.

Her long blonde hair cascaded over one shoulder and revealed one big hoop hanging from the visible ear. She sauntered into the room and placed her basket on the machine beside a washing machine Kincaid wasn't using, all the while, staring at him—appraising him for value. He had only attended meetings on one Fast Sunday, but her stare made him feel like a cheeseburger on fast Sunday.

Once she put her basket down, Kincaid could see she wore fancy, tan-colored, skintight leggings, and a light blue leotard with cheap, clear plastic high heels on her otherwise bare feet, with a delicate gold chain around one ankle.

Kincaid stared back at her, but with less appraisal in his eyes. "My name is Kincaid," he said, softly.

"I'm Lauren. Nice to meet you, Kincaid," she said as she loaded her machine. "You're new here, aren't you?"

"Yep. Just arrived today." He wanted to be friendly with his new neighbors, but this one made him feel uneasy. An idea suddenly popped into his head. "What time do worship services start on Sunday? And where's the chapel?" he asked with an innocent smile.

The combined questions were like a one-two punch, taking the wind out of Lauren's sails. She sneered at him. "The Westminster Young Singles Ward meets at the chapel across the highway from here, 10:00 am to noon." She pointed to the piece of paper on the wall that gave the same information. The paper included the name of Bishop Carson Brock and a telephone number. "Follow the trail of people from here at about 9:30." She looked him up and down again, shaking her head. "I'd never have figured you for a Mormon."

"Really? Why not?"

"You just seem... different."

"This is Utah." Kincaid was surprised at her attitude. "Isn't everyone Mormon?"

She closed the lid, pushed the button, and started toward the door. "First time in Utah, honey?" she asked, shaking her head.

"Yep, and looking forward to every day, too."

Her eye suddenly turned sad. "You *look* like a nice guy. Don't let the church change that."

Kincaid suddenly saw a different side of her he hadn't expected. For just one quick moment, she had dropped the baby doll routine. "What do you mean?" he asked.

She modestly bent down to get another load of her clothes from a dryer. "I mean, don't let the social side of the church become the reason you keep going. People can be brutal when they think no one else is paying attention."

Kincaid squinted as he studied her. The last he saw of Lauren, she walked out the door, with her basket full of dried clothes that had finished before Kincaid started his laundry. She looked back once more and smiled when she caught him watching her.

Although Kincaid did not appreciate the exchange, at least he got the intelligence out of her he needed: location of the chapel and times of the meetings. Now, all he needed was a suit of Sunday-go-to-meeting clothing.

*****

He hated to drive back into the city on Saturday afternoon, but he needed to purchase clothing for church. He remembered seeing a clothing store right around the corner from the COB. What was it called? Mister Mac's? It seemed to have a lot of men's clothing in the window, and Kincaid figured he couldn't go wrong if he bought his clothes from the same place the general authorities purchased theirs.

That evening, after completing ninety minutes of shopping in Mister Mac's, Kincaid lugged his purchases back to his truck. A young salesman inside had offered to help him carry his bags, but Kincaid said he would manage. The salesman had done a good job and had probably earned a whopping commission off the new kid in town, but, out of habit, Kincaid schlepped everything by himself.

~Chapter Twelve~

Sunday morning, Kincaid drove to the chapel. What would have been a two-block stroll turned into a ten-minute drive, trying to find a way across the highway, without getting lost. Then, when he saw the chapel's full parking lot, he had to search for a parking spot. In the Sugar House Chapel, there was one ward's meetings starting at 9:00 am, his ward started at 11:30 am, and another ward started at 2:00 pm. The parking lot was too small to accommodate all the individuals and families who drove. Many of them just had to walk the distance of one or two city blocks to the chapel, anyway. He determined his own two feet would be his mode of travel to church on Sundays from now on.

As Kincaid approached the door to the building, he heard the steps of someone behind him, so he pulled the door open and stepped aside to hold it for the next person. As he turned to look at the recipient of his gallantry, his mouth fell open. "Special Agent Parker?"

"Kincaid? What are you doing here?"

"This is my new ward. I took an apartment across the highway." He gestured in the direction of his new apartment building, then motioned for her to enter while he held the door for her.

As soon as they were both in the lobby, she tugged on his shirt sleeve and took him aside. "Lay off the *special agent* stuff with these people. Okay?"

"Why? It's not as if you're undercover."

"No. But it's hard enough to get a date in this singles ward, without everyone expecting me to flash my badge and frisk them before accepting an invitation to dinner."

"What do you tell anyone who asks about where you work?"

"I just say I work in Church Headquarters. Most people think that means some kind of administrative job for the Church, so they don't ask any additional questions."

Kincaid nodded his understanding. "So, I guess you also live in this part of town?"

"I know. Right? There must be fifty singles wards in the Salt Lake City area. How did you happen to pick the same one I was in?"

"I don't know. Just fate, I suppose. So, what do we do, first?"

Parker started walking through the foyer to the chapel doors. Kincaid followed her. "The first meeting is Sacrament Meeting. So, everyone goes into the chapel for announcements, business, the passing of the bread and water, and inspirational talks."

"Sounds like the ward, back home." He stopped after several steps inside the chapel and stood still. The folding wall between the chapel and cultural hall was open, and five rows of folding chairs were set up to accommodate the number of attending members in the singles ward.

"Home? I thought you weren't a member."

"I'm not. But I attended meetings for two weeks in the Fayetteville First Ward in North Carolina."

"How does *that* work? Not being a member, I mean."

Kincaid started fidgeting, then quickly changed the subject. "Say, I need to talk with the bishop. Where would I find him?"

"Oh, yes, Bishop Brock..." Parker turned, craning her neck, looking around the chapel for him.

Without warning, a heavy hand landed on Kincaid's shoulder from behind. By reflex, Kincaid grabbed the hand, spun, and locked the elbow, twisted it behind the back of the owner, driving him to his knees. He stopped himself just short of snap-kicking his assailant in the throat.

"Orson!" Parker exclaimed, grabbing his sleeve.

The efficient but short-lived violence in the chapel earned immediate and total silence from everyone within eyesight. Even the organist—who had been playing the spiritual prelude music—stopped and stared at him in shock.

As soon as he realized what he had done, Kincaid relaxed, let go of the hand he held in an arm-bar, and glanced around him. The other ward members were gawking at him with open mouths.

"Uh, Orson Kincaid, meet Bishop Carson Brock. Bishop this is Brother Kincaid," Parker said, not knowing how the Bishop would respond to the sudden violence.

The man in a dark suit straightened up, turned around, and smiled, trying to ignore the pain in his elbow and shoulder. "I heard a new young man had moved into this area, but I wasn't sure you would know about our meeting schedule in time to join us, today," Bishop Brock said to Kincaid, as he rubbed his arm to work out the kinks. "Sorry I snuck up on you like that, Brother Kincaid. I should have known better."

Kincaid was stunned into silence, aghast at what he had just done. He wanted to run, to hide, to get away from his embarrassment. "No, no, I'm the one who should apologize," Kincaid stammered. "I haven't been away from the military long enough to forget the muscle memory, I guess."

Bishop Brock moved forward and extended a conciliatory hand toward his new ward member. When Kincaid put out his own hand, they shook, and Bishop Brock threw his left arm around him in a warm embrace. "Nothing to worry about," he said, as he turned and walked toward the front of the chapel with his arm still around his newest lamb.

Kincaid looked back at Parker. She motioned for him to go, and she would find a seat with friends.

"The ward members may be a little stand-offish now until they get to know you better," Bishop Brock said with a low chuckle. "I'm sure *none* of them will approach you from behind."

Both men stopped short of the steps to the podium. Kincaid checked around him, not knowing what he was supposed to do, now.

"*You* can sit anywhere you want," Bishop Brock said. "Bishops have assigned seating. We'll talk more after the second meeting. Okay? So, stick around after the last *amen*." He slapped Kincaid once more on the shoulder, let go, and walked to his seat, still massaging his tender elbow and shoulder.

Kincaid nodded, still numb from his initial exchange with his new priesthood leader, and took a seat in the shorter side pew, second row from the front.

True to the bishop's prediction, members smiled and nodded at him in the minutes before the meeting started, but no one else came to introduce themselves to him and no one sat within three rows of him during sacrament meeting.

*****

After Sacrament Meeting, Kincaid followed the largest group of young adults and ended up in the Relief Society Room for the Sunday School Class. The room filled in just minutes, except for the front row. It remained empty. He figured that must be a Mormon idiosyncrasy, so he looked at an empty seat in the second row, beside his new partner at work.

"May I sit down?" he asked Parker.

"Yes, please," she replied with an easy smile.

As soon as Kincaid settled into the cushioned folding chair, he looked at her and suddenly could not think of anything to say. After a few uncomfortable moments, Kincaid opened his mouth to speak, but stopped again, when a man stood at the front of the room.

"Good morning, brothers and sisters," said the instructor. "Welcome to Sunday School. I see we have at least one new member in our midst. Would you mind standing and introducing yourself, so we can avoid tittering during the class among the young sisters, wondering who you are?" He gestured toward Kincaid with a tight smile.

Kincaid stood and rubbed the sweaty palms of both hands on his pants. He glanced down at Parker, who smiled at him with encouragement. "Uh, my name is Orson Kincaid. I was born in St. David, Arizona, but I recently got out of the Army and found a job at Church Headquarters. I live just across the highway," he said, motioning out the window toward his place. He paused and looked at the instructor. "Is there anything I missed? I mean, I've never done this before."

"I suppose you could add your cell phone number or your Snapchat," said the instructor with a wry smile.

"Uh," Kincaid began, his face flushing.

"I was just joking, Brother Kincaid. Welcome to our ward."

With that, Kincaid took his seat, again.

Parker leaned to the side and nudged him, like a punch to the arm, but with her shoulder. "You did that well," she whispered.

Saying nothing, Kincaid nodded and pulled out his iPad, as the instructor presented the lesson for the day.

*****

After Sunday School class, Kincaid walked out with Parker. She held her scriptures with one hand, against her breast.

"I'm not sure where the bishop's office is located," he said, as they entered the busy hallway. "I'm supposed to meet him for an interview. Can you point the way?"

"Sure. I'll even walk you there," she replied, changing direction.

Kincaid quickly caught up with her and strolled at her side.

They both walked in silence, with only the noise of the children from another ward going to their Primary classes.

When they passed the Primary rooms, Kincaid had to dodge one little child who was running and seemed to be late.

Kincaid did a double take as he saw a woman exiting, who looked somewhat like the woman he had met in the laundry room. Her name was Lauren. But this woman looked quite a bit more conservative than Lauren had been in her skin-patterned leotards and hoop earrings. Could it actually *be* Lauren?

"How is it you are *not* a member of the Church, yet most church employees *have* to be members with a temple recommend getting hired?" Parker asked.

"I had an interview with the Prophet, and he offered me the job. I mean, I needed the job, and I didn't want to turn him down, so I took it."

"And how come you haven't been baptized, yet?"

Kincaid shrugged his shoulders. "My best friend was a Mormon when I was growing up, and we became partners in the Army." Kincaid tried to smile.

"And he didn't *convert* you?"

Kincaid laughed uneasily. "He always tried. But when he saw how angry I got every time he brought it up, he stopped. That's when he became my *best* friend."

Two padded folding chairs were sitting at the end of the hallway, across from the bishop's office door. The door was closed. Parker sat first, gesturing for Kincaid to sit in the chair beside her. "We'll wait here until he comes out. Then you can go inside."

"Where is he, now?" Parker asked.

"The Bishop?" Kincaid grinned, playfully.

"No. Your best friend."

Kincaid got a vacant stare on his face. "He died in my arms a few months ago." As the words spilled from his mouth, he remembered the blood and wiped the palms of his hands on his trousers without thought. He suddenly recalled the smells of the sweat, the blood, and the early morning desert air.

"That's horrible! What happened?"

Kincaid adjusted his position in the folding chair, deciding it was not as comfortable as he thought it would be when he sat down. The picture of Ted's body on the chopper slammed into his head, and he flinched. "Can we talk about another subject?"

"Uh, yes! Sure. I'm sorry. I let my curiosity overwhelm my sense of decency."

Kincaid studied a picture on the wall beside the door to the Bishop's office. It was a painting of a temple of the Church. Grasping for another topic, he landed on that. "Have you been to the temple?"

Parker looked confused, then followed his stare to the picture on the wall. "I've been going since I was twelve. Why?"

"I bet it's beautiful inside, isn't it?"

Parker also stared at the picture and smiled. "Yes, it is." Pleasant memories of her temple service instantly came back to her.

"Once a person becomes a member of the Church, when can they go to the temple?"

"Well, after baptism, talk to the Bishop about getting a temple recommend interview—so he can decide whether you're worthy to go to the temple."

"When can I talk to the Bishop, to do that?"

"You have to wait a year, to make sure your testimony is strong enough."

"A whole *year*?"

"You'd be surprised how many people get baptized, and then stop coming to church, and just disappear." She suddenly frowned and stared directly at him. "By the way, we can have this *friendly* relationship at church, but I am not this girl at work. If you can't cut it in Personal Services, I'll be the first one to help get rid of you. Got it?"

Kincaid fought the urge to smile at the pure schizoid manner in which Parker switched from a simple Mormon girl, who secretly carried a sidearm, to a straight-laced businesswoman, who would not be afraid to shoot him in the face if she thought he posed a threat.

Before he could answer, the door to the Bishop's office opened.

Bishop Brock held the door open as another member stepped out of the office. They shook hands, and the other man walked away with a humble smile on his face. The Bishop then turned toward Parker. "Is this already *your* guy, Haley?"

"*No*, sir." She winced with a nervous smile. "We work together in the COB and I thought I'd keep him company until you were ready to take over."

"Are you two traveling together, today?"

"No, of course not." Parker screwed up her face at the suggestion. "I won't even be waiting for him."

Bishop Brock laughed and turned his attention to Kincaid. "Brother Kincaid, come on in so we can get to know each other better."

Kincaid shook the Bishop's meaty hand and allowed himself to be pulled inside the small office.

"Welcome to our ward," the Bishop said, again. "Tell me a little about yourself and your experience in church callings."

"Uh, I've never had a calling in the church," Kincaid slowly replied. "I'm not a member, yet. I talked with the missionaries almost a year ago, and because of my job, they said I would have to speak with the Prophet or one of the apostles before I could get baptized. I spoke with *him* last Friday. He and I agreed I should wait one year, to see if I can adapt to a more *peaceful* life as a civilian."

Bishop Brock smiled. "I'm glad you came to our ward. In keeping with the spirit of the Prophet's recommendation, I would like to speak with you every month, between now and your baptism. That way, you can tell me about your progress, and I can give you pointers, if that's all right," he said.

For the next hour, the Bishop and Kincaid engaged in a warm and uplifting conversation. Kincaid told him some details of his encounter with the missionaries, leaving out his paramilitary rescue mission at the time, and the country in which it had taken place.

At the end, as Bishop Brock opened his door, he heard the choir practicing in the chapel. "Do you have a ride?"

Kincaid nodded.

"Then I think I'll go to choir practice. Interested?"

"Thanks for the offer, but I want to give the members a week or two to forget their first impression of me."

"I understand. But it may take more than a few weeks to forget seeing their *bishop* getting trounced by a stranger."

"Why's that?"

The Bishop seemed to redden. "I, uh, teach martial arts to children, as a part-time job."

"Oops! At least none of those kids attend this ward."

"By the grace of God," he said as he turned, opened the chapel door, and walked inside.

Kincaid paused at the phrase, by the grace of God. He had heard it before and wondered if it was a standard Mormon phrase.

~Chapter Thirteen~

Farouk Ali Farhan had come to America from Iran, for a western education at his parents' insistence and expense. They were wealthy and wanted the best of life for their only son. He had been raised in a well-to-do, Sunni Muslim family, and he had listened to all the extremist rants about the evils of the west. Yet, he came to America with a mind open to making his own assessment. He had seen poverty and evil in Iran and knew it must be everywhere. But he had come to the United States to find out for himself—as part of his education. He promised his parents he would not allow himself to be *corrupted*.

On the campus of Wayne State University, in Detroit, Michigan, Farhan sat alone in the open quadrangle, eating a light lunch as he read his assignment for his European History class. The sky was clear, and the air was warm with only the hint of a breeze. Quite a few of the other students were also taking advantage of the fair weather.

Professor Fredrickson was a good instructor, but he always gave his students too much to read, as if his history class was the only class for which they needed to prepare. Farhan had fallen behind, but he was trying to make up, because the lectures were always so fascinating. Professor Fredrickson seemed to find at least one special perspective in every class that made Farhan think, wonder, and wish he had been born in that time and place to help fight for such a great cause—whatever the cause might have been.

A shadow fell across Farhan's book and remained. He looked up feeling a little irritated, to see who was blocking his light. He saw two college-aged men with backpacks over one shoulder and helmets in one hand. Cuff clips were secured to one ankle of their dress trousers, so they must have secured bicycles, nearby. They wore short-sleeved white shirts, neckties, and name tags on their shirts with the largest letters saying: JESUS CHRIST.

"Hi," said the first young man. "My name is Elder Monroe, and this is my companion, Elder Brickey."

Elder Brickey nodded as Farhan looked him over. "We're missionaries for The Church of Jesus Christ of Latter-day Saints."

"Yes, yes," said Farhan, waving them off so he could return to his studies. "I am Muslim, and I'm not interested in any Christian religions."

"That's okay," Elder Monroe said as he sat beside Farhan. "We've noticed a lot of Muslim students at this school, and we were wondering if you might tell us about Islam."

The request would have knocked Farhan over if he had been on his feet. "If I tell you about Islam, do you have to tell me about *your* church?" he asked, hoping he could talk them into leaving him alone.

Elder Brickey shrugged. "No. We just want to know more about Islam because it's such a major religion in the world. It seems like the Detroit-Dearborn area is where a *lot* of Muslims settle. We just want to understand more about the major religions of the world."

"Can you meet me back here tomorrow at this time?" Farhan asked. "I have to be at my next class in a few minutes, but we can talk more then."

Both missionaries grinned as they stood. "You bet," said Elder Monroe. "We'll be back here—right here—tomorrow," he said, pointing to the grass under his feet. "What's your name?"

"Farouk Ali Farhan. But you can call me Farhan."

"Thank you, Farhan," said Elder Brickey. "We'll see you

tomorrow, then."

*****

The next day, Farhan, sat in a different location, hoping the Christian missionaries would not find him. What he did not count on was that he happened to sit near the bike rack they used. He watched, dumbfounded, as they locked up their bikes and walked to their pre-arranged meeting spot. When they did not find him, they looked around, and finally located him with his face in a textbook. Farhan tried to appear like he had been studying his book, but he suspected they knew what he had tried to do.

They both took off their backpacks and clipped their helmets to a shoulder-strap so they could hold everything in one hand when they approached.

"Hello, Farhan," Elder Monroe said.

Farhan looked up in a mock surprise.

"Sorry we're a few minutes late," Elder Brickey added as if they had connected as planned. "Do you still have time to share with us?"

Farhan's mouth hung open for just a moment, then changed to an expression of resolve—a resolve born of delayed integrity. He had agreed to talk with them, so he would do just that. He relaxed as he sat in the shade with his back against a large tree, his books scattered around him on the grass. Smiling, he closed the book he had been studying. "So, what can I tell you about Islam?" he asked, bracing himself inside to defend his faith from their challenges.

"We are full-time missionaries for a Christian church called The Church of Jesus Christ of Latter-day Saints," Elder Brickey said. "Our leaders have advised us to search for common ground with other religions so we can eliminate contention and arguments between us."

"Yes?" Farhan asked, waiting for them to preach so he could

get up and leave, as soon as possible.

"Well, the little we know of Islam makes it impossible to find common ground until we learn more about what Islam teaches."

For the next thirty minutes, Farhan told the two Elders about how the angel Gabriel appeared to the Prophet Mohammad and told him to write what the angel would reveal to him, and how the Koran, their scripture, came from those monologs. Farhan read short passages from the Koran to them, and it astounded him that they listened with such rapt attention.

Both missionaries asked questions, not trying to disprove the story, but to clarify their understanding. Farhan talked about Father Abraham, and how he had almost sacrificed his son, Ishmael, before an angel stopped him. He then added the Christian Bible was wrong when it said Abraham almost sacrificed his son, Isaac. Farhan referred to the Hebrews and the Christians as the *people of the book*. He told them how these people had originally been the chosen people of God and described how each group had turned their backs on God—known to all Muslims as Allah—and how Allah had rejected them because of their sins and had sent the Angel Gabriel to Mohammad, with specific instructions to build up another people unto himself.

Farhan finished relating the story of Islam. Then, he searched the faces of the two missionaries for their reaction. "Well, do you believe me?" he asked them.

Elder Monroe was first to speak. "I find it amazing how similar our two stories are," he said.

"Similar? How can they be similar?" Farhan asked, almost insulted to think that any other story could be as beautiful.

"Well," said Elder Brickey, "We believe similar events happened in the year 1820, in the state of New York, when God the Father and His son, Jesus Christ, appeared to a young boy named Joseph Smith."

For the next thirty minutes, the missionaries related the

story of how a fourteen-year-old boy wanted to know which church to join. Jesus Christ had told him not to join any church, but to wait, listen, and learn, so God could perform a mighty work and a wonder through him. Then, the complete Gospel, which Jesus Christ had taught when he was alive in mortality, was restored to the Earth, through Joseph Smith. This restoration was necessary because of the lost and corrupted parts of the Bible that had occurred over the centuries.

Farhan could not help himself, but he interrupted the story several times to ask for clarification. The two missionaries had listened to the story of his religion, and now he truly felt obliged to understand their story.

When Farhan's smartwatch alarm sounded, he reached up to turn it off. "I am sorry, but I must go. I have an exam in my next class, and I should not miss it."

"That's okay. We understand," both elders said, amicably.

While Farhan gathered up his books, he spotted several of his Muslim neighbors standing nearby, watching him. They were talking among themselves. One was talking on his cell phone. None of them appeared very happy. He returned his attention to the two missionaries, but he was distracted. "Can we, uh, meet and talk again—at a place more... *private*?" Farhan scanned the area around him, furtively glancing again at the men as they began walking toward him.

"Yes, of course," Elder Monroe said. "We'd like nothing better. When and where?"

Farhan quickly gave them a date and time just a few days away and also gave them an address. Elder Brickey wrote the information in his appointment book. Farhan shoved the last of his papers inside his backpack and walked away from the missionaries. He tried to walk past the small group of his Muslim acquaintances, without comment but they stopped him with a hand against his chest.

Farhan stopped, then turned and watched the two

missionaries retrieve their bikes. These three young men confronting him had been watching him carry on the conversation with the Americans. He knew them but he was not friends with them. They were always surlier than most Iranians, and he never felt good after speaking with any of them.

"What were you talking to those two men about?" asked the largest one, as he stared at the departing missionaries' backs.

"They wanted to know more about Islam," Farhan responded.

"And what did you tell them?" another asked.

"I told them about Mohammad and the Koran."

"You shouldn't talk to them. They will corrupt you and turn you against Allah," the third one warned. "They don't care about Muslims unless they think they can turn us into Christians."

"We need you to come to the *Center* with us," the largest one said. It sounded more like a demand than an invitation.

Farhan was afraid for his safety if he were to refuse. He just nodded and went with them as they walked. After all, they said they were going to a place where other people would be attending, and what could happen inside the *Center*? It was almost time for afternoon prayers, so he thought nothing else of it—except that he would have to make up the test he was going to miss.

The *Center* was only a few blocks away. When Farhan turned to enter, he bumped into the others, who had not turned to go through the door.

"No. We're going into the side door, into the basement." He was referring to a place with which Farhan was not familiar. It was supposed to be a place where young men went to argue and debate politics, mostly.

The mosque was for daily prayers. The *Center* was more of a place of informal education and light recreation for the entire Muslim community in the Detroit area. It was near enough the WSU campus that many of the Muslim students went there after their daily prayers at the mosque.

Farhan was not personally familiar with the place, but he had heard rumors that college students and professors with extremist views, often met there after school hours to discuss subversive ideas and to plan hypothetical activities. He had also heard tales they stored weapons and ammunition inside the *Center*, locked away in the basement. But everyone was hesitant to say much about that topic in public.

Farhan did not like entering the *Center* now, with these men. He had come to America to get a quality education, and he felt getting involved with any subversive types could jeopardize that. But he went along with them because they had just seen him in conversation with Mormon missionaries and he didn't want to risk becoming a target for the subversives. He hoped he could convince them he was not a threat by attending this one meeting.

As they entered through the single door, the largest one turned and put a hand against Farhan's chest. "All cell phones have to stay here." Another of them pointed to a wooden framework hanging on the wall. It was divided into small cubby holes, just large enough for a cell phone or smartphone—one hundred of them. The cubby holes were each numbered. Most of the cubbies were empty.

Farhan reached into his pocket, fished out his smartphone, and placed it inside cubby hole number three. The others also placed their phones in holes near Farhan's phone. As a group, they walked down the stairway, toward the basement of the *Center*, the largest of them leading the way. Another young man Farhan didn't recognize, came out from a side room and walked past them, toward the stairs.

Farhan and the small group walked through another door, into the same side room. Before the door closed, Farhan looked back and saw the single man reach up and take a smartphone from a cubby hole where he had left his phone. He thought about protesting that a stranger might steal his phone, but the door shut before he could say anything about it.

"Don't worry," said one of the men who accompanied him. "Your phone will be safe."

*****

One hour later, a panicky Farhan walked out of the *Center* alone and grabbed his smartphone. He was happy no one had stolen it, but he noticed it was not in the same position he had left it. *Or maybe it was.* As he recalled what he had seen and heard in the meeting, he was so upset he struggled to maintain an outwardly calm appearance. The situation upset his stomach, which threatened to bubble over. He could not allow those feelings to show—at least not yet. He left before the others, who remained behind in social banter.

Farhan knew he had to get in contact with those two missionaries soon. But he couldn't remember their names. They had name tags on their shirts. Why did he not study them with greater care? Why hadn't he *tried* to remember their names? How would he *ever* get in contact with them if he didn't know their names? He didn't know where they lived, their cellphone numbers, or any other way of contacting them.

Within a city block from the *Center*, Farhan ran into the same three men with whom he had gone to the *Center,* who had caught up with him by running. They had been talking amongst themselves, but he had been lost in his fearful thoughts and hadn't been listening to them. He was glad they had not asked him any questions, because his mind was a thousand miles away. He knew he could probably find a telephone number for a local Mormon chapel and maybe he could convince them he told the truth. But if the religious leaders in the Mormon Church were *anything* like the *Muslim* leaders Farhan had known, they would not forward a message like his, with any urgency, and all would be lost.

Farhan jerked himself back to reality when he heard

someone behind him call his name.

"Farhan, are you going back to school or your apartment?" one of them said.

"Uh, no... uh, yes," he tried to answer but had not heard the question. "I'm going back to my apartment to rest."

They said their farewells, and the men broke off in different directions, smiling and joking among themselves.

Once at his apartment, Farhan punched the numbers 4-1-1 into his smartphone and asked for the number of the LDS Church leader in Utah. The computer voice switched his call to a human operator who was flustered, for a moment. Farhan remembered the Latter-day Saint Church was in Salt Lake City, Utah. The operator gave him a number and connected him. He did not request a text message with the same number, thinking it would be evidence he had called the Mormons.

When Farhan was finally connected to a real person in Utah, he realized he did not have enough information to be helpful, and what he told the man on the telephone only made him suspect Farhan might be involved in the plot of destruction, himself.

After the first unsuccessful call, Farhan decided he would try once more before taking a more drastic course of action. It wouldn't be the quickest way, but it would be the surest course of action for saving many lives—Mormon lives.

~Chapter Fourteen~

The Personal Services Director, Jedediah Tanner, sat at his desk, reading through his scriptures during his lunchtime. He had seen several other employees bring *digital* copies of their scriptures on a tablet, smartphone, or laptop and use them at church headquarters or in their wards during Sunday meetings. But he was not yet ready to make that jump into the 21st century. He still preferred his paper copy. It had body and weight that seemed to give it more authority and power. He kept a copy of his patriarchal blessing inside the cover of his quad and regarded it as scripture from a loving Heavenly Father directly to him.

He unfolded his blessing and again read the part that had confused and concerned him over the years.

Tanner tried in vain to remember anything in his job in the past several years that might fit that description. He knew he had little energy left for the physical labor required in *this* job and did not look forward to the challenge described in his blessing.

His wife had been ill for the past several years, requiring a full-time nurse to care for her during the workday. He took care of her each evening, bathing and dressing her every morning before he went to work. He loved her with all his heart but feared his energy and failing health might not be enough to continue taking care of her for a few more years. He didn't want to end up having a stroke or a heart attack, like other working men his age.

He opened the center drawer of his desk, withdrew a thin packet of papers, and gingerly placed it in front of him. He lost himself for several minutes as he again contemplated submitting his retirement papers.

In the church, the leadership always preached that family must come first. But even in the church, there were pressures to perform between the hours of eight to five, and then take care of the family the rest of the time. It was becoming tougher and tougher for him to do both.

He dreaded having to travel on business trips. It always required him to ask his children to come for a few days to take care of their mother while he was away. He knew they loved her, and they *would* come whenever he needed them. But taking care of her was *his* job. So, he had cut back on his travels as much as possible. However, managing the best security program for a worldwide church was not possible from a desk. It took hands-on, face-to-face interaction to do it right, correctly.

The phone on Tanner's desk rang. He picked it up before the second ring.

"Director Tanner," he announced.

"I need to speak with a person in Mormon Security," said a male voice with a thick Middle East accent.

"Yes, sir. That would be me. How may I help you?"

"Some bad people plan to destroy your Mormon temple, soon," the voice warned. "And many of your leaders will be killed along with it."

"Sir, are *you* planning to destroy our temple?" Tanner asked, his pulse elevating.

"No, no. I have heard other men—bad men—talking, and they are planning to do this destruction. I am *not* in their group."

"Which temple are they planning to destroy?"

"What do you mean? How many temples do you have?"

"Well, sir, we have over 200 temples around the world, right now. If you will tell me which one is in danger, we can take measures to protect it."

"I—I don't *know* which one." The voice was suddenly

flustered.

"Do you know *when* they plan to destroy a temple?"
"No, I do not know that, *either.*"
"Sir, if you will give me your name, I can verify--"
Click...
"Sir? Hello?"

The stranger on the other end of the line had ended their connection. Tanner took out a ledger from his desk drawer and recorded the date and time of the call, with a summary of the threat. He also made a note for himself, to tell Special Agent Parker, later today. There was not much else he could do with the little information he had to go on.

The church received this kind of call at least once or twice each month. Most of the time, they turned out to be crank calls. Thank goodness for that, Tanner thought. If even half of the threats had any substance to them, he feared the Church would not be prepared, manned, or equipped to protect itself. But it was his job to try.

Tanner knew giving the information to Special Agent Parker was necessary so she could alert the FBI to gather their resources to either protect the church or to go after whoever made or carried through with such threats.

*****

Special Agent Haley Parker sat at her desk, tapping with vigor on her computer keyboard. She was fuming. Once again, she had been turned down for a request to transfer to an undercover position. She'd had enough of desk work and escort duty in her current position as the FBI's Liaison Officer at LDS Church Headquarters. Now, she wanted to do *real* FBI work. Parker felt she had earned that right—and now they wouldn't allow her!

Submitting three separate applications for re-assignment, the FBI HQ had returned each one, replying she was too valuable in her current assignment. They continued, saying they could not find a suitable replacement for her, to reassign her. The replies returned did not even have the decency to include the word *yet*! She did a copy-paste from her previous reclamas to inform them she *was* qualified for each of the positions for which she had applied.

Parker didn't hate her job as Liaison Officer to the Church, but it burned her insides to have been turned down for other positions when she knew she was better qualified than the men—*all* the men who ultimately had been awarded the positions.

She struck the Enter button with more force than she had actually intended. Then she stopped, took in a slow breath, and blew it out, hoping to blow out all the hostility inside her at that moment.

*****

When Orson Kincaid left North Carolina, the Army had paid him for his unused vacation days, and Harris' contract company paid him handsomely for the one mission he completed with them. It all went straight to his bank account. He drew out what he needed in cash and let the rest of it sit there to gain interest.

With all that money, he had planned to travel to Utah and set up housekeeping, until he could find a new job. Now, he had to use some of that money to buy more clothing. He was sure they would not approve of him wearing his blue jeans, t-shirts, and cowboy boots—his normal off-duty apparel—to work, every day.

The first day at work, however, he wore a polo shirt, cargo pants, and hiking shoes, thinking, at least, they would be better than blue jeans and a tee shirt. Only when he approached the building, did he realize his mistake.

As Kincaid entered the COB, he carried a 10-ream paper-sized box of his office and personal items. The box was not heavy.

He had never been interested in starting an *'I-love-me wall'* and had never worked a job where he'd had his own office. But he owned framed photos of his parents, his baby sister, and him with their favorite horses in the Dragoon Mountains, a picture with his first ODA—operational detachment alpha—posing before his first sniper mission, and a photo of Ted and him before their last mission together. It still hurt to think of Ted as being deceased. But he wanted to remember their friendship, so he brought his picture to the office with the others.

It was 8:02 am when Kincaid rounded the corner and entered the small office. He put down the box, looked at his phone, and winced. He had been taught better than to be late for anything. But it was only two minutes, and he had not considered the parking problem, or how long it would take him to walk from his truck in the underground parking lot to his new office.

Special Agent Parker was already at her desk and looked like she had been there for some time. Kincaid knew his desk was the empty one with the flat screen computer monitor and keyboard beckoning for him to sit and work. The two desks were katty-cornered to each other in the small office and had only about three feet between them. It was small but the ten-foot ceiling made it look bigger.

Parker looked up and offered him a forced smile as he entered. "Good morning," she snipped.

Kincaid put the box on his desk. "Morning," he replied, confused about the sudden attitude. He looked around the room, taking in his new digs. At least it had a real window and wasn't the corner of a cube farm, he thought.

Parker's sad puppy eyes flashed. "The dress code in the office is coat and tie. Coat on, shirt sleeves rolled down, and tie secured to the neck, snuggly. While you are at your desk, you may take off your coat, loosen your tie and roll up your sleeves, if you feel so inclined."

"Yes, ma'am," he replied, realizing he had just met the

military working dog. Kincaid looked down at his clothes. Aside from what he had purchased to wear to church meetings, this was about all he had until the moving company delivered his belongings. He smiled cockeyed and gave himself another mental note to return to Mister Mac's before heading home.

Allowing the scolding to roll off his back, he did a quick assessment of his work area. He would have to sit with his back to the window, which made him feel a little uneasy—tactically. But the only other choice would force him to sit with his back to the door. After thinking it over, he left the furniture the way it was. But he still worried about the attitude of his new partner.

Parker and Kincaid looked at each other over their desks, for an awkward moment. Kincaid started the conversation. "So, what's this job like?" he asked, off-handedly, as he emptied his box and put his belongings on the desk or in the drawers.

Parker's conservative lipstick did nothing to soften her tight-lipped smile."Well, *my* job is kind of a nothing-liaison job," she said, with some bitterness. "I'm a fully trained FBI Special Agent. But here, I follow up on crank or threat telephone calls, or escort visitors and advise the general authorities on law enforcement issues which apply to their travels and other activities. But *you're* officially with the Church's Personal Services," she continued. "They like to call it *the Service*, to give it mystique. For the others working in that department, it includes bodyguard escort work, building security, and the occasional investigation of *whackos* claiming *revelation* by saying the church has gone astray, or by men using their *priesthood authority* to curse the GAs—general authorities." She stopped and took a deep breath. "You're also my partner, so, together, we will conduct the *rare* serious investigation."

Kincaid chuckled under his breath. "That sounded rehearsed. Have you given that speech to other new employees?"

Parker smiled with no visible warmth. "You think I'm being *funny?*"

"Uh, no-o." Kincaid shook his head, looking at the door in case he had to escape, in short order. "I just thought Personal Services meant putting together birthday celebrations, getting plaques for people leaving the Church's employ, and sending cards in condolence of lost loved ones. Now, you tell me it's actually the Church's *security* department?"

Parker lowered her gaze and shook her head. "Admit it," she said, "you don't belong here. I read your jacket this morning. You're a combat vet with absolutely no security experience."

"How much experience could it take to guard a door and flash the magic wand over people who set off the alarm?"

"You've got this all wrong," Parker replied, feeling the heat coming forward again. "*Your* job is to conduct investigations and interview suspects. You're not *trained* for that."

That set Kincaid off like a bottle rocket. "Lady, I didn't *ask* to be here. The Prophet decided *this* is where I should be. I don't understand why, but he must know a few of the facts you and I missed," Kincaid's voice rose to meet her attitude in intensity.

Parker didn't back down. "I know of several good people who lost out when *you* took this position. I don't like anyone unqualified taking a job this good and this important,"

Kincaid sighed. There would be no reasoning with her on this topic—not while she was so keyed up. He paused for a few beats. "Okay, so, let's start over. You mentioned bodyguard escort work. Do the general authorities travel much?"

"Are you kidding?" Parker said with a cynical chuckle, trying to simmer down. "They travel all over the globe for stake conferences, creating new stakes and missions, breaking ground and dedicating new and renovated temples, and many other reasons to get out among the people."

"Do they take security with them? I mean, will I travel much?"

"When they travel stateside, they might take one or two security people. But when they travel overseas, they rely upon the local church members of whatever country they're in to provide law enforcement and translator experience," she explained.

"Local members with security experience?" Kincaid tried to understand how effective such a program could be.

"Yes, U.S. military members, when possible, or Church members who are local constables or police officers of a non-military nature or in other jobs that might keep the GAs safe."

"That sounds kind of careless. How many have been shot at or abducted?"

"You mean in the last hundred years?" Parker said. "None. The last place they might have had problems would have been in Missouri."

"Why Missouri?" Kincaid asked, thinking Missouri, the Heartland of the USA, would not be an especially dangerous place for anyone.

"In 1838, Missouri Governor, Lilburn Boggs, issued the 'Extermination Order' that made it legal to shoot Mormons on sight, anywhere in the state and for any reason."

"Wait. What? How'd he get away with that?"

"The federal government didn't want to interfere with states' rights, and they saw no need to rile the good voters of Missouri before an election year, so they let it slide."

"So, when did the law get rescinded?" Kincaid asked.

"Not until 1978." Parker let that hang in the air between them for a few seconds.

Kincaid shook his head in disbelief. "And now?"

Parker shrugged one shoulder. "Now, there are wards, missions, and stakes all over the good state of Missouri. The residents have no problem with Mormons at all. In fact, this is the best time in the entire history of the church for public relations concerning missionary and member safety, worldwide."

"If that's true, why do they even need security?" he asked.

"A few of the general authorities take no security with them, anywhere they go."

"When can I expect to get called on, to go with them?"

"You? Only when I travel. Partners. Remember?"

"Do you carry a weapon?" he asked.

She nodded and shrugged again. "I'm a Federal Agent, so I carry *everywhere* I go."

"How about the other members of the Service?" Kincaid tried not to smile as he used the department's self-proclaimed nickname.

"A few of them do. Director Tanner and the entrance security supervisors always do. Mostly, the longer they work here, the less they carry," Parker said. "You carry?"

"I didn't today because I didn't know what the regulations required," Kincaid explained. "But I have my SIG Sauer P-226 locked up in my truck."

Parker nodded her approval. "Good weapon. Is that what you used in the Army?"

Kincaid nodded.

"I thought all you guys used the Beretta M9."

"The *regular* soldiers do, I guess. Special operators use the SIGs as much as possible," Kincaid explained. "It's a better fit in the hand and doesn't take up as much space on the hip or under the arm."

"So, you weren't a *regular* soldier?" Parker asked, using the same words Kincaid had spoken.

Kincaid squirmed as he sat on the edge of his desk. He realized, too late, he'd walked into that one. He didn't mind answering the question, but he didn't want to highlight his past, since he was trying to put it all behind him.

"Never mind," Parker pointed to the box he had brought into the office. "Is that *all* your stuff?"

"Yep. And the box is only half full," he said. "What's your story? I mean, what brought you here?"

Parker smiled wryly before answering. "I was the *only* LDS Church member in the Salt Lake City FBI Office—and the only woman. They put me over here so the big boys could run all the investigations that would help them get transferred to a plum assignment like Los Angeles, New York, or Miami."

"They don't *like* it here?"

"No. There's not that much to do, I guess. Now, there're quite a few real cowboys in that office. They would rather be anyplace else—you know, where the action is."

"How long have you been with the FBI?" Kincaid asked.

"Almost two years. This is my first assignment. Before attending the FBI Academy in Quantico, Virginia, I served a mission in the Michigan Detroit Mission. Before that, I spent two years on the Draper Police force."

"So, you were a missionary?" Kincaid asked, but he filed the other information in the back of his mind, for later.

"Yes," Parker said, perking up at the change of conversation. "Yes, the best year-and-a-half of my life—so far. How did you get here?"

Kincaid shrugged and continued looking preoccupied with adjusting his seat. "Like I said, the Prophet recommended me for the job... So, what's Tanner supposed to do, tell him I wasn't the right fit for the Service?" He tried to make it sound casual, but he could already feel the air between them filling with dozens of unspoken questions.

Parker gave him a strange look. "Well, we're supposed to be partners, so when we get a call to go, we both go, together—kind of like missionaries."

"What happened to your *previous* partner?" Kincaid wanted the question to come out smooth and well-timed. When he saw her face harden, he realized he had just struck another one of her hot buttons.

"He was an older man, about the director's age, not in good health, and he had a stroke during Priesthood Meeting one Sunday. The hospital kept him for more than a month. One day, his wife came in and handed the director her husband's retirement package. I haven't seen him since."

"Wow, tough job, if it gives people strokes," Kincaid said, trying to lighten the mood.

Parker ignored the sarcasm.

"If I get to carry a sidearm, I guess I have to qualify. Right?" Kincaid asked.

"That's right. And I'm your qualifying officer. Take care of the rest of your in-processing and we'll go to the range after that," Parker promised.

Kincaid stiffened, scrutinizing her when she returned to her paperwork. He was trying to figure out his new partner. Was she as good as she thought, or was she trying too hard to be a *big boy*?

*****

Farouk Ali Farhan got off the airplane at the Salt Lake City International Airport and took an Uber to Temple Square. He asked several people where to find the Mormon church leader and got strange looks in return. A Visitor Center tour guide offered to help and pointed him to the Church Office Building instead of the Church Administration Building.

Farhan was angry at himself to no end with the several telephone calls he had made, trying to warn the Mormon church of an impending attack on them, with no positive results for his effort. There was more at risk than the destruction of buildings and the murder of its church leaders with this attack. That kind of incident could make life more difficult for all *honest* Muslims living in the United States who wanted nothing more than to earn a college degree and make a straightforward salary for themselves and their families. He felt he needed to do more to make sure his extremist acquaintances did not upset that status quo.

Entering through the glass doors of the Church Office Building, he immediately asked a nearby guard where he could find the church leaders. He claimed he had to warn them about a plan to assassinate the leader and destroy a temple.

Several guards with warm smiles surrounded Farhan. One guard took his bag with patient firmness and rifled through its contents. Two other guards politely put him up against a nearby wall and searched him for weapons, bombs, or other dangerous items. Farhan did not resist. He realized just how suspicious they must be of him.

"Not! No!" he protested, as they searched his bag. "You do not understand. It is not me. I came to warn you so you can protect your leaders."

The guard supervisor had two of his people escort Farhan to the nearby interview room where Farhan told them his story about what he had heard and experienced in the Islamic Center, in Detroit.

That stymied the guards. They didn't know what to do. Nothing like this had ever happened at the entrance of church headquarters. The supervisor remembered that *when you don't know what to do, always pass it up the chain of command.* He got on the phone and called his boss.

"Director Tanner?" the guard supervisor asked.

"Yes," Tanner said.

"We have a man at the front entrance who claims to have information regarding a plan to assassinate as many of the church leaders as possible and destroy a temple of ours," the supervisor said.

There was silence on the line for several seconds. Finally, Tanner replied. "Escort the gentleman to the interview room. Make him comfortable, stay with him, and I will be right there."

~*Chapter Fifteen*~

Director Tanner walked out of his office and turned toward the elevators. He hesitated, stepped into the office of Special Agent Parker and the new guy. What was his name? Orson... Orson *somebody*. His desk was empty, but there were papers, books, and other office paraphernalia spread over the top. "Parker, get your new partner and meet me downstairs at the interview room," Tanner commanded.

"You bet," Parker said. "What's up?"

"We have a walk-in downstairs, and he might be a hot one *you'll* have to handle. You and the new guy... What's his name?"

"Kincaid. Orson Kincaid."

"Yeah, him. I'll talk to the walk-in. You two stay behind the glass. If there's anything to his story, I don't want this guy to see either of you—at least, not yet."

*****

Tanner walked into the interview room carrying two bottles of water. The walk-in sat at the table. There was a small microphone on a plastic stand and a blank pad of paper already waiting for him. Two video cameras recorded different angles of their interview as it proceeded from two corners of the room.

The walk-in was a male in his early twenties with a haircut that was conservative. He was clean-shaven and wore no eye glasses. He was either Middle Eastern, Israeli, or Latin American. Tanner didn't trust his ethnic recognition of non-American. His western khaki trousers, black leather shoes, and a plaid, long-sleeve shirt said nothing about him that screamed *terrorist*.

Kincaid and Parker stood at the glass inside the dark viewing room. They watched Director Tanner's interview through the one-way mirror. Kincaid wondered why a young Muslim male would come to LDS Church Headquarters. He panicked for just one moment, thinking the young man could be a suicide bomber. But he saw none of the signs of a bomb in the man's clothing or in any mannerisms of a bomber on a suicide mission. Finally, he relaxed so he could watch the Director interrogate the man.

Parker peered through the glass. "He's sweating in an air-conditioned room," she observed aloud. "See how he's looking around so furtively? He almost jumped out of his skin when Director Tanner opened the door. I'll bet he's a provocateur, sent to test our security."

Kincaid suspiciously kept his eyes on the suspect stating, "You're right about that, but he's a Muslim, alone in the headquarters of a major Christian religion. He just doesn't know what we'll do with him, that's all. He might be afraid we'll hogtie him and dunk him in a baptismal font before letting him go."

She smiled at the visual image of such an outrageous event.

Tanner took a seat across the table from the walk-in. "My name's Tanner," he said without inflection. "What's your name?"

"My name is Farouk Ali Farhan. I live in Hamtramck, Michigan," he said, with a thick Middle Eastern accent.

Tanner noticed the man's nervousness. "Settle down, Farouk," he said, passing a water bottle across the table.

"My friends call me Farhan," he said, reaching for the bottle. He twisted off the cap and took a big slug of water.

"What can I do for you, this morning?" Tanner asked, opening his bottle, and taking a light sip.

"They are going to assassinate your leadership and destroy

your temple," he blurted out.

Tanner realized this must be the same man who had telephoned him several days earlier. He pulled the pad of paper closer to himself, opened it, and said, "Tell me everything you know, and I'll take notes. When you finish, I'll ask some questions, okay?" He pulled out a pen from his coat pocket and prepared to write.

"I was in a meeting in Detroit two days ago when they said your church has no security, and your leaders have no protection. They called you a… *soft target*, and said they wanted to show the world they were courageous and strong enough to kill your leaders—your prophet." He stopped.

Tanner looked up. When Farhan did not continue, he asked, "Is that all? Don't you have anything else?"

Farhan gave him a blank stare, not knowing what else to say.

"We have temples all around the world. Which one are they planning to destroy and who are *they*?" Only then did Tanner realize he had forgotten his training. "Let me start from the top."

"The top? The top of what?"

"I mean, let me ask my questions again. Who did you hear making this threat?"

"There is a new Muslim man in Detroit who wants to make a name for himself. He is an extremist, and he wants to show the Muslim world he can work with the bigger groups that have the same politics as Al-Qaida and ISIS. The man wants to strike against a Christian religion known around the world. He identified you Mormons as a church that is growing too fast for his liking. He wants to teach you—and the world—a lesson so no other people will join your religion. There are others who have agreed to follow him into a holy jihad against your church."

"Can you give me the names of these men?"

Farhan's eyes drifted upward, as he tried to recall any of their names. "No. I know *none* of their names." He searched the eyes of his inquisitor. "You must *believe* me," he said, panic creeping into his voice.

"Did they say *which* of our leaders they wanted to kill?"

"Your prophet! Yes. They want to kill your prophet," Farhan said, thrilled to have a specific answer to a question.

"When? Where?" Tanner asked in a voice that made it sound like a demand. He cleared his throat. "Did they say when or where they would try to kill him?"

Farhan panicked, knowing he had not given enough information. "No," he said, his voice crackling with despair. He put his elbows on the table and rested his face in his hands. "Maybe when he is inside your temple."

"*Which* temple?"

Farhan didn't trust his voice, so he just whispered the words, "*I don't know*." He let his forearms fall onto the table with his palms turned up and opened.

Tanner took a deep breath and let it out. He thanked Farhan for his information, but his voice belied his lack of enthusiasm. He slid the second bottle of water across the table, stood, and started toward the door. Turning back to the informant, he said, "I'll be gone just a few minutes. If you can think of anything else about any attacks or assassination plots against our leaders or temples, please write them on the paper."

Farhan nodded his head and looked at the paper on the table. He picked up the pencil, hesitated, and then dropped it on the pad of paper, again, in frustration.

*****

Tanner entered the observation room, shaking his head as he turned toward his two neophyte investigators. "I got nothin'," he said with a hopeless rasp in his voice. "I don't know what to make of this guy. Either of you?"

Parker was first to reply. "I think he's telling the truth," she said. "I don't think he's hiding anything from us. He really either *can't* remember or never knew anything else in the first place." She turned to her partner. "Orson?"

Kincaid stared through the glass at the young man sitting alone inside the interrogation room. He didn't answer for several seconds. Then he shook his head. "I don't know, either." He turned to face his new boss. "Mind if I try, Director?"

Tanner stepped back without a word and waved an arm toward the door. "Be my guest," he said, wondering what this new guy thought he might get out of the informant.

Kincaid entered the room and walked toward Farhan, putting his right hand over his left breast. "Wah salaam Alay kum," he said, greeting the young man in Arabic.

Farhan jumped to his feet as this stranger spoke to him in his own tongue. "Alay kumwah salaam," he replied.

"My name is Orson," Kincaid said in English, then switched to Farsi. "You caught me in my first month on the job and my boss is watching me," he said, cocking his head toward the one-way mirror. He walked around the table, grabbed the empty chair, and moved it so the table was not in between them when he sat. "I heard what you told my boss, so there's no need to go over that information again. But I have a few additional questions to ask you."

"Yes, please. Ask me anything. I came to help, and I feel that I have only caused concern without enough facts for you to act upon."

Kincaid switched to speaking English. "Are you a Latter-day Saint?"

"Me? No, I was born and raised a Muslim. I am a *good* Muslim," he corrected himself.

"Where's home? Where were you raised?" Kincaid asked.

"Iran. A little village north of Tehran."

"Did your parents bring you to the States?"

"The United States? No, but they sent me to college so I

could get a good education and help our people when I return home."

"What are you studying?"

"Microbiology. I want to become a doctor and help protect my people from the many diseases in my country."

"It sounds like your parents love you—and your people—to send you so far away, and to trust the United States to educate you so you can return home to help your community. I am sure you miss them."

"Yes, I do," Farhan replied in a whisper, relaxing his hands on the table.

"How did you find out about the Mormon Church?"

"I spoke with two missionaries. They came to my campus—the college where I attend classes."

"What college is that?"

"Wayne State University, in Detroit, Michigan."

"I've never been to Michigan; is the school any good?"

"Oh, yes. I'm getting a wonderful education there."

"Yeah? What year are you in?" Kincaid adjusted his chair again, closer to Farhan.

"This is my first year, so I am a freshman. Did you go to college?"

Kincaid shook his head once. "No, not yet. If I can save enough money from this job, I hope to go to college in a few years." He paused. "There are thousands of Muslims in the Detroit-Dearborn area, aren't there?"

"Yes, there are."

"So, most of your friends are Muslim?"

Farhan shook his head as if trying to avoid embarrassment. "No, I stay to myself. But I go to morning and evening prayers with a few of the men I see on campus."

"Are there any extremists at that university?"

Farhan almost leaped from his seat. "*That* is what I am trying to tell you," he almost shouted in Farsi, turning his chair to face Kincaid in his excitement. He quickly remembered where he was and switched back to English. "There are a few extremists in Detroit, and they want to kill your prophet and destroy your temple," he exclaimed.

"But you can't remember *any* of their names, and you don't know *which* temple they want to destroy, right?"

Farhan fell back on his seat like a deflated balloon. "Right."

Kincaid reached forward and slapped Farhan's knee. "Hey, don't let it get you down. At times, my memory fights against me, too. What are your plans once you leave here?" Kincaid asked.

"I plan to fly home later today and return to my regular class schedule as soon as I get back."

"I think that's a *great* plan," Kincaid said with a reassuring smile. "I would like to talk to you again, in Michigan. Would that be okay?"

"Yes, of course," Farhan said with sincerity. "Let me give you my address and cell phone number so you can call me when you arrive."

"That would be fantastic," replied Kincaid, sliding the pad of paper and pen toward Farhan. "Maybe you could point out these extremist men who want to hurt my church leaders."

"Yes, I hope we can stop them before they do any real damage, too."

"Me, too." Kincaid glanced toward the mirror as Farhan wrote his information. Then he looked at his cell phone. "This is Monday. I'll call you at your number on Wednesday, and I'll give you a time and place for us to talk again. Okay?"

Farhan nodded.

After a few more minutes, Kincaid walked Farhan out of the interview room and toward the front entrance of the building, past the contingent of security guards. He retrieved Farhan's bag from security and handed it to him. He opened the glass door and stood back, so Farhan could exit.

"I will wait for your call on Wednesday," Farhan said,

beaming.

"I'll see you then," Kincaid affirmed. "Can I help you get a taxi to the airport?"

"No, thank you. There are many taxis in this city, and it will not be difficult."

Kincaid and Farhan embraced, which is customary of Muslim friends. Farhan walked out the door with his bag and immediately hailed a cab for the airport.

*****

When Kincaid turned to go find his boss, he almost bumped into Director Tanner, who had been standing behind him with Parker by his side. Tanner was flushed with excitement. "You get the airline tickets and make the hotel and car rental reservations," Tanner ordered Parker. "I want you two on a plane to Michigan to follow up on this threat—tomorrow."

"Tomorrow?" Parker asked.

"That's right. Before you leave, I want you both to go to the local FBI office and get an updated counter-terrorism briefing for Detroit."

"I'll set that up, too," Parker said.

"Oh yeah, get Orson qualified at the FBI's indoor range, too, while you're there. Just in case."

"Yes, sir."

Kincaid clenched his teeth, turned to Parker, and bobbled his head. "Let's go, partner." He turned and gave another quick nod. He felt like he was about to go swimming in a shark tank instead of qualifying at the shooting range with his partner as his range officer.

*****

The Federal Bureau of Investigation took up residence in their building in Jordan Heights, Utah, in 2010. West of Salt Lake City, it had the best indoor shooting range in the state. Special Agent Haley Parker used her FBI credentials at the gate to the indoor parking facility and parked her car two levels below the street. Kincaid was riding with her.

When she and Kincaid exited the vehicle, they both took their briefcase-size Pelican cases and walked to the indoor range. Again, Parker showed her creds. Not because the man didn't know her, but because that was the protocol.

"Who's he, Haley?" the gatekeeper and range master said, giving Kincaid a once over.

"Fred, meet my new partner, Orson Kincaid. Orson let me introduce Fred Radichal. Once we put you in the computer, you'll be able to come train by yourself and to qualify as needed. If you bring your own ammunition, make sure it's not pre-load. If you use the FBI's rounds, they will charge the church. That is not a big deal unless you're firing a thousand rounds every day," Haley said. She looked at Fred. "Did I forget anything?"

"You can use your own eye and ear protection, but don't expect us to pay for any injuries with your own equipment," Fred added. He looked Kincaid up and down once again. "You're a SIG 9-mil man?"

"Yeah, P226. How'd you know?"

"You smell like a covert action man," Fred said with a hint of disdain.

"And just what do they smell like?" Kincaid tried to smile.

"Death." Fred gave them each a box of ten pre-loaded magazines across the counter. One was marked as *.40 caliber Glock* and the other as *9mm SIG*.

Fred walked into the back room, leaving them to start on their own.

"That guy's real cheery," Kincaid said as he took his box of ammo from Parker.

Parker took the other box and led the way to the shooting lanes. "Fred's been here since the range opened in 2010. His sense of humor is dry, but he's a good man. You can count on him."

They put their ammunition boxes and Pelicans on the prep table, donned their eye and ear protection, and opened their cases. They were the only two on the range at the moment. Parker took out her Glock and looked at Kincaid's open case. "You use two SIGs?" she asked.

"One's my primary, and the other's my backup," Kincaid replied.

"Most people carry a *smaller* backup."

Kincaid shook his head. "Not in special operations." He put his backup in a compact, leather holster and clipped it to his belt at the small of his back. He laid his primary weapon on the counter, with the slide retracted and the magazine well empty. He then waited for Parker.

They each took their life-sized silhouette target sheets from a nearby stack, connected them to the clips on the cables, and sent them downrange to the twenty-five-foot mark.

"The FBI made this range for shooting small arms. They have another range for shooting rifles and larger caliber firearms out on the Salt Flats."

Kincaid simply nodded his understanding. His focus was already on his target.

"Let's do it," she said, locking the magazine in place and releasing the slide to put her first round in the chamber.

Kincaid did the same, lifted and aimed his SIG at the paper target. He hesitated and fired each round with three seconds between shots until the magazine was empty. By then, he was sweating and trembling. He could taste the bile creeping up into his throat. He was more than glad to put the empty SIG on the counter in front of him when the magazine was empty. He wiped his forehead and willed greater control of himself before Parker finished her first magazine. It actually surprised him he hadn't heaved yet. He thought maybe the information he got from his missionaries in Mexico, and the boost from the Prophet, had helped him manage his demons—no such luck.

Both shooters flipped the switch and brought their targets back to them, so they could compare. Kincaid's shot group followed around the shape of the silhouette's head, from ear to ear. He had not hit the target once—as planned. That would have earned him hoots and hollers from his old unit. But he had hit exactly what he aimed for.

He glanced over at Parker's target and saw a tight shot group. All rounds in the same area of the silhouette's chest, that one fist would cover. Her shooting impressed him.

"Not bad shooting, soldier." Parker snickered after seeing the results of his shooting. "Are you afraid to kill a piece of paper?"

Kincaid ignored the jibe. "You're not so bad, yourself. That's good shooting."

"I thought you special ops boys could put three shots in the size of a quarter," Parker said.

"The Army trained me to be a sniper. I can put three rounds through the same hole with a rifle and scope at two hundred meters," he said. "But I tried to leave the handgun shooting to the knuckle draggers."

Parker turned away and rolled her eyes.

Kincaid leaned forward, put both hands on the counter, and hung his head, to regain his composure.

Just then, however, Parker looked around the lane divider and saw him leaning.

"Are you all right?" she asked.

Kincaid pushed himself up and looked at her. "It must be a stomach flu," he lied.

"You want to quit?"

"No, no. I'll be fine. Let's get ready for the next mag load."

They both put up new targets and shot the other nine magazines of ammunition downrange. Each time, Parker's shot groups were tighter than Kincaid's. But his became tighter the more he shot. He didn't let it get to him because this also happened in his old unit. They had never used him on the assault teams because they liked and trusted his ability to shoot the long distances—and that was what he did best.

*****

Parker and Kincaid took a few minutes to clean and secure their weapons in their vehicle before heading upstairs for their FBI briefing on potential threats to the LDS Church.

"These guys can be a little obnoxious, so let them give us their briefing. If you have any questions, let me ask them. Okay?" Parker knew how the FBI unofficially treated outsiders—especially people not trained in law enforcement.

Kincaid nodded his head.

Dressed in a three-piece suit, a man in his early thirties approached them. "Good morning. I'm Special Agent Collins. I understand you want a current threat briefing for potential threats against the LDS Church. Right?" he said, officiously, speaking with a deep Texas accent, with a suggestion of disdain in his demeanor toward them.

Parker and Kincaid both nodded.

"Come with me. I think I've got what you need."

He led them to a conference room with a long faux-wood table and a projector hanging from the ceiling. There was a single keyboard on the table and a large screen on the wall at one end of the room. There were at least twenty chairs around the table—all of them leather and cushy.

"Please, take a seat," Collins said as he waved toward the

seats, he preferred they take.

Collins sat at the keyboard, hit a few keys, and turned on the projector.

The first image that came on the screen was a map of the United States.

"Currently, there are three off-shoot groups from the LDS Church that would love to upset the order and progress of the main Church," Collins said. As he spoke, the map zoomed in on southern Utah. "However, we have no sign that they plan any destruction, at this time. They would love to embarrass the Church in the public eye, but they seem to conduct most of their hijacks on the internet."

The map zoomed out and showed the entire United States again. "There are two major militia groups in the country that make threats against *all* organized religions. But we have no indications either of them has targeted the LDS Church. If they were to target the Church, it would probably be with guns blazing and bombs exploding. But we have no indicators of that, at this time."

The image zoomed in on the northern half of the country and highlighted both Oregon and Michigan. "Oregon's militia groups recently suffered from an internal struggle which left them weak, so we don't think they will cause any mischief for at least two more years."

The image next zoomed in on Michigan. "Now, the State of Michigan has only one large militia group and a few smaller splinter groups. The big one is well armed and equipped, its leadership is competent, and the rank-and-file members are loyal to the end. However, they lean more toward Ku Klux Klan-type activities. They don't regard the LDS Church as a threat because church members generally vote Republican and reflect conservative values. They don't regard Mormons as either ally or enemy as of last week."

The image again zoomed out on the entire United States.

"Believe it or not, that is *all* we have. If you believe any of these groups could be your threat, we have more information on each of them. But otherwise... any questions?"

It was clear by Collins' attitude he was not LDS and that he had been told to give them this briefing only as a professional courtesy. Parker wanted to jerk him around by the lapels and shake some sense into him until he could see the urgency of this issue. But she didn't.

"Yes," said Kincaid, hesitating for just a moment. "What about Muslim extremist groups? Our source has indicated an Islamic extremist group has identified the LDS Church as a *soft target* and plans to attack a temple to make its point."

Special Agent Collins didn't miss a beat. Placing one thigh sideways on the edge of the table and facing toward them, he replied. "I wouldn't doubt it. The church keeps a low profile and uses few security escorts, so it isn't seen as an armed organization ready for battling its enemies. That means *any* group would have an easy time attacking the church during meetings, at large activities, or events where thousands gather—like for general conference. They could probably even try to *kill* a general authority or take them hostage for ransom, and kill them just to make a point."

For several minutes, Special Agent Collins talked to them about the major Muslim population centers in the Detroit area and the suspected hot spots of which they should be aware.

Collins stood from his seat at the table and brushed away imaginary wrinkles in his trousers. "I have heard nothing in the traffic that would indicate a specific threat, but we would love to hear what you know," he said.

"I'll send you our report later this afternoon," Parker jumped in.

"Thank you. Now, anything else?" Collins asked.

There was nothing.

~Chapter Sixteen~

The next day, at the Salt Lake City International Airport, Parker showed her badge at the security station. The TSA supervisor flipped a hidden switch as Parker went through the metal detector with her weapon holstered beneath her jacket. The metal detector alarm did not sound, and the other travelers were none the wiser.

Kincaid had to declare his weapons at the baggage counter and leave them in a locked container inside his suitcase. The ticket agent placed a long sticker on the outside of his suitcase, stating a weapon was inside.

Once they landed at Detroit Metropolitan Airport and disembarked the plane, Kincaid and Parker picked up their suitcases from the turnstile. They then took the shuttle to the car rental company.

After filling out the paperwork, they walked out to the lot and placed their bags in the trunk. Before shutting the trunk, Kincaid opened his suitcase, unlocked the small Pelican case inside, and took out both of his SIG Sauers and their holsters. He inserted a full magazine into each SIG, chambered one round, and put the safety on. He put one into the shoulder holster and the other at the small of his back. He clipped an extra magazine into the small pocket beside the primary gun, shut the suitcase, and closed the trunk.

There was no question about who would drive the car. Parker knew the area, so Kincaid casually slid into the shotgun seat. He wanted the chance to look around as much as he could, to familiarize himself with the area.

"So, this is where you served your mission?" Kincaid asked. As they drove up the on-ramp of eastbound I-94, he looked out the window at the passing landscape.

Parker gave him a sidelong glance. "Yes, I spent eighteen months in this part of the world, preaching the Gospel."

"I went on a mission, too, you know," Kincaid said, still looking out the side window.

"What do you mean, you went on a mission?" Parker chuckled. "Was that before or after being a trained sniper for the Army? I just can't picture you in a white shirt and a tie for two years."

"I didn't," Kincaid answered. "I wore a white shirt and tie for about six hours and my name was Elder Gomez."

Parker's mouth fell open. She looked sideways at him again, while driving, trying to catch the joke. "You're serious, aren't you?" she finally replied, laughing as she shook her head. "Now, you will have to tell me *that* story." It was an unwritten law between partners all over the world, if one partner brought up a subject, it was fair game for the other partner to interrogate, until the whole story came out. "Come on. Out with it."

Enthralled by the potential of his story, Parker almost missed her turn onto eastbound I-96. She drove onto the ramp and kept driving without letting him know she almost missed their turn.

Kincaid started with the part where the enemy chased him, trying to kill him. He told her how he had stormed into the apartment of two missionaries and how they cut his hair and dressed him up in the clothing of a missionary who had completed his mission and returned home, leaving a few of his belongings behind—namely his name tag. He included how they had tricked him into listening to their discussions and how he had come to believe their message.

He told her about his interrogation by the main cartel bad

guy and how he had preached the Gospel to the sleazebag with boldness. He ended by telling her how his Mormon partner in that operation—not his missionary companion—had been killed from gunshot wounds before the six-hour missionary experience had even begun.

Throughout the entire story, Parker listened, intently. When Kincaid started the story in the middle, she at once realized it must be related to one of his military missions. When he finished, she didn't ask any questions about *where* it took place, *why* the bad guys wanted to kill him, or *why* he had been there in the first place.

Parker kept her eyes on the road, but her mind raced with amazement. "That has got to be the *wildest* conversion story I have ever heard," she said while laughing aloud. "You have to write that one up and send it to the Ensign Magazine."

"Nope. There are too many details I would have to leave out, so it's best not to tell anyone else."

"*Except* your partner," Parker added.

"Except my partner," Kincaid repeated with a grin. "You should know my history so you know you can trust me."

Parker turned on her blinker as she approached their exit. She got off at Woodward Avenue and drove north through downtown Detroit so Kincaid could get the lay of the land. "I trust you," she said, defensively, still amazed that anyone could have had so many wartime experiences in his young life.

"I've arranged for the Detroit Temple President and the Michigan Detroit Mission President to meet us at the stake center, later today. The stake center is another few miles down the road, so we'll stay here for the night." Less than a mile from the off ramp, Parker drove past the Marriott Hotel and turned right two streets farther down, pulling into the parking lot of a Motel 6. She parked the car outside the motel office and lobby.

Kincaid watched as they drove past the Marriott but only commented when she parked the car. "Are you kidding?" he insisted.

Parker knew what he meant, but she still turned off the engine and opened her door.

"Isn't the Marriott family a super-Mormon family?" Kincaid asked. "Why aren't we staying *there*? Church employees must get a great discount."

"Yes, we do. We get a free Book of Mormon in every room." Parker grinned as they both stepped out of the car. She punched Kincaid in the arm when he showed no sign of understanding her joke.

"Wait... What?" Kincaid asked before he saw the grin creep onto her face.

"Don't worry. There's a Tigers game in town tonight, and all the rooms in the Marriott are taken," she explained.

"How far away is the stadium?" Kincaid asked.

"Only about five or six miles," Parker replied.

"Are you kidding? And all the hotel rooms for six miles are taken by baseball fans?"

"No, all the rooms for *ten* miles are taken," Parker clarified. "I could only get us these two rooms because two of their customers canceled out at the last minute. This was the best we could do on such short notice. But don't worry. I'll take you to a special place for dinner, to make up for it."

"What does *that* mean?" he asked, skeptical of the fiendish tone in her voice. "Where do you plan to go for dinner?"

"Have you ever had a Coney Dog?"

"What kind of hot dog is that?" Kincaid asked.

"Good. I'll introduce you," she replied, ignoring his question.

After checking in and getting their room keys, Kincaid took his bag to the room. Parker dragged her wheeled suitcase with one hand, looping her free arm through Kincaid's free arm as they walked.

"C'mon, now. What's so special about a Coney Dog?"

Kincaid asked, bringing them back to their conversation before they checked into their motel rooms.

"You have not lived until you've eaten a Coney Dog," she said, almost drooling as she spoke. "But first, we can rest in our rooms for about an hour. Then we have an appointment with a mentor of mine."

*****

An hour later, Parker turned into a large parking lot flanked on both sides by two Mormon structures. One structure had a tall steeple topped with a golden statue of a man blowing a long horn; he faced east. The other looked like so many other LDS chapels around the world. One story, steeped roof, with a spire that pointed to the heavens.

"Is that a statue of Joseph Smith blowing the horn on top of the temple?" Kincaid asked, still staring up at it.

"No, that's the Angel Moroni. That same statue is on top of all the temples, worldwide. Keep asking your questions, and we'll turn you into a real Mormon before you're even baptized."

There were quite a few parked cars as Kincaid and Parker pulled into the lot. One sign said *Detroit Temple, The Church of Jesus Christ of Latter-day Saints*. The other sign said, *Bloomfield Hills, Michigan Stake*.

Parker pulled into a spot near the stake center building.

"Aren't we here to visit the temple president?" Kincaid asked, wondering why they parked so far from the temple.

"Yes, but you don't have a temple recommend, so we'll meet him here, in the high council room," she replied.

"Hey, I've only been an investigator for a few days. It takes a year after baptism before I can go inside there, doesn't it?" he asked, walking backward so he could continue staring at the temple. Although he hadn't spoken about it to anyone else, Kincaid was already looking forward to his baptism and the end of the subsequent one year of probation, so he could see why it was such a popular place for long-time LDS Church members.

"I guess it's possible to get a temple recommend in less than a year, but only to do baptisms for the dead," she said.

Kincaid was still walking backward and almost tripped over a large rock at the junction of the sidewalk and the walkway to the entrance of the stake center. "What? What are baptisms for the dead?"

"God has commanded us to do all the ordinances for everyone who ever lived on this planet. That starts with baptism and ends with sealing them to their parents, spouse, and children."

Kincaid hesitated as he looked at the chapel doors. "I've got more questions, but it looks like they're waiting for us," Kincaid said, pointing to the entrance.

Parker turned and saw two men standing inside the building's foyer as she and her partner approached. "Whenever we have time to ourselves, I'll be glad to answer them," she said, as a man opened the door for them.

"President Rutherford," Parker said, holding out her hand to the man who was holding the door for them.

"Sister Parker," the man replied, shaking her hand with vigor, and giving her a big hug. "It's good to see you again."

"Same here," she said. "But aren't you about ready to go home?"

"My wife and I got extended for a year because my replacement had health issues that delayed him. The brethren didn't want to cancel his calling, so they asked me to hang in there," he explained.

"Hang in there?"

Hearing Kincaid's voice, Parker remembered she was not alone. "I'm sorry. President Rutherford, this is my partner, Orson Kincaid. He's with the Service."

Orson stepped forward and extended his hand. "Glad to meet you, sir."

"Oh, a military man," Rutherford said as he shook Kincaid's firm hand and observed his straight shoulders and short hair.

"Is it that obvious?" Kincaid said. "I spent ten years in the Army before I got out earlier this year."

"I'm a retired Marine myself," Rutherford said, chuckling. "You know what they say: 'Once a Marine...'"

"Always a Marine. Yes sir," Kincaid, finished the popular saying for him.

President Rutherford almost jumped. "Now, where are *my* manners," he said, stepping aside and gesturing to the other man, who stood quietly behind him as he spoke with his former sister missionary. "Brother Kincaid, Sister Parker, let me introduce President Dorn—Detroit Temple President."

"I have come to the stake center because you are not yet endowed, am I right, Brother Kincaid?" He smiled. "You have a special look about you." He stopped and studied Kincaid from his cowboy boots to his cowboy hat, in hand, and nodded. "Now I see it. You already *know* the Gospel is true, but you are still *learning* about the Gospel, am I right?"

Kincaid looked at the man who President Rutherford had introduced. He wore a white suit coat and tie along with the white shirt and trousers—neat, but not military crisp. Even his shoes and socks were white.

President Dorn stepped forward and extended his hand to both of the visitors.

Parker was the first to pull out her badge. As she did so, Kincaid reached into his pocket and pulled out his credentials.

"President Dorn, I'm afraid we're here on official business. I'm an FBI Special Agent and liaison to Church headquarters in Salt Lake City. My partner is an agent of the Church Personal Services," she explained, with an air of formality.

"Please, come inside so we can talk turkey," President Dorn said as he walked past the chapel and down the hallway. The others followed as President Rutherford and Parker continued catching up on old times.

Before long, they came to an open door, and President Dorn stepped inside the room. The others followed. "Please. Let's sit in here, where we won't be disturbed." He gestured them all to a chair.

The room was dwarfed by two large tables. One was long and wide and took up the length of the room. The other table was shorter and narrower and sat at one end of the longer table like the cross on a 'T.' On the wall at one end of the table was a framed painting of Jesus Christ at His second coming.

At the other end of the dark wood table was a large photograph of the current twelve apostles. On the same wall as the door were three framed photographs arranged in a triangle. At the top was the current prophet. A little lower and to each side were his two counselors. Kincaid had seen all of those pictures in the COB.

He smiled at seeing the photo of the prophet who had defined for him, his path toward baptism. He knew the two counselors by name but realized he had already met one counselor. He was the elderly man in the wheelchair who came into the Prophet's outer office while Kincaid was there.

The two presidents took seats on the far side of the table; Parker and Kincaid sat near the door, facing them.

"So, how can we help the Service and the FBI?" asked President Dorn, taking the lead.

Parker looked over at her partner and nodded to let him know it was his show.

Kincaid began. "Brothers, we believe a threat to the church leadership exists, and to at least one temple somewhere in the world, from a group of either international or home-grown terrorists." He looked at the two older and wiser men for a reaction but saw none.

He continued. "We wondered if you might have noticed any strangers lurking around the buildings, or experienced any vandalism, graffiti, or threats by anyone at any of the church buildings in the Greater Detroit area?"

Presidents Rutherford and Dorn looked at each other in confusion and finally shook their heads.

President Rutherford turned to Parker, then to Kincaid. "Can't say we have," he said with a shrug.

"Do you think *this* temple is in any danger?" President Dorn asked.

"No, we haven't come here because we believe *this* temple is in danger," Kincaid explained. "We came here after discussing the matter with the FBI, so we could follow up on a few leads they gave us. We thought we would ask you both whether you have experienced or heard of any members experiencing these kinds of problems."

The four people discussed the volatile issue for several more minutes. Parker explained what they might look for and advised them to call her or her partner if they discovered anything off-kilter.

Both Parker and Kincaid slid two of their business cards across the table toward the brethren.

Kincaid recommended they inform the local church leaders to be on the lookout for problems but advised them to keep this information from the regular membership until they could get a better handle on the situation. "No sense scaring people who do not need to be afraid," Kincaid solemnly said.

When their business was finished, Parker and Kincaid stood, shook the presidents' hands, and walked back to the door with them. Parker and President Rutherford continued their personal discussion, bringing each other up to date on their lives. Before they reached the door, he advised her to find a good priesthood bearer husband and settle down to raise a family. Parker laughed and assured him she would try.

Before this meeting, Kincaid hadn't known much about how the LDS Church worked behind the scenes. Now, he realized it worked similarly to the military, with a chain of command and an alert roster, to contact all leaders in short order. In some ways, the church seemed to work *better* than the military, when an emergency made it necessary to get a message to the people.

Parker and Kincaid returned to their vehicle.

"So, are you really *looking*?" Kincaid asked.

"Looking for what?"

"A good Priesthood bearer, so you can raise a family?" Kincaid said with a big grin.

"Yeah, right! No, I'm stuck here with you, instead of looking for a husband. If I ever get *selected* for a good FBI assignment, how would I take care of a family?"

"I'm just sayin'…" Kincaid laughed, knowing he was putting undue pressure on his new partner on a personal matter.

As Parker drove the car out of the lot, Kincaid noticed two identical, black SUVs parked together in the lot. He looked at the license plates and recognized New Jersey plates. The windows were tinted dark, but he thought he saw one driver and at least one passenger sitting inside both vehicles. He thought it strange in several ways, but the moment quickly faded and soon they were in traffic, heading back toward Detroit.

"Where to, now?" Kincaid asked, considering the two SUVs as coincidental and most likely non-threatening.

"Now, we go to the Islamic Center of Detroit, to see what kind of cooperation and information we can get from them," she said. "It's almost a straight shot from here, closer to the city."

Kincaid recognized the name of the center from their FBI briefing. Special Agent Collins had identified that center and mosque as having more activity than all the others combined. "Let's go shopping, first," Kincaid said, looking over at his partner.

"Shopping? Why?"

"I think we might get more cooperation from the Mullah at the mosque, if we show respect for their customs when we arrive," Kincaid responded. "I need to get a pair of loafers instead of these boots, and you need a Hijab to cover your head."

"A what?" Parker asked in confusion.

"A Hijab. It's the head covering traditional Muslim women wear," Kincaid said. "If we go to a mosque, we will gain points up front if you wear one. You know a place we might buy items like that?"

Parker thought about it for a moment, put on her left blinker and turned the car when traffic cleared. "We need to go to Hamtramck for Muslim clothing articles," she said. She turned left off Woodward Avenue and to the Edsel Ford Expressway eastbound on-ramp.

"Hamtramck? What kind of store is that?" Kincaid asked.

"It's not a store. It used to be a ghetto of Detroit where all the Polish immigrants settled when they came to this area. It's more of a Muslim community now, so we should be able to find the store we need in that area. It's right near here."

They parked the car in a large, public lot and walked down the street until Kincaid saw the store he wanted.

"Let me do the talking," Kincaid said. He entered the store without waiting for his partner. Parker followed behind him. The small shop displayed women's Hijabs, men's Kufias, slip-on shoes, and other clothing traditionally worn by Muslim men and women in Arabic nations. In the US, some women wore the entire burka in public, but most of them just wore the hijab when they left the house.

They went inside the shop and Kincaid greeted the storekeeper, in traditional Arabic, placing his right hand over his heart and bowing, slightly at the waist, as he spoke.

The sales clerk had been sitting by herself behind the counter. As her customers came in, she quickly threw on a hijab to cover her head. Other than the hijab, she was dressed conservatively, but in a manner common to American women. She wore loose-fitting slacks and a thin cardigan sweater with long sleeves, over a plain white blouse.

The woman expressed her surprise at hearing the correct greeting from a Caucasian. She replied in kind, shifting to Pashtu, as a sign of friendship, and asked what she could do for them. Kincaid continued speaking in Pashtu.

"We plan to visit the local mosque and would like to purchase some items so we can honor your customs while we are there."

"Of course." The woman walked to a shelf and showed Parker several styles and colors of Hijabs.

Parker took several colorful Hijabs from the shelf. "These are beautiful!" she exclaimed.

"Thank you," said the saleswoman.

After ten minutes—and the purchase of three Hijabs and a pair of slippers for Parker, a kufia and pair of slip-on shoes for Kincaid, they thanked the woman. Kincaid handed the bags to Parker and walked out the door.

Parker started to bristle at being considered a workhorse, but let it slide as soon as she remembered the customs.

"We're only going into the Mosque this one time. Why'd you buy three Hijabs?"

Parker thought for a moment, then shrugged. "I couldn't decide which one to buy. They're all so pretty."

Kincaid shook his head. "Even when you give a woman a gun and teach her to shoot, she's *still* a woman."

Parker glared at him. "I should *hope* so."

As they walked back to their car, Parker couldn't hold off any longer. "You are one surprise after another, aren't you?" She stared in amazement at her partner. "That didn't sound like the Arabic you spoke with that walk-in, at the office." It was more of an accusation than a mere statement.

Kincaid smiled as he opened the car door and sat with his feet still on the ground. "It wasn't. It was Pashtu or Farsi. They're almost alike," he said over his shoulder. "What was I supposed to do–introduce myself on day one and say, 'I also speak Arabic, Spanish, and Farsi,' while shaking your hand?" He reached into the shopping bag and extracted the outdoor slippers he had bought. He took off his boots, tossed them in the back seat, and put on the slippers.

"Well, uh, no, I guess not," she blustered, searching for a point of logic to pull her out of the mess she had caused herself. "Wait, What? Where did you get time to learn those languages? You were a soldier who went to combat."

"I was in the Army for *ten* years. I guess I'm a quick study," he replied. "I learned Spanish in high school while living in southern Arizona and Arabic and Farsi while I was in the Army."

"Well, you could have *told* me," she settled on saying.

"It's *all* in my jacket," Kincaid said. "I thought you said you *read* it?" He smiled as he swung his feet into the car and shut the door behind him.

~Chapter Seventeen~

When they arrived at the Islamic Center, Parker stopped the car across the street from the center and left it in a free, public parking lot. There was a large and ornate mosque beside the Center, with a breezeway running between the two structures. Before getting out of the car, Parker changed into the new slip-on shoes she had purchased for the occasion and struggled with the Hijab.

Kincaid reached over the seat and helped her arrange it properly. "You won't have to cover your face, but let me do the talking," he said as he swung the long end of the Hijab across her throat and back over her right shoulder.

"As long as you talk in English," she replied. "This is an official investigation, and I want to know what's going on during an interview."

"Of course," he replied. "In fact, I don't want these people knowing I speak their language. We might get a little intelligence out of them while they're speaking among themselves if they think we don't know what they're saying."

Parker agreed. They both tossed their smartphones in the console and got out of the car. As they walked across the street, Kincaid had a little more to add. "This shouldn't get ugly, so keep your shield in your pocket. Let me show my credentials so they don't throw up a wall of resistance at talking to a fed. Okay?"

Parker scowled. She didn't like it, but she saw the logic in his plan. "Next, you'll be telling me to walk behind you and to keep my mouth shut."

"Only for the next half hour," Kincaid said with a grin. He picked up his pace to walk several paces in front of her. "After all, it is for the sake of the investigation." He turned his head forward and walked straight toward the front entrance of the mosque beside the center.

A large, golden dome adorned the top of the mosque, with a crescent moon at its peak. It was flanked by two long, slender minarets from which the call to prayer was issued five times each day. The entire mosque was painted in impeccable white and was lit between sundown and sunrise each day so that all might see and appreciate its majesty.

As they stepped inside the mosque, an elderly man with a long, white beard began walking toward them. He was dressed in the robes and accouterments of a Muslim religious leader. Kincaid led Parker to a bank of cubbyholes along one wall. He took off his shoes and placed them in a cubbyhole. Parker did the same as the man approached them.

"Assalamu alaikum," the elderly man said to Kincaid, placing his right hand over his heart.

"Wa alaikum salaam," Kincaid replied in the traditional response.

The elderly man asked Kincaid in Arabic how he could help him.

"Yes, please. My name is Orson Kincaid," he said in English, reaching into his coat and pulling out his credentials. "I work for the security service of The Church of Jesus Christ of Latter-day Saints, in Salt Lake City, Utah.

"Yes, of course. I am Mullah Abd al-Salim al-Ahmad. Your office said you would be here today or tomorrow. How may I help you?" he added, more cordially. He glanced at Parker, but quickly returned his attention to Kincaid after giving her a cursory look.

"We have received word of a plot to destroy one of our

temples and we—"

"So, of course, you thought it must be a Muslim that would want to do this destruction?" the Mullah accused, the cordiality instantly gone from his voice.

"No, sir. We will also follow up on other leads. But it would be reckless of us to automatically assume the perpetrators were not Muslim, don't you think?" Kincaid had meant no offense and did not want the Mullah to perceive any, where none existed. He stopped to gauge the response of this Muslim spiritual leader.

The Mullah took in a deep breath to compose himself. "I am sorry. The hatred between your people and mine seems to build every day."

"My people? Do you mean Christians in general, or Americans, or Mormons specifically?" he asked, only half jesting.

Before the Mullah could respond, a door opened from the breezeway. Two men looked around and hurried toward the Mullah. A third person remained standing in the shadows, holding the door open and watching from a safe distance. Kincaid could see nothing of him except a human shape in shadow. It appeared to be the shape of a thin young male.

As the two men jogged up to the Mullah, Parker pressed her elbow against her ribcage where the holster held her Glock .40 caliber handgun. It was more of a habit whenever she felt threatened.

Kincaid caught a quick, faint aroma on the men, but was not sure of what it was. On the right side of the neck of each man was a tattoo—written in Arabic which said, "Allahu Akbar."

"We have brought the man you told us..." a man began in Arabic until the Mullah held up his hand to silence him and glanced back at Kincaid with a smile.

He switched to Pashtu. "I have guests here," he said, in a calm voice, indicating both Kincaid and Parker. "Hold him downstairs until our friend can talk to him. He will know how to handle the dog."

The Mullah's voice was smooth as cream, but Kincaid understood one of their workers must have made a big mistake. He would most likely be detained until an "enforcer" could arrive to deal with the infraction—whatever it was.

Both men turned to Kincaid and studied him, assessing him for usefulness and as a potential threat. After a friendly smile and nod from Kincaid, they brusquely turned away, thanked the Mullah, and returned through the door from which they had come. The shadowed silhouette held the door open for them and shut it after they had all exited.

The movement of air in their wake brought the faint smell back to Kincaid's nose. Only this time he recognized it from his military experience—cordite.

"I am sorry," the Mullah apologized. "The boy who cleans up after each prayer session did not appear this morning, until now. I must go and chastise him for his waywardness."

Kincaid held up one hand as the Mullah turned to walk away. "One more question," Kincaid said. "We don't know that any enmity exists between our people, but if you hear of anything that could harm us, would you call me?" he said, handing the Mullah a business card.

For a mere second, impatience flashed in the Mullah's eyes. Then it evaporated, and he spoke cordially, as he had, earlier. "Of course," he said, reaching out and accepting the card. "We have no extremists in our mosque. I would not allow it. I want only peace between the Mormons and the Muslims, and I would do anything to help support that feeling of friendship between us," he said. He bowed, extended his hand, and shook Kincaid's. For the first time, the Mullah turned toward Parker and gave a slight nod, acknowledging her existence, before hastening toward the door of the breezeway.

Parker and Kincaid retrieved their shoes and walked back toward their car.

"Did you understand any of what they said?"

"Oh, yeah," said Kincaid as soon as they were outside the sanctuary. "Those two men were up to no good. As soon as they spoke in Arabic, the Mullah shut them down and switched to Farsi, thinking we wouldn't understand them."

"And...?" said Parker, needing him to explain. "Did you understand *them*?"

Kincaid brushed off the question. "Did you smell anything on those other two men when they walked up to the Mullah?" Kincaid asked.

Parker shuttered. "You mean, other than several years of accumulated body odor?"

"No, that part is normal. There was also another smell."

When they both got into the car, Parker took off the Hijab. She folded it, neatly, and placed it in its box on the back seat. "So, what was the odor?"

"Cordite. Gun powder." Kincaid retrieved his boots from the back seat and put them on, tossing the slippers in the back. He also took off the kufia and retrieved his cowboy hat.

As Parker pulled out of the parking lot, Kincaid looked over at the mosque and the Islamic Center. To the rear of the structures were two black SUVs, parked as if loading or unloading supplies at the back entrance of the mosque. He remembered the two black SUVs parked in the temple parking lot. Coincidence? Maybe... Maybe not. "Hey, turn left here. Quick!" Kincaid commanded.

She swerved the vehicle where her partner had indicated, and they drove along a side street one block away from the Islamic Center. That block was an empty field and allowed them to keep watching the mosque as they turned again and drove toward the back side of the Center.

"What did you see?" she asked, looking for anything unusual.

"See those SUVs?" Kincaid asked.

"Yes, of course."

"I saw those same SUVs at the temple parking lot, this

morning."

"They can't be the same ones," Parker assured him.

"I don't know. Drive slowly past them. The ones this morning had New Jersey license plates on them. In Michigan, that can't be too common." Kincaid scrambled to take out a small notebook and pen.

Parker kept driving unhurriedly and read the license numbers as she saw them. Kincaid wrote them in his book. They then drove past the backside of the mosque and turned away from it. "Are those the same numbers as this morning?" she asked.

"I don't know," Kincaid replied. "I didn't get the numbers this morning, but I'm sure they're the same vehicles. How many people with black SUVs would drive from New Jersey to Michigan, anyway?" He tried to make his point, as they drove back to their motel rooms.

Parker shook her head once. "Keep those numbers handy and we'll see if they appear again."

*****

"It's about dinner time," said Kincaid. "Is there a good steak house around here?"

"Uh-uh," corrected Parker. "I promised to give you a real Michigan treat for dinner, and I won't let you leave this state until you taste your first Coney Dog."

"What kind of dog?"

Parker glanced impatiently at her partner as she changed lanes and slowed down to pull into the parking lot of a National Coney Island Restaurant. "These restaurants are all over southeast Michigan, but *this* one is the best—and it's less than one mile from our motel. *This* is where we will eat dinner, tonight."

"I've eaten dog on two continents, but never in a restaurant," Kincaid said to himself.

"Dog? What are you mumbling about?" cried Parker.

Realizing her partner was ribbing her, she said, "No, not *dog* meat, a *Coney* Dog. It's a hot dog the way the good Lord intended hot dogs to be prepared and eaten." Pulling into the restaurant parking lot, she turned off the engine and opened her door.

They both walked inside. Flat-screen televisions were mounted on every wall. They were all tuned to the last inning of the Detroit Tigers' baseball game. People gathered around the monitors, more interested in the game than the beers in their hands. They all spoke to each other in loud voices, pointed to the screen, then cheered as their team got another hit, putting two men on base.

The Tigers were playing the Texas Rangers, and the Rangers were ahead by two points. At the bottom of the ninth inning, the Rangers' pitcher hurled a fast ball, low and inside. The umpire called it a strike, and the people in the restaurant booed the call.

Of course, they could all see better than the umpire, Kincaid thought.

The next pitch was right down the middle. The batter struck that ball so hard it hit the roof above the upper deck in right field, without even slowing down. Home run! The entire room erupted in cheers with people jumping up and down, throwing their fists into the air, exchanging high-fives and hugs with anyone close to them. The two runners on base and the hitter leisurely ran around the bases until they scored. The Tigers won the game by a single point.

"What's the big deal?" asked Kincaid as the hostess led him and Parker to their booth. All the tables near the bar and the televisions were taken, so they got a booth near the back wall, which was fine with Kincaid.

"The Tigers have now won their last seven games straight, and they've got a good shot at the World Series, this year," the hostess said, with pride. She put two large and colorful menus on the table. "Lonni is your waitress this evening, and she'll be right with you."

Kincaid chose the bench which put his back to the wall, so he could monitor the entire room. Personal security habits were hard for him to break. Sitting where he could watch the whole room—especially the door—may not be important in *this* job, but then again, he was not so sure about that.

Kincaid opened his tri-fold menu. It was plastic coated, all in brilliant colors to show their entire variety of hot dogs—Coney Dogs—and to make the customers salivate even more than when they had come in. "I've never been much of a hot dog person," Kincaid yelled above the continued cheering and loud talking throughout the establishment. They sat on opposite sides of the wide booth table which forced them to lean closer toward each other so they could carry on a decent conversation.

"Let me order for you," Parker yelled back with a big smile.

When the waitress came to their table, Parker motioned for her to bend down. She yelled their order into Lonni's ear. At one point, both women looked over at Kincaid and smiled. Parker went back to whisper-yelling, and Lonni nodded her understanding.

When Lonni left to turn in their order, Haley Parker called her back, held up one finger, and mouthed the words "One check." She then stood, stepped around the table, and pushed her new partner over, to share the bench with him.

"It will be a little easier for us to talk, this way," she said.

Kincaid nodded his approval. "How did a sister missionary find a place like this?" he asked in amazement, as the noise in the restaurant began to diminish. With the game over, many of the customers quieted down and others even paid their bills and left.

"Two of the Elder missionaries told us about the place during a Zone Conference," she said. "My companion and I came here once for lunch, and we were hooked. Neither of us could afford to come often, but in the four months we were together, we must have come five or six times."

"Did you eat the same kind of Coney Dog every time?"

She laughed. "No, that wasn't our choice. We decided everything looked so good that we ate different entries every time."

"So, what's on the menu, tonight?" Kincaid asked.

Parker cocked one eyebrow and glared at him. "It's called the Bull Dog, and it's got *everything* on it."

"Yum," said Kincaid, with half a smile. "I can hardly wait."

Parker elbowed his shoulder. "Oh, come on," she said. "You've got to at least *try* it."

When Lonni brought their meals, she lingered to watch Kincaid's reaction. Kincaid was awed by the size of the meal and intimidated by the number of condiments on it. The Bull Dog must have had everything except chocolate syrup on it, but he dove in, anyway. This was the food of the indigenous folk and he didn't want to shame or anger them by turning down their offering.

Parker ate her favorite Coney Dog with chili, cheese, onions, and mustard on the dog. When she picked it up and put the bun to her mouth, she accidentally elbowed Kincaid as he was eating his own dog. Globs of condiments fell onto both plates. They tried to laugh, and their mouths were so full, it just made the mess even worse.

After Kincaid chewed and swallowed, he said, "You did that on purpose."

Parker hooted. "Honestly, I didn't. I just didn't have the space for that first bite. That same thing happened to my missionary companion and me when *we* came here."

The ballgame and after-game critique were over, and the monitors went back on mute as they all showed different sports or news shows. The noise level lowered, so the patrons could all talk to each other without hollering.

Kincaid finished his meal by using a spoon to scoop up all the condiments he'd dropped on his plate.

"Now you're getting the hang of it," Parker said. "No need

to waste any of it."

Kincaid smiled but remained silent for another moment. "You know, this is a nice family restaurant. I could see how it might become a favorite of young soldiers if it was near a military base. Thanks for recommending this place."

"It *has* been nice, hasn't it? Before this, the closest we've come to having any social time together was on the FBI's shooting range."

"You're right. We better not let it happen again, or we might lose our edge as a dispassionate partnership. I'd hate to think we might start treating each other like brothers and sisters in the church."

"All right. So, I did come on strong in the office that first day."

"Strong? You almost had me crying and running into the street to look for someone more *qualified* for the position, so I could turn it over to him—or her."

Lonni appeared with their bill on a small tray.

Parker blushed, salvaged a small dab of chili from her plate, and sucked it off her spoon. "This meal is on me," she said, grabbing the bill as fast as Lonni could put it on their table.

"I'll *let* you get this one," Kincaid said. "The next one is on me. I heard there are still a few White Castle hamburger joints in the state."

"Don't you *dare*! Five-for-a-dollar hamburgers? Uh-uh! If we're going to play *that* game, then I'll pay for *all* our meals. That'll still be better than having our stomachs pumped at a hospital."

~Chapter Eighteen~

After paying for their meals, Parker drove them back to their motel. They were both full after eating. Kincaid was afraid if he spoke, he would either belch or puke, which would probably not impress his new partner. He had even turned down the chocolate mints the restaurant offered at the cash register.

Maybe it was the full stomach that made him wonder. "What's life like as a missionary?" he asked Parker while they drove down Woodward Avenue.

"You mean for more than six hours?" she replied, poking fun at him for his story earlier in the day.

"Yeah." Kincaid got a dreamy look in his eye. "I wish I could have served a full two years as a missionary."

Parker's eyes lost their focus for a moment. "It was the most wonderful time of my life. I learned and grew so *much*," she emphasized, looking right at him.

"Did you get many baptisms?"

"Well, yes, I did. But that's *not* what it's all about," she said. "It's about giving people the chance to listen to the message and choose for themselves. And when they listen, we teach them what they need to know to return to Heavenly Father."

"Now I *really* wish I could have gone on a mission," Kincaid repeated.

"I wish we had received more intelligence information from the Mullah at the mosque," Parker said, changing the subject. "Today, we can't even say the threat is a Muslim threat, or even that the threat is in Michigan."

"Yeah, I know what you mean," Kincaid agreed. "There's a problem in that Center, but we can't prove it has anything to do with our investigation."

Parker pulled into the motel parking lot and stopped the car in the only available parking space, around the corner from their first-floor rooms. The parking lot was full because of the Tigers game and the nightclub attached to the motel. As they stepped out of their vehicle, the sound of club music filled the air.

They were both quiet as they rounded the corner toward their adjoining rooms. A slight breeze blew the intense smell of body odor, cordite, and something else into Kincaid's nostrils. He stopped mid-stride and motioned for his partner to stop. He looked at the door to his room. "My door's open," he whispered as he pulled out his SIG Sauer.

Parker also pulled out her gun. She held it in front of her with both hands and signaled her partner that she would lead the way through the door and into the room. Kincaid prepared to follow close behind. Although they had never practiced this before, they both knew how it went.

At that moment, a black SUV drove past the motel's parking lot with an open sliding door. Weapons extending through the open door sprayed automatic gunfire at Parker and Kincaid. They both dove to the asphalt behind two parked cars. In seconds, dozens of bullets riddled the windows, walls, and doors of the cars near that part of the motel.

As the SUV sped away, they jumped to their feet. Instantly, several more gunshots sounded from inside Kincaid's room. They hit the ground again and heard the sudden crash of glass and metal from inside. Parker pulled out her badge on its chain around her neck, then nodded that she would lead the way inside. Kincaid prepared to follow her into the room, his weapon at the ready.

Rushing inside, Parker went right. Kincaid followed, going

left.

"FBI!" she yelled, checking the room as she rushed inside.

"Hands! Show me your hands!" Kincaid hollered, scanning left and center. He rushed to the bathroom and looked through the broken glass window. The room's coffee maker laid on the grass and gravel of the alley, outside the window, amidst the shards of broken glass from the window.

Three more shots rang out, and bullets struck the window frame near Kincaid's head. He dove for the floor, waited two seconds, and rose again, the muzzle of his gun leading the search for the culprit. All he saw was a light-weight figure wearing dark clothing and a black baseball cap, racing down the alley, away from his room. As the suspect ran beneath the glow of a streetlight, Kincaid saw the cap fly off his head in the wind. His flowing long, straight, black hair and what looked like a white streak on one side of his head instantly brought back memories that shocked Kincaid to the core.

"No way!" he exclaimed to himself, as he climbed onto the sink and dove out the window. Gun in hand, he sprinted after his suspect.

Parker ran to the window and watched as her partner raced after a suspect dressed in black. She remained in the room, which was now, officially, a crime scene. She was shocked at what she found on the king-sized bed.

As Kincaid ran down the alley, the other black SUV stopped at a cross-street. Kincaid fired three shots at the back of the running suspect. Three men threw open the SUV's doors and fanned out from the vehicle.

Kincaid immediately recognized the compact SR-3 Russian automatic weapons they fired in his direction, giving their compatriot a chance to get to the vehicle. Kincaid knew their distinctive sound. He had familiarized himself with the 9mm SR-3s in his unit. They were great in close quarters—but only for targets closer than twenty meters. Otherwise, they were impossible to aim and almost useless unless the shooter sprayed a magazine of rounds—the way these guys were spraying.

Kincaid immediately dove behind a nearby trash dumpster. He waited a few seconds, then raced again toward his man, while the others changed magazines. He shot another three-round burst at his target. The first one caught him in the heel. The man fell from the bullet's impact, before reaching the vehicle, skidding along the asphalt.

Kincaid's two other rounds impacted in the side of the vehicle, right where the man's head had been before he tripped. The wounded man got to his feet and limped around the SUV to the open door, jumping into the back seat.

As soon as the man with long black hair leaped into the back seat, the same shock of long white on the black hair came out the front passenger window with his gun. He swiped his jet-black hair out of his face, took aim through the open window, and shot at Kincaid. This time he held a simple semi-automatic handgun, not the SR-3 he had used moments earlier. The snow-white streak of hair fell forward, getting in the man's eyes.

How did he do that? Kincaid wondered to himself as he kept running and shooting at the three men giving cover fire. Why would his man race around the SUV to get into the back seat, then use a different gun from the front seat?

Kincaid ducked behind a car in the alley for cover. Ejecting the empty magazine from his handgun, he slammed a full one in its place. Popping up, he shot three times and wounded one shooter in the shoulder. He shot at another one and dropped him in place. The man fell and stopped moving on the old and cracked blacktop beside the SUV.

Kincaid felt the bile creeping up into his throat as he considered shooting more at these men. He disregarded it and swallowed hard, to put it back down. He had a job to do, first.

At a signal from the SUV driver, the two remaining gunners raced back to the vehicle and jumped inside. The driver sped away in a trail of smoke and black rubber along the pavement, leaving their fallen compatriot behind.

For good measure, Kincaid emptied his magazine at the fleeing vehicle, hoping to hit a tire or gas tank. No luck. At least three rounds slammed into the tailgate and rear window without any crippling effects.

Two blocks away, the SUV skidded left around a corner and was gone.

Kincaid raced to the body lying in the street. He kicked the SR-3 out of reach of the dead man and searched the body for any clues to his identity. No wallet, no keys, a thin wad of cash, and an extra full magazine—nothing else.

He looked around the area for anyone who might have witnessed the gun battle. Again, nothing. He reached into his back trouser pocket, pulled out his cell phone, and called his partner.

"Parker."

"Was that you shooting? Are you all right?" she asked.

"Yeah, yeah. I'm fine. Our perp got away, but I have the body of another of their people here, in the alley. What should I do with it?"

"Pull the body out of the way of any foot and vehicular traffic. Collect any weapons and bring them back here. You have to see what our guy left behind, in your room."

Kincaid agreed. While searching the area, he noticed a video camera perched on the roof of a two-story brick building across the street. He filed that information in the back of his mind. hoping it was still being maintained. But he would have to check on that, later.

Kincaid dragged the dead body out of the street and dropped it next to the building at the entrance to the alley. Picking up the abandoned SR-3, he ran back to the motel room with it. He stopped short, outside the open door to his room. "Parker. It's Kincaid. Don't shoot," he yelled.

"Come on in," said the tired, familiar voice of his partner.

Kincaid entered the room, holstered his weapon, and handed the SR-3 to her.

She stood at the foot of the king-sized bed. The single light was from a bedside lamp. Parker was on her cell phone, giving directions for the police and the coroner to come to the crime scene.

On the bed was the body of a man, lying on his back, dressed only in his shorts. His face was turned to one side. It was bloody, bruised, and broken. Finally, he had been shot twice in the chest and once in the face. Both his wrists and ankles were bound and tied to the bed corners with electric cords.

"Do you know who this guy is?" Parker asked as soon as she ended her phone conversation.

"Should I?" Kincaid replied, looking at the beaten face with no idea of his identity. He realized not even his family would recognize the man this way.

"That's the guy Tanner, and you interviewed back in Salt Lake City," she said. "Farhan. The guy who told us about the threat to the church."

Silent seconds hung in the air between them like a blackout curtain.

Kincaid looked closely at the man who had flown to Utah just to warn them of a threat. The sight of blood was not new to him, but this kind of death for a man who just wanted to keep peace, created a profound sense of sorrow in Kincaid's heart. They had no time to discuss that topic now. They could talk about it later. He had work to do, now.

"I guess this confirms the threat," Kincaid said, stating the obvious. "And I *might* know who's behind it."

Just then, the shrill sound of multiple sirens filled the air as several of Detroit's finest surrounded the motel. Kincaid and Parker both went outside, into the parking lot, to greet them. Parker holstered her gun and held her badge visible around her neck, for all to see. "Now the circus starts."

*****

Detroit Police Detective Lamar Morehouse was the lead investigator on the scene. He arrived within twenty minutes of Parker's call to 9-1-1. He had taken his family out to dinner and just got them home when his cell phone rang. The dispatcher's voice directed him to go to the crime scene at the Motel 6 at Woodward Avenue and Champion Street.

He wore an old cap to cover a bald head. With a clean-shaven face and about twenty to thirty pounds of excess baggage, wearing a herringbone wool sports jacket and shoes that were attached with Velcro, he completed the picture of a big city detective.

Because of the number of calls to 9-1-1 reporting gunshots, and the estimated high number of gunshot injuries in Detroit, the nearby Oakland County Sheriff's Department also sent two squad cars. Their job was to help with protecting the crime scene and conducting traffic control, nearby.

Morehouse rolled half a toothpick in his mouth as he approached two people. When he saw her badge, he walked straight toward Parker. He didn't yet know which agency she represented, but he could smell a fed from twenty feet away. He wondered what it was about *this* crime scene that made it a *federal* case.

"I'm Police Detective Morehouse," he said to Parker, glancing at the male, Caucasian who accompanied her. He didn't wear a badge, so Morehouse was interested in who the shmo was.

"I'm FBI Special Agent Haley Parker. This is my partner, Orson Kincaid," she said.

Morehouse cocked his head toward Kincaid. "He a fed, too?" he asked.

"No, he's an agent of The Church of Jesus Christ of Latter-day Saints. We're both from Salt Lake City, Utah," she clarified.

"So, is this a hate crime against Mormons?" he asked, in sarcasm. He quickly realized the humor was a swing and a miss when they didn't respond.

Parker sighed. She told Morehouse why they had come to the Detroit area and what had happened when they returned from dinner. Kincaid added his report about the shootout in the alley. The other body was still in the motel room untouched.

As Morehouse sauntered toward the crime scene, he fumed and muttered to himself about a Bonnie and Clyde shootout in his town by two Mormons—one was a *security guard*, and the other a female Fed, for cryin' out loud!

After giving his oral report, Kincaid remained silent unless someone spoke to him, while Morehouse walked around his crime scene, through the room, into the alley, and back to the room again. The detective thought the only way his evening could have been worse would have been if the Tigers had lost their game.

Kincaid pointed to the weapon on the bed. "I took that off the dead body in the alley. When I returned fire, I killed one gunner and wounded another. I thought I might have also wounded the primary suspect in the foot or ankle, but he got away in a black SUV."

Morehouse nodded and checked his notebook. "My FCS—Forensic Crime Scene—techs need this room to process it. I think I have everything from you, but I want you to follow me down to the precinct and make your written reports."

They nodded and followed Morehouse out to his car. "I'd like to get copies of our written statements for the Bureau, if that's all right," Parker said.

"Ain't that the way locals and feds are supposed to work?" Morehouse said. He spit out an errant piece of his toothpick as he lowered himself into his unmarked police car. "Get your car and follow me downtown."

*****

After submitting their reports and being released, Parker and Kincaid returned to their vehicle. As soon as they shut both doors, they clicked into their seatbelts and sat there.

Kincaid took a deep breath. "I think I know who might be behind the shooting," he said. "And I think I know how we can prove it, too."

Parker stopped at a red light and turned toward her partner. "What do you mean, you *think* you know who's behind this?" she demanded. "How can you *prove* it and why didn't you include this little tidbit in your report?"

"I didn't tell Morehouse because the newspapers would have gotten hold of it and we would have lost our only suspect."

"Go on," Parker said crisply, beginning to feel the pain of lost sleep.

Kincaid pointed toward the traffic light. "It's green."

Irritated at having to be told, she continued driving back to their motel rooms.

"Do you remember, about eighteen months ago, two fanatic Muslims in Syria, were beheading hostages with a dull knife?" he asked, keeping his voice calm.

"So...?" Parker prompted him to continue.

"Well, I killed one of them. The other was called Mohammad Sayf al Din, which means *Sword of the Faith*. I was sent in with my team to rescue more of his hostages before he killed them, too. When I had Mohammad in my sights, I balked and shot his dominant hand, instead. Everything went to hell after that, so I didn't get another shot. We took control of the hostages and got out of Syria, but Mohammad got away. My first mission as a contractor was in Mexico."

"Contract killer?"

"No, more of a merc. It's a long story. Let's stay on topic. All right?"

"Okay, for now. Another rescue mission?"

"Yes. We suspected Mohammad was in Mexico, but we had no evidence. Once the assault began, I saw him through my scope. I *swear* it was the same guy. I shot him in the shoulder that time."

"To make a good Mormon, you shouldn't *swear*. Tell the truth all the time so you don't have to swear to tell the truth," she chided him with a broad grin.

"Really? I didn't know that," Kincaid confessed, a tad irritated at the interruption. "What about shooting people? Will I also have to stop that, too?" He knew she had been joking with him, but he upped the ante to his other ethical problem.

"Yes, *especially* shooting people." She was suddenly serious. "Shooting *innocent* people is a definite no-no."

"I ain't never shot any innocents. All my targets were as guilty as sin."

"Not until a court of law says they're guilty."

"That's not the way it's played in combat. If they shoot at us, they're guilty. Quick and easy."

"Well, this isn't combat. So, get used to *not* killing people—as least not while you're partnering with me."

Kincaid pursed his lips in silent frustration.

"So, what's Mohammad doing in Michigan?" Parker demanded, getting their conversation back to their current business.

"I don't know. I took his photo in Mexico and ran a check on facial recognition, but I never heard back on whether they found anything."

"Why not?"

"I was wounded in the firefight and ended up in a hospital. When I was healthy again, I left the contract company. They wouldn't tell me now, even if I asked *pretty please*," he said. Kincaid got a devilish look in his eye and smiled at Parker. "But I'll bet they'd tell an FBI Special Agent."

"That's quite a story, Kincaid," she said. "We don't have a good track record for getting anything from the Department of Defense—especially from the special ops guys. You said you can *prove* who he is?" It was more of a question than a statement.

Kincaid grinned his boyish smirk, again. "After the firefight in the alley, I saw a video camera looking straight down the length of the alley. Mohammad was running right toward the camera. If we can get the video from that camera, we might run another facial recognition on it through the local FBI office, to prove I'm right."

"Early tomorrow morning," Parker said, as she walked toward her room, "We'll give the results of our search to Detective Morehouse on our way out of town. Right now, I'd love to get at least two hours of sleep."

The morning sun was just peaking over the Detroit River.

Kincaid nodded, knowing she wouldn't see the tired, up-and-down movement of his head as they trudged toward the motel office. He had to get another room—this one on the second floor—since his first room was now taped off as a crime scene. Anyway, he had decided he didn't want to sleep in the same bed a dead man had been killed in, a few hours previously, anyway.

Earlier, the manager had said Parker could have the last two rooms in the motel. But this time, he conceded the motel manager told him he always maintains two rooms in reserve, just in case of emergencies. He dubbed this an emergency and gave her two other keys.

~Chapter Nineteen~

"We are a *religious* organization, not law enforcement, and we are definitely not the Military! We don't go around *shooting* people. It's bad for public relations, and it sends the wrong message toward our missionary work," yelled Tanner as soon as Parker and Kincaid walked into his office. He had heard of their escapades from Detroit Police Detective Morehouse, who had called to confirm their identities.

"I am still an FBI special agent," Parker spat back.

"Yes, in a *liaison* position," Tanner shot right back at her. "How can you *liaise* with people if you're *shooting* at them?"

Several people down the hallway stuck their heads out of their offices and cubicles to find out what all the ruckus was about in this otherwise sedate floor of church offices.

Director Tanner took a small pill from a brown prescription bottle on his desk and swallowed it without water. He jerked downward on the hem of his suit coat, then sat back in his semi-plush chair. He tried to put on a façade of being calmer, like a fire burning above a stash of explosives. "Now, tell me what happened," he said, simulating a more relaxed voice. "I need to know how to present this to the brethren."

Special Agent Parker gave Kincaid a direct order to sit in the only other chair as she briefed Director Tanner on the same information she had included in her official report to the Detroit Metropolitan Police and the FBI office. In Detroit, Kincaid had let *her* take the lead in the investigation. He simply filled in the parts in which he was involved, in the alleyway. Now, in Director Tanner's office, he was happy to let *her* do all the talking, again.

When they finished, Parker gave her final assessment of the events. "Sir, it looks like a Church building in New Jersey will be the main target of this extremist Muslim group, whoever they are."

When she finished, Tanner shook his head. "This is not good. This is not good at all. For the life of me, I can't find any fault in how either of you reacted, but that doesn't mean I have to *like* it."

"I'm confused, boss. What would *you* have done?" Kincaid asked. The question was soft and sincere.

Tanner flushed, looking like he might launch into another diatribe on shooting people while working for the Church. He restrained himself before coming up out of his seat. He braced himself with his hands flat on the desk. "All right. I just wish the world was an easier place to live in so we wouldn't have to make these kinds of decisions."

"But isn't that why you get paid the big bucks?" Kincaid said, using an old saying to Army officers. "To make the *hard* decisions?"

Parker instantly shot her partner a glare that could have pierced him like a laser.

Kincaid saw her scowl and ignored it. "These guys *must* be from New Jersey because of the license plates we saw on the same SUVs three times. Terrorists wouldn't want to blow up a *chapel* in New Jersey. They would want to make a big killing, at a place like a general conference or a temple. We don't have any temples in New Jersey, do we?" Kincaid added.

"No, the closest one is in Manhattan," Parker said.

Director Tanner stopped, slowly sank into his seat, and stared at them both. His reaction was like a sluggish lightbulb that had just turned on above his head. "A new temple in Camden, New Jersey, just finished construction. Its open house, cultural celebration, and dedication are ten days from now." His voice was soft and submissive. "The trouble is, we still don't have enough information or evidence of any impending attack to take positive action to protect the temple or the authorities who will visit the site for the dedication."

"Who will preside?" Parker asked.

"The Prophet, himself."

Knock, knock, knock.

Tanner looked at his door as Sister Christian passed a note to Parker, who stood closest to the door. "I'm sorry, sir," she said, looking at Director Tanner. "The FBI Office called for Special Agent Parker. They confirmed the results of her request for facial recognition and left a name and last known address of a suspect she had mentioned in her report."

Parker unfolded the paper and looked at the information. "The name means nothing, but the address is in Camden, New Jersey," she said, handing the paper to Director Tanner.

Tanner studied the information on the paper. "Kenneth Droggan." He pursed his lips and shook his head. "Nope. It means nothing to me, either. But the address in New Jersey now gives me enough to act on." He looked up at Parker and Kincaid. "I'll take care of security for Temple Square. I want you two on a plane to New Jersey, the day after tomorrow. Visit this address and find out if Droggan still lives there." He handed the paper back to Parker. "Check the set-up for the cultural celebration and dedication. Do what you can to fill in any security gaps and watch the temple site until I arrive." He stood as if to leave but remained behind his desk.

"I'll be there early next Friday to inspect the security arrangements for the celebration. I plan on staying for the dedication. If this guy would strike at a brand-new temple, just because the Prophet will be in attendance, and because he will get the most news coverage, then we *have* to stop him. Any questions?" He looked at both of them. "I'll see you there."

Taking their cue to leave, Kincaid stood, and both he and Parker left the office.

"Does trouble follow you wherever you go?" she asked her partner.

"It seems like I am meant to deal with this guy, Mohammad. We have to stop him for real, this time."

*****

After landing at Trenton-Mercer Airport, Kincaid picked up their luggage while Parker rented a small SUV for them. She also put Kincaid's name on the contract as an authorized driver. The drive to Camden wasn't as long as she thought it would be, and it was easy finding the address, once she plugged it into the vehicle's GPS.

Parker took the lead and knocked on the front door. Kincaid stood at her right and half a step back, so he could be seen when someone opened the door.

The house was an older, single-family, two-story, brick dwelling with a full driveway that led to a large metal warehouse or workshop in the backyard. Kincaid could not see the entire structure from the front porch, but it appeared to be large enough to hold a fleet of vehicles.

A thin, middle-aged woman with straggly, graying hair answered the door. She was dressed in modest, older clothing meant for working around the house, or for mere comfort when not expecting guests. For a moment, she looked at them with, what, disapproval? Parker wasn't sure.

Parker flashed her badge and credentials. "Good afternoon, ma'am. My name is Special Agent Haley Parker, of the FBI. This is my partner, Orson Kincaid. Are you Mrs. Hillary Droggan?"

Slowly, the woman relaxed her shoulders and smiled with muscles not used in years to produce a smile. "Yes. I'm Hillary Droggan," she said in a raspy voice. She stepped back, holding the door open. "Won't you come in?"

Hillary Droggan pointed them toward the living room as she shut the door behind them.

The living room had several pieces of nondescript, older furniture, and doilies on the end tables. There were family pictures that must have covered a lifetime, on the mantel, end tables, and coffee table. It was evident she was proud of her children.

Parker tried to place the photos in chronological order in her mind, based on the maturation of the little boy in the photographs. As he got older, he changed, as if a part of his life bothered him. He wore traditional Muslim garb in one photo and appeared more hostile and rebellious as a high school student than he had been as a young boy. In almost every picture of the boy, there was also a girl. She had the family resemblance but was smaller or younger. In one photo, she looked up at the boy, either admiring or adoring him. Her smile confirmed they were brother and sister.

Hillary sat in the plush easy chair and lit up an unfiltered cigarette with a silver-coated lighter. As soon as she sat, both Parker and Kincaid took seats on the sofa.

"How can I help you, Special Agents?" she asked, cutting right to the matter at hand.

Parker noticed the overpowering smell of tobacco and old cigarette butts in the ashtrays around the room. She suppressed her gag reflex. Kincaid must have been exposed to the smoke by working with his team in the Army and with other armies overseas, so it didn't seem to bother him.

"Are you the mother of Kenneth Droggan?" she asked.

"Yes. Well, I'm his adoptive mother. Has Kenneth gotten himself into more trouble?" Hillary asked, before taking a small piece of tobacco from her mouth and delicately dropping it in the nearest ashtray.

"Adoptive mother?"

"Yes, I adopted him when he was an infant."

"How did you come to adopt him?" Parker asked, looking at the photos again.

"My husband and I couldn't have our own children, and we wanted to adopt children from a culture that was under fire, so we chose Syrian children. We sent a few emails, filled out a few applications, and were finally selected. It wasn't difficult."

"You mentioned Kenneth has been in trouble before. What kind of trouble?"

"When he was in high school, another boy made fun of his Dishdasha and Kufia—his Muslim clothing. So, when the biggest bully wouldn't leave him alone, Kenneth followed him home and threw a homemade smoke bomb through the boy's bedroom window. The house didn't burn down, but the boy's hands got burned when he threw the bomb back out the window. Neighbors of the bully saw Kenneth running from the scene and testified against him. Kenneth ended up in juvenile detention for almost two years."

"When was he released from juvi?" Kincaid asked.

"Oh, let me see. That must have been about four or five years ago," she replied, looking up at the ceiling for the answer.

"What did he do after they released him?" asked Parker.

"He tried to return to high school, but he must have had an unpleasant experience in juvenile detention. I think he met up with at least one radical Muslim youth because, after his release, he was always talking about killing the infidels and destroying the infidel society. It wasn't long before he announced he was going to the Middle East, to fight for Allah. At that point, there was nothing else I could do with the boy." Her voice was calm, and she told the story as if she had resigned herself to Kenneth's self-chosen fate.

"When was that?"

"That he went overseas? Oh, about three years ago, I think."

"Have you heard from him since he left?" Parker asked.

"Well, he used to send postcards for several months, maybe

even a year. But he stopped. I didn't know if someone had killed him, or if he had just put his 'infidel history' behind him."

"Have you heard from him recently? Has he called or visited you in the past month?"

Hillary began absently tapping the heel of her right foot on the floor. "Why, no. He hasn't. Why? Is he back in the United States?" Hillary asked, looking from Parker to Kincaid and back again.

"Would you call us if he contacts you for anything?" Parker asked.

"Yes. Of course. But what's going on? Is he in more trouble?"

"No, ma'am. We just want to ask him some questions about a case we're working on," Kincaid said.

Parker stood and handed Hillary her business card. "You can contact me at this number," she said. "May I ask who the little girl is, in the photos with you and your son?"

Hillary remained seated and took another draw on her cigarette. "She's my daughter. Kenneth's sister. They're twins," Hillary said.

"Twins?" both Kincaid and Parker said together.

"My husband and I adopted twin Syrian children when they were still infants. Have you heard anything about my daughter?" Hillary pressed.

Kincaid had to work to keep his mouth from hanging open. "Twins?" he repeated, while his mind raced.

"What did your daughter do when Kenneth went to the Middle East?" Parker asked.

"Kathryn stayed out of trouble, graduated from high school, and worked at a local Muslim daycare center for two years. About a year ago, she got a letter from her brother, inviting her to come join him in the fight against the infidel forces in their mother country—Syria."

"Did she go?" Kincaid asked.

"Yes, she did. She took about a month to make all the arrangements. But she left last year, and I haven't heard from either of them since her departure. Before she left, she said she and Kenneth had taken Muslim names."

"Do you remember those names?" Parker said.

"Yes. I told Kathryn I thought that was silly, but the names they took were Fatima and Mohammad."

Parker wrote down the names in her notebook.

"Do you have any recent photos of either of them?" Kincaid asked.

Hillary seemed to think about the question for a moment and tapped her foot again. "No, I have nothing more recent than four to five years ago. Would that help?"

"No, probably not," Kincaid replied, watching the woman's tapping foot.

Parker seemed deep in thought, while studying all the photographs, again. Only one photograph included a father with the rest of the family. Parker recognized the building in the background, and was about to ask about it, when Kincaid stopped her.

"Please call us if either of them contacts you," said Kincaid. He nudged Parker out of her reverie and they both stood to leave.

"Yes, I will," Hillary agreed.

~Chapter Twenty~

Three years ago, Kenneth Droggan left home to find himself in the Middle East. He had no idea exactly where in Syria that journey would take him, or how difficult the path would be to walk. He wanted to find his biological family, to meet his blood relatives. So, he traveled to Syria—the land of his birth. The first major obstacle in his path was that he had no idea what the family name was, or in which village or city they resided.

Without knowing of his relatives' whereabouts, he knew of their existence. With that knowledge, he determined to fight against the threat that overwhelmed the nation, the people, and the hearts of all who called themselves Syrians.

After a short search, he found the Army of Allah and joined their ranks. Although he was accepted into the AA from the start, he still had to prove himself worthy and loyal to Allah before they would trust him sufficiently to take him into combat.

His heart was true, and his strength was born of love for his people, his loyalty was for Allah, and the cause of overcoming the resistance from the infidels of the Earth. After several combat missions where he used a rifle, handgun, and knife, he found he took the greatest joy in killing with the blade. He felt an inner, spiritual joy in killing infidels and wanted to experience more of it. In his search for more inner joy, he began carrying out executions in public, as a message to the survivors that they, too, would end up at the wrong end of a dull blade if they offended Allah.

In less than one year, he became known as the executioner, as he executed hostages over a live feed on the internet.

He, himself, made the arrangements for the formal executions and advertised them on all the Al Jazeera websites. The response was so overwhelming, thirty minutes before the scheduled time for each execution, he had more than one million viewers signed in online.

When his mother sent him a message requesting they both return home, he was irritated. But her explanation made sense. Within one week, he and Fatima packed their bags and flew a circuitous route home, so no one would realize they had come from Syria.

*****

Once Special Agent Haley Parker started up the engine and placed the car in gear, she said, "Did you notice the pictures on the walls and mantel?"

"I did. How could you miss so many of them? I was also surprised that a Muslim family would have *any* photographs in the house," Kincaid replied.

"Really? No, I mean, did you look closely at them?"

"I noticed an angry boy growing into a troubled youth," Kincaid said.

"One photograph at the Los Angeles Temple."

"Wait. What? How is that possible? Aren't they a *Muslim* family?"

"I doubt it," Parker said. "In fact, that was the only picture I saw with a man in it. Did you notice that?"

Kincaid thought about it for a moment. "Come to think of it, I don't remember a man in *any* of the pictures."

"Except the one with the Los Angeles Temple in the background."

"Why would they visit the LA Temple?" Kincaid asked.

Parker shook her head. "Maybe they took the missionary discussions and went to see the temple? Or maybe they used to be members of the LDS Church? I'll phone back to Salt Lake and have the records office check for a Droggan family in California about... what do you think? Twenty or twenty-five years ago?"

"That should cover it. And maybe we can find out what happened to the husband, too," Kincaid added. "By the way, she lied to us on several matters."

"How do you know that?" Parker asked.

"When we asked if she had heard from either of the children lately, she started tapping her foot. When I asked if she had any recent photos, she tapped that foot again. I think there's more to her than we already know," Kincaid said.

*****

On the day of the cultural celebration, Mohammad drove his old, brown van up to the temple grounds gate and stopped. He wore khaki slacks, a royal blue BYU polo-style shirt, and carried a clipboard with a few official-looking papers on it. A mechanical pencil behind one ear completed his disguise.

The van he drove had magnetic signs on each side that identified it as the "Temple Sound Installation Company." He anticipated no problems getting inside.

An elderly man dressed in a short-sleeved white shirt and tie, sat in the shade, near the gate. He was whistling a catchy tune to a song Mohammad did not recognize but would remember. He looked at the signs on the van and walked over to talk to the driver. "Howdy. I thought you boys came and installed everything yesterday."

"Yes, sir. We did. But part of our service is to handle any unforeseen problems that may develop during the performance."

"You bet. That sounds good to me. Will you please park the van *behind* the temple, on the side of the dirt road?"

"Sure. After I make a quick side trip to the dignitary seats and the lectern, I'll park it in back."

"Great. Thanks," said the old man. As the van slowly continued past him, the old man took up whistling the same tune as he walked back to his seat in the shade. The day promised to be sunny and warm.

Mohammad maneuvered his van toward the dignitary stage, dropped off two coils of cable and a footlocker-sized box. He then drove the van to the back. When he found a place to park, he took off the signs so no one would look for the sound technician.

Walking among these Mormon people gave Mohammad a peculiar feeling. They reminded him of the students in his school when he was a child, and his neighbors in Camden. They were friendly and kind as long as they thought everything around them was status quo. But as soon as he put on the clothing that identified him as different, they changed. Seeing something they did not understand made them furious. Suddenly, he was worthy of their bias. These people would be the same, if he were wearing the same kind of Muslim clothing now. He was sure of it.

As he walked around the area, among the performers and technicians, Mohammad could see he had chosen his trousseau wisely. Other young men dressed in similar fashion, were working on last-minute fixes to the scenery, or painting final touches to the large backdrops and flats to be used in the show.

Wandering among the costumes and props, he spotted a police trailer, still attached to a pickup truck, with a sign on it that read "TACTICAL OPERATIONS CENTER." A small satellite dish and two other omni-directional antennae of different types sat perched upon the roof of the trailer. So, now he knew their communication capabilities. He was sure they would raise no problems for him.

Mohammad snorted in derision and continued his stroll among the many racks of costumes and various pieces of stage scenery for the show. No one stopped him, but several people smiled and greeted him as he walked by. He always smiled and returned the greeting before moving on.

When he discovered the first video camera on the side of a light pole, he looked for others. There were six in total. They were the type that could each be remotely activated to follow a moving person or vehicle, probably from the Tactical Ops van. Each of them had blind spots. Before long, Mohammad found paths he could walk, without fear of being seen on any of the cameras.

How easy it will be to wreak havoc among this crowd. They did not understand what it was like to live every day in fear for the morrow, like his people in so many countries around the world. How hypocritical and arrogant they were to think they would always be safe in the shadow of their precious temple. Well, he would soon change that perception for this and all future events.

*****

Kincaid and Parker arose early and skipped breakfast so they could get to the temple grounds just after sunrise. Kincaid had decided today was not the day to wear a suit, so he had chosen a dark blue polo shirt, khaki cargo pants, and hiking shoes. He threw on a heavier long-sleeved plaid shirt and left it untucked and unbuttoned to conceal his shoulder holster and the secondary holster at the small of his back. He was pleased when he saw Parker had dressed in a similar manner. That meant he had chosen wisely.

The sun was cresting over the horizon when Parker pulled their vehicle into the temple parking lot. She flashed her badge at an old man at the gate, and he let her past with a smile and *move-along* gesture. She drove around the temple once to get the lay of the land then settled on a parking space in the rear, where the most action was bound to take place.

Kincaid grabbed his backpack as he exited the car. As

early as it was, there were already several other vehicles on the grounds. People skittered around the ten-acre property, capturing wind-blown trash, placing large vases of fresh flowers, testing the sound equipment, and connecting and setting the special effects lighting for the show.

One man laid on his back under the VIP stage, like a mechanic under a car. Several rolls of cable sat beside his legs. He whistled a hymn Kincaid remembered having sung in church. *We Thank Thee O God for a Prophet*. It was a catchy, upbeat tune to work by.

"Umm. This is nice. Do you smell the fresh flowers?" Parker asked her partner.

Kincaid inhaled a deep breath, then shook his head. "Nope. I do smell sawdust from the circular saws still cutting frames for the scenery." He pointed ahead of them where workers still prepared for the celebration.

They both scanned the area for anything looking suspicious or out of place.

"These people are sure working hard, for this early in the morning," said Kincaid.

"There's a reason the beehive is the symbol of an industrious life," said Parker.

"Huh?" Kincaid didn't know what she was talking about.

"Never mind. I'll explain it later," Parker said. "It would probably be better if we split up."

"Put your cell on vibrate, so it won't make a sound when you least want it to," Kincaid advised.

Without a word, Parker reached into her pocket, made an adjustment to her phone, and slipped it back inside her jacket.

"I'll go clockwise," Kincaid said, moving toward the front of the temple.

Parker nodded and went in the opposite direction.

As Kincaid came around to the front of the temple, he saw a bell tower about three hundred meters away—with a straight-line view of the VIP seating area and podium. He walked a straight line over the freshly plowed field, looking for any other tracks in the loose dirt. The field was about a half mile long and a quarter mile wide. A highway ran along the far edge of the field. Kincaid also took his time, scanning each direction to get more familiar and comfortable with the area as he hiked.

When Kincaid arrived at the tower, he discovered it was connected to an old and deserted red brick church. Although abandoned, the door was locked. He pulled a small pouch out of his backpack and withdrew two wire tools. Putting both tools to the lock on the door, he popped it open in less than a minute. That was good, he thought. Maybe if Parker could have seen that, she would consider him an asset worthy of the position.

The main room was deserted, except for a few pews that had been tipped over, and lay unceremoniously among the dust and dirt after years of disuse. He found the inside door nearest the bell tower, opened it, and went inside. The only way to get to the top of the tower was to climb a thirty-foot wooden ladder attached to the outer brick wall inside the tower. An old, braided rope hung from the top. Kincaid supposed it was connected to the bell's tongue, but he didn't want to test it. He studied the first few rungs of the ladder and saw they were also covered with years of dust. As he climbed to the top, he kept watching the rungs. No one else had been up this ladder in a long time, he realized as he saw bird droppings along several of the rungs.

At the top of the ladder, he came to an open brick watch tower. About thirty feet above the ground, he could see everything in the front of the temple with no obstructions. As a sniper, he appreciated the amount of damage and mayhem he could cause from this site. The tower also had one deadly negative attribute: the only escape route was down the same ladder.

Kincaid reached into his pack again and pulled out two miniature motion-activated video cameras. He placed one camera to show the inside the watch tower and the front of the temple in the distance. He placed the other one in a shadow, facing downward from the top of the ladder.

Syncing the cameras to his smartphone, he adjusted the motion detector alarms to notify him if anything bigger than a bird or rat moved, in the tower. If anyone else came up that ladder, he would find out about it when the app on his phone vibrated.

After he set everything in place, Kincaid descended the ladder and returned to the temple grounds, noticing his tracks were still the only ones in the morning dew. He followed his own tracks as closely as he could along the way back.

"Where have you been?" Parker demanded. Her voice had an edge of impatience in it.

Kincaid jerked his head toward the bell tower. "I checked out the best site for a sniper. If our man is good with a long rifle, that tower would be the most logical place for him to set up."

Parker looked over at the tower and back at the seating area and stage. She nodded. "Good call. What did you do about it?"

"Do about it?" Kincaid shrugged. "I placed two miniature video cameras up there, so I'll know if anything moves in the top of the tower."

"You're pretty good with technology?"

"And you're not?"

"Yes, but I'm surprised a combat veteran like you would be tech savvy," she said with a grin.

Kincaid noted her sarcasm and thought he might get through to her, eventually. "What have you found?"

"There's a trailer over on the south side of the temple that is set up to monitor several cameras they placed around the area. They're high res, movable, and zoom capable, but there aren't enough of them, unless our guy steps up to a camera and smiles."

"What about personnel?"

"The Camden County Sheriff's Department is running the Tactical Operations Center—TOC—and they have three uniformed deputies roaming the grounds. There will be three more for a total of six, during the celebration. The fire department has also detailed an ambulance and two paramedics from two hours before the celebration until two hours afterward, just in case. Make sure you introduce yourself, so they don't think you could be a terrorist."

"Yeah, okay. I've got four more cameras in my bag," Kincaid said. "I thought of setting them up in high-traffic areas and potential dead spots where any bad guys might try to hide."

"Okay, I'll leave the video surveillance to you, and I'll keep in telephone contact with you *and* with the TOC. As long as you and I stay in contact with each other, we should have the area covered."

*****

Fatima walked through the front gate with a group of college students who were happy beyond measure and talking about their new temple. Several of them wore BYU t-shirts and caps. She was dressed modestly and fit in with the group so well, some of the girls actually believed she was one of them. When they passed by the gate guard, the tempo of their excitement increased so the guard simply waved them through.

Once on the temple grounds, Fatima laughed bitterly to herself as she separated from the group and went backstage. She had arranged to avoid meeting up with her brother until they were ready to leave the area—after their work had been set and they could leave before the fireworks.

Being a twin, she had always loved her brother. When he had gone to Syria in search of himself, she had missed him. But she kept her eye toward the target and completed her schooling. After graduating, she got a job at a Muslim daycare center, taking care of the children. She also met many of the parents and realized how apathetic they were toward the Syrian cause. That sickened her, but they were still her brothers and sisters in Islam.

When her brother sent for her, she wasted no time in leaving the US, even though their mother was upset at being left alone.

Her greeting with her brother had been wonderful. She saw how he had changed and how devoted he had become toward the cause of the Syrians. She also became devoted to the cause. Not because she cared so much for the Syrians, but because she loved her brother and wanted to share his joy in the cause he had chosen.

Now they were both back in the US, this was their chance to find glory in their work and further the Muslim and Syrian cause by taking down this prideful religion and their secrets in their precious temple. After completing this operation, they would both be recognized around the world as pro-active Muslim extremists. What glory that status would bring upon them!

In order to get more familiar with the area, she walked around the stage and performing area, went to the back of the temple and among the many young performers and technicians prior to their performance—and her moment of exaltation.

~Chapter Twenty-One~

Fifteen minutes before the pageant was scheduled to begin, several large, black sedans drove onto the temple grounds. The drivers all stopped as close to the dignitary seating as they could. They were all dignified men dressed in dark suits. Their wives dressed modestly in their Sunday best.

At least a dozen young, smiling escorts stood at the base of the steps to the seating stage to assist the dignitaries to their seats. In every case, the men deferred to their wives, allowing them to ascend the steps first and to sit in the padded chairs.

Next, two tour buses drove in, and the members of the Tabernacle Choir, already in costume, stepped off and took their places in the arena-type seats at the back of the performing stage.

At 11:00am, the show began with music, singing, and several elaborate acrobatic moves couched in the dance routines. Without counting the Tabernacle Choir, there were over one-hundred people taking part in the performance. Jessica Brock, a member of the same ward Orson and Haley attended, did her part with dancing and singing in a quartet, to the great pleasure of both her parents. Kincaid was surprised that her voice was so fresh, beautiful, and coached. When he met her at the chapel, they had spoken briefly. But she had not mentioned she was part of this festival.

Behind the temple was a frenzy of activity as performers rushed onto the stage, performed their parts, and rushed off to change their costumes, so they could rush back on stage again, to take part in the next routine.

Orson Kincaid watched the bustle from an inconspicuous position near the many racks of costumes. He didn't want to get in the way, but he wanted to watch the show, to make sure nothing improper or dangerous took place.

Mohammad and his sister, Fatima, were the targets of his search. Kincaid thought back to how strange it was that he and Parker were actually looking for two look-alike terrorists—instead of just one—along with anyone else they might have working for them on this mission. Kincaid flinched at the thought of how much damage three terrorists with assault rifles, or just one suicide bomber, could do.

Kincaid's cell phone vibrated in his pocket.

"You have a visitor coming your way," said Parker, at the opposite end of the grounds.

"Who?"

"Director Tanner. I told him where he could find you, but in case he misses you on the first pass, step out and get him, okay?"

"I sure will."

"No, that's 'You bet.'"

"What?"

"You bet. That's what Utah Mormons say instead of 'Okay," or "I sure will,'" Parker said.

"Is that for real?" asked Kincaid, wondering if she was messing with him.

"You bet."

"I see him, now," said Kincaid. Tanner looked like a man on the verge of a heart attack or stroke. Being past his middle age, he carried around too much weight and tried to do a job that inherently brought a lot of stress along with it. Now he was trying to walk medium distances for several hours, in coordinating the security efforts for this event. Kincaid shook his head. Tanner was a cardiovascular accident waiting to happen, he decided.

Kincaid stepped out from his position and greeted Director

Tanner. "Howdy, boss."

Tanner startled but recovered quickly as he turned to face Kincaid. "I parked my rental car nearby but must have missed you when I arrived. I only noticed Special Agent Parker in front of the temple. She told me where to find you." Tanner was breathing hard from the walk and looked flushed. "Have you covered all angles, looking for our guy?"

Kincaid's cell phone vibrated again.

When he looked at the screen, the cameras from the bell tower showed him movement. "Here's what I've done," he said, as he handed the phone to the Director and reached down to open his long, flat Pelican case, on the ground. "Stand here, please, director," Kincaid said, showing him where to stand to block him from passing performers or technicians.

Kincaid laid down on the ground between two of the higher costume racks, picked up his AR-10 rifle, Leupold scope, and sound suppressor, and quickly assembled them. He locked and loaded a magazine of five rounds into the weapon and sighted in on the tower. He estimated it was a little over three hundred meters' distance. The ambient light was good, and he sensed the breeze was minimal. The scope's viewfinder told him the distance was three-hundred-twenty-five meters.

Kincaid was sure he could make this shot, but he still missed having his spotter-partner. Although he had already thought it a thousand times, he thought it again, how much he missed his partner and friend—Ted Pineda.

"Just one man in the tower," said Tanner, still looking at the live video images on the phone. "He seems to be checking his field of fire. I can't see anyone else in the tower or on the ladder."

"Do you see a weapon?" Kincaid asked.

"No. Not yet. Won't he see us looking at him?"

Kincaid looked up at his inexperienced spotter with a half grin. "No. He's looking for his targets on the VIP stage. He's not even checking out this area in back of the temple."

Tanner slid behind a tree, anyway, putting his back to the tower. He was less than an arm's length from Kincaid.

A covered rental truck innocently drove onto the grass and stopped, blocking their view of the tower and the enemy sniper.

Director Tanner ran over, shouting at the driver, ordering him to move the van and park it elsewhere. At first, the driver wanted to argue with Tanner, but then Tanner flashed his credentials.

"All right, Brother Dude," the driver said, backing up the truck. "I guess I'll just leave these flowers up front, near the microphone."

"Yes. You do that," Tanner said, as he watched the driver closely.

Returning to Kincaid, Tanner said, "Wait a minute." His voice had gained an edginess to it. "I've lost him. I've lost him."

"What do you mean you lost him?" Kincaid said in a stage whisper. He still laid on his side on the grass, under the costume racks, looking up at Tanner for orders. While waiting for Tanner to explain himself, Kincaid took a quick look around the immediate area to make sure no one was watching them.

"I mean he's not in the tower or on the ladder," Tanner replied. "Wait! Wait! There he is. He's climbing up the ladder again. This time it looks like he's hauling a duffel bag up with him."

"All right. That's his rifle and gear. He's getting ready to set up for his shot. Tell me what he does next," Kincaid said, getting into a good prone position.

Silence.

Kincaid rolled to his side again and looked up at Tanner.

"Okay, he unzipped the bag, and he's taking out a rifle stock," Tanner said in a stage whisper. "Now, he's taking out the receiver and barrel. He's putting the pieces together. Now, he's snapping a scope in place and screwing on a long sound suppressor."

Kincaid rolled back into position and sighted in on the

top of the bell tower, waiting to see movement. He saw the top of a head, with a lot of black hair, as it appeared and looked downward at his equipment in front of him. The hair was thick but short—and there was no white streak in it; he also wore a thick mustache. "Okay. I have him," he told Tanner. "But it's not Mohammad."

"Then who is this guy?"

"He's just a hired gun," Kincaid replied. "A terrorist mercenary. Isn't that a scary thought?"

"Yeah, but how many of them are there?"

Kincaid shook his head. He watched as the man laid down a towel on the edge of the tower, doubled it over and laid his rifle on top of it. There was no doubt this was an experienced sniper, Kincaid decided. He waited patiently, squeezed the trigger.

*Pfft!......*The silenced shot made little noise and the costumes on the end of the rack nearest Kincaid, fluttered in the gas escaping the muzzle of his weapon. Director Tanner jumped even though he realized the silenced shot had been coming.

The man in the tower reached for a couple of bricks to block the sun, and his movement took him out of the path of Kincaid's shot.

The round impacted against the bricks behind the sniper, sending shards of brick and mortar careening around, inside the tower. The man instantly recoiled, then reached up and casually brushed the debris off his arms and shoulders with his hands. He then rolled over and looked up and behind him.

Kincaid gritted his teeth and snarled to himself. "Tell me what he's doing now," he said to Tanner, treating him as he would his spotter, in combat.

"He's lying on his back, studying the impact area of your first round."

Kincaid chambered his second round and waited.

"Now, he's..."

"Never mind," said Kincaid. "I've got him."

Tanner smiled. "How's it feel to be back in the zone?"

Kincaid glanced over at him with sadness etching his face. "I'd hoped to leave all this behind me." He glanced back through the scope.

The man in the tower rolled to his stomach again, holding a small handheld scope. He put it to his eye, searching for his foe among the costumes and props at the back of the temple. He must have judged the direction of his would-be killer by the angle of the first shot, Kincaid realized.

The man disappeared again. When he reappeared, he aimed his rifle in Kincaid's direction. He fired quickly, to avoid giving his foe any chance to return fire. Kincaid saw a small burst of smoke from the muzzle of the man's rifle. There was no sound. A round impacted two feet short of Kincaid's position, kicking up dirt and debris from the ground.

"He's *shooting* at you!" Tanner growled. "The nerve of him!"

The shooter disappeared from view again.

Kincaid waited. "Tell me the instant he moves. Got it?"

"Got it... Now!" said Tanner.

Pfft!..... The man in the tower rolled back into position. He started to take aim at Kincaid.

Kincaid had shot before the man even appeared in his sights. The watch tower was small. He was sure where he would appear. He took aim for that spot.

The sniper in the tower stiffened, then collapsed in place without a sound.

"You got him! You got him!" Tanner whispered excitedly, kneeling beside Kincaid, slapping him on the back and continuing to watch the smartphone screen.

Kincaid nodded, watched for a few more seconds, to make sure his shot had been true. He had aimed for the sniper's left clavicle. In a prone position. The bullet should have hit his collar bone, splintered, and pinged around the inside his torso, causing death within seconds. Kincaid silently disassembled his weapon and put it back inside his Pelican. Then he stood and brushed off his clothing.

Tanner handed Kincaid's phone back to him and pulled out his own phone. He took a few deep breaths to compose himself before dialing. "Sheriff, this is Director Tanner. East of the temple grounds is an old church tower. Please send two of your men and the ambulance to that tower. At the tower top, you'll find a body and his weapon. He was sighting in on our visiting dignitaries when we eliminated the threat." Tanner listened for a couple of seconds as the Sheriff started asking his questions. "That's right... I'll tell you everything a little later," he said, and hung up.

Kincaid's smartphone vibrated again. He didn't recognize the number on the screen. "Yes?" he answered.

"Mr. Kincaid?" asked an older male voice with a Middle Eastern accent.

"Yes," Kincaid repeated, without giving away any more information than absolutely necessary.

"This is Mullah Abd al-Salim al-Ahmad, from the Islamic Center in Detroit. Do you remember we spoke when you visited our mosque last week?"

Kincaid stood and moved farther away from the few people nearby. He dragged Tanner with him. Then he put his phone on speaker. "Yes, Mullah Abd al-Salim. I remember you well. What can I do for you?"

"No, it is a matter of what I can do for *you* that prompts me to call."

Director Tanner's eyes bulged, looking at the phone.

"Yes? What is that?" Kincaid asked.

"There is a man who came to the United States. He has fought valiantly for Islam and executed many infi—I mean, many non-Muslims. Now, he is here to conduct more mayhem. I believe you are already familiar with this man. Am I right?"

Tanner looked at Kincaid and nodded his head several

times, quickly.

"Go ahead," Kincaid said, again, with caution.

"I need to tell you that Mohammad is no longer a sanctioned fighter in *any* jihad around the world. He has disgraced himself and shamed Allah, and he will not receive any protection or support from Muslims anywhere, once they discover who he is."

Kincaid was now confused. "You mean, whatever he is now working on is not part of any jihad?"

Kincaid's mind raced. Why would Mohammad have targeted the LDS Church? And why here, in New Jersey? Then he remembered his talk with Mohammad's mother—she raised him in New Jersey. Kincaid recalled the photograph he had discussed with Parker after their visit—the boy must think he's getting revenge on the church for a personal issue, maybe from years ago.

"That's right," replied the Mullah. "There is already too much hostility between our people and yours. We do not need a truly evil man making life worse for all of us."

Kincaid wasn't sure if he should accept the Mullah's word or not. This was crazy! "It would help me if you could tell me what his plans are, or even his time schedule for his current project." Kincaid was out of his realm. Major Harris had done all the planning for his operations. Now, Kincaid had no one else to go to, and he had to figure out which questions to ask for the most information—how to protect his people. He turned to Tanner and saw the Director furiously writing in his notebook.

"I heard Mohammad say he had built in redundancy in case of unanticipated problems. He is a man who is good with a blade in close quarters, and he is also an expert at explosives."

Tanner shoved the notebook in Kincaid's face.

Kincaid scanned the page. "How many of your men came with him?" Kincaid read from the notebook page.

"He asked for only two of my men. One long-range shooter and the other a close-range expert with the handgun."

"No suicide bombers?"

"No, the Muslims living in the United States will take risks, but they do not want to lose all the advantages they have, for a cause that is so fanatical."

Tanner flipped the page and shoved it back at Kincaid. Tanner's hands visibly shook.

"Can you give me a physical description of Mohammad? We have never seen him, and we have little time left."

"He is in his late twenties, about one-hundred-eighty centimeters tall, thin, and in good physical condition. He is clean-shaven, has long black hair with a white streak running through it."

"Did he say anything about a sister, or a woman by the name of Fatima?"

"No, I have never heard him *speak* of her, *either*. I know nothing else of his work except that I would execute him myself if I could find him. Two of my men hired on with him for the money. I have called them both back."

"Only one will return," Kincaid said, solemnly, showing no compassion or weakness.

The Mullah sighed. "Yes, I suspected as much when he did not answer his phone."

"Shukraan, almala," Kincaid said in gratitude, only now, his heart pumped quicker than normal as he realized he would still have to confront Mohammad.

"Marhabaan bik."

"Wadaeaan," said Kincaid in farewell. Kincaid pushed the disconnect button on his phone and turned to Tanner.

"That confirms it," Tanner said in a higher and faster voice than normal. "We have a bona fide terrorist plot to kill the Prophet and blow up the temple. Are you sure that wasn't Mohammad in the tower?"

"I'm positive. He was just the sniper paid to kill the Prophet. That guy had a mustache and short black hair," Kincaid said. "Wait, a minute. Our guy isn't working with any Muslim extremists or jihadis—anymore. They've excommunicated him, in a way of speaking."

"Then, why does he want to kill and destroy the LDS Church?" Tanner asked.

Kincaid ignored that question for the present. "We've still got to find the close-up shooter."

Saying nothing else, Tanner and Kincaid both looked around, trying to find the remaining hired assassin.

"We might consider him a non-asset, because the Mullah said he called the man off," Kincaid offered.

Tanner pulled his phone down from his ear. "We can't afford to assume that. We have to find him and confirm that he's gone."

"I'll contact Parker and bring her up to speed, so we can all find this last guy," Kincaid said as he walked toward the TOC.

"I've got to get word to the Prophet," Tanner said, reaching for his phone and walking toward the front of the temple.

"Understood," Kincaid replied as he reached Parker on his phone. "Parker. Meet me at the TOC. We have to talk." He listened, then took off running. "Now! I'm on my way. I'll see you there."

Kincaid reached the TOC right before Parker. Both were out of breath.

"What's the hurry?" Parker asked.

Kincaid told her about the call from the Mullah and the sniper he killed in the tower.

"I wondered why the Sheriff's vehicles all took off in that direction," Parker said.

"We still have to find Mohammad and there's one other Muslim assassin moving around the temple grounds."

"Where's Tanner," Parker asked.

"He should be here, soon. He walked that way around the temple." Kincaid motioned toward the far side of the temple.

"I don't think we should wait for him," Parker advised.

Kincaid shook his head. "Neither do I. But you and I should stick together because there are still two of them."

"What about Mohammad's sister, Fatima?"

"We haven't even confirmed that she's part of this."

Parker looked at her partner, shocked at what he had just said. "We need to operate as if she *is* in on it. Where would *you* go to do the most damage?"

"I would go to the platform where the VIPs will be seated. But I would stay in the back until that time. There are enough people moving around back there to hide one or two men for an hour or more. But there's one more hired gun. If we find him, we might find Mohammad. Let's go to the backstage area and look."

"I agree. Let's do it," Parker confirmed.

The constant coming and going of performers, technicians, and other stage crew members, had formed distinct pathways around the racks of clothing, tables of props and dressing rooms for the actors.

Kincaid and Parker split up and walked either side of the main trail leading back to the parking area. They didn't want to spook anyone in the cast or crew, so they kept their guns holstered. But they both had a round chambered, ready to fire, if necessary.

The dressing rooms had doors that left the bottom eighteen inches open and visible. They could see everyone there was busy changing. Kincaid looked at each of the people at the table full of props and saw one man just browsing like a person might do at a bazaar or craft festival. Kincaid walked toward the table but couldn't get Parker's attention.

When he got within twenty feet, the man looked up and saw Kincaid staring at him. He instantly bolted away from Kincaid, pulling down racks of hanging costumes and pushing people out of his way, so Kincaid would have to negotiate the mess before getting to him.

Kincaid saw Parker also running after the man from another

direction. She pulled her weapon as she ran.

Kincaid pulled his SIG out and flicked the safety off, as he ran.

The man they pursued pulled out his own weapon and fired it twice in the air, then ducked behind a full-sized sedan.

Dozens of people nearby screamed and ran or hit the dirt as if they had been raised in a large urban area and were familiar with exactly what that sound was.

The man threw the car door open, jumped inside and started up the engine. As he put the car in gear to take off, Kincaid fell to one knee and skidded a short distance as he leveled his gun at the back of the car.

Parker ran up to her partner and holstered her weapon. "That wasn't Mohammad, was it?"

Kincaid shook his head. "No. That must have been the last of the hired guns. Since the mullah already called him off, he didn't want to take the risk."

Tanner showed up as Kincaid stood back to his feet. He was breathing hard, but still functioned the best he could. "Did you get the plate number?" he asked Parker.

"Yes, sir. We can give it to the local Sheriff, but this is now officially a danger zone." Tanner jabbed his finger downward towards the ground on which he stood, to emphasize his point. "We should call off the celebration and get all these people to safety."

"But we still don't understand *why* our guy wants to destroy the temple and kill innocent Mormons," Kincaid said.

"No, and I want you to stay alert and do whatever you can, to keep this celebration safe for everyone until I get the authority to call it off," Director Tanner said. "I'll go make a long overdue report to the local sheriff." He looked across the furrowed field, then shook his head. Thinking better of it, he pulled out his car keys and walked toward his rental vehicle.

Kincaid noticed Tanner was sweating more than normal

for the temperature. But he understood that personality type. He realized warning him would not stop him.

~Chapter Twenty-Two~

Kincaid tapped his partner's number into his phone. "Parker, where are you, right now?" He had to cover one ear and yell into the cell phone because of the loud noises around him.

"I was about to call you. I found Mohammad near the VIP platform and figured I better not lose him. I'm following him now, heading toward the back of the temple. Why?" Parker reported.

"Are you sure it's Mohammad? Or is it his sister?"

"What? I, uh, I'm not sure. They both might have the same body type."

"Stay with whichever one you are following. I'm already in back. If I see him, I'll pick him up. Catch up to me. I've got to talk to you and can't do it over the phone." Kincaid paced the ground near the main path all the cast and crew used. So much adrenaline pumped through his blood, he thought he might burst. "What side of the temple was he coming around?"

"The north side. He's at the northwest corner now and walking toward the back."

"Don't lose him. We have a better chance of shutting these two down if we can do it together."

"Okay, I'll be there as soon as I can." Kincaid turned around to walk when he stopped abruptly to avoid bumping into someone.

"Oh! I'm sorry," said a young woman who looked familiar to Kincaid. He just couldn't place her face. She was dressed in the costume of a Native American, or someone else from that time period.

"I'm sorry." Kincaid started to walk away.

"Do you remember me? My name is Jessica. Jessica Brock. We met at church last Sunday." She extended her open hand, and they shook in greeting.

Kincaid fought to shift his mental gears. "Yes, I remember, now. What are you doing here?"

She gestured to her costume. "I'm a performer in the cultural festival."

"Great! I had no idea they recruited actors from so far away." Kincaid tried to avoid getting distracted by her, or by their conversation. His eyes darted around the area, looking for Mohammad or Parker.

"They sure do."

Kincaid's cell phone vibrated, and he looked at the screen." He put his hand up to stop her talking. "Just a minute."

He put the phone to his ear. "Parker, where are you?" He listened to the response. "I'll wait in back. Keeping walking."

"I guess I came at a bad time. Are you working?" Jessica asked.

"Yes. I am. Can we talk later? I'll find you before you leave the temple grounds. Okay?"

"Yes. I guess so. I'll wait right *here* for you after the show," she said with a tinge of hope in her voice, pointing to the ground, and smiling.

"Then it's a date. I'll see you then." Kincaid smiled at her, but quickly returned to his phone.

*****

Fatima recognized the man she had seen at the mosque in Detroit. She had been standing in the shadows at a short distance, but now she saw the same man, here. He must have made the connection and followed them here. But it didn't matter. He could not stop her and her brother from conducting their business. She moved to the side, to observe him, when a young woman approached him and greeted him with a friendly handshake. She didn't recognize that woman, but Fatima realized they were familiar, and instantly decided to use her to get at the man.

Fatima watched them from her semi-concealed position behind the dressing rooms. They appeared to be talking casually, but the man kept looking around him. Was he looking for an escape route? Or another person? Fatima didn't know.

The man checked his phone again while the woman tried to speak with him. He put one finger in the air to shut her up as he answered the phone and looked in one direction for someone. Who? His partner?

Fatima stepped out from behind the dressing rooms and stood beside a rack of costumes among several racks and hundreds of costumes. She saw an angel's robe on the end of one rack and a wisp of irony whipped through her head.

*****

After finishing his business with the local sheriff at the church tower, Director Tanner drove back and parked his car on the dirt road at the rear of the temple where all the action—performance and security—took place. He was less than one hundred meters away from where Kincaid had shot the sniper.

Kincaid's cell phone rang. "Director Tanner. Where are you, now?" he asked above the din of the surrounding crowd.

"I'm driving back from the church tower. You've got the local constable in a genuine dither," Tanner said with the hint of a chuckle. "They want the details of how we knew the man was in the tower and how we realized he planned to shoot at our people. Even though they have pieced together his mission themselves, they want to know how *we* fit in."

"That's okay. They can have a copy of my video feed. It's

recorded on my smartphone."

"That might pacify them for a little while. But they also want to know by whose *authority* you placed the cameras in the tower. They took the cameras as evidence, by the way, because they were on private property." Tanner hated to be the one to deliver the bad news, but he had no choice.

"For crying out loud! I wasn't about to stop and call 9-1-1 and *watch* the man shoot the Prophet before stopping him. And I *wasn't* about to take the time to submit a request for a court order to legally install the cameras. We had no time to do it any other way. You *know* that."

"I know, I know. Don't worry. I'll take care of it," Tanner said, already planning that meeting with the Sheriff in his mind. "I have no juice with these people as the mere Director of Church Security."

"Give them Parker's name and authority so she and the FBI can handle it."

Silence.

"I think I just saw Mohammad," Tanner said in a loud whisper, stepping out of his parked car and walking around to the side of the temple building. "Where are you now?"

"I'm in back with the cast and crew. Have you seen Parker?"

"I thought she was with you." Tanner panicked. He didn't want this terrorist plot to be the last operation of his career. He had to find Parker, soon.

"No. She said *she* was following Mohammad. Look around for her now, please."

Tanner checked his immediate area. "No, I don't see her—oh, no! Now, I've lost Mohammad. He's working alone now, right?"

"No. Parker and I discovered he has a twin sister who is just as fanatical as her brother," said Kincaid. "Oh, snap!"

"What's going on?" Tanner asked into his phone, hoping he wouldn't have to deal with any more negative issues.

"I'm not sure, yet. Let's find Parker before we do anything else." Kincaid broke the connection.

Tanner and Parker ran up to Kincaid from different directions. Parker pointed over Kincaid's shoulder. "Mohammad just got into that brown van," she said, out of breath and pointing at a vehicle about thirty meters away.

Kincaid spun around to see an old model Ford van, medium brown, with no side windows. The engine started. He moved toward the van before it could drive away.

"Orson! Help!" Jessica screamed, from behind him.

Tanner and Parker both turned toward the scream.

Kincaid skidded to a stop when he heard a woman's scream.

Dozens of people milling in the area stopped and looked toward the disturbance. Not knowing what else to do, they pulled out their smartphones and started taking a video of the screaming girl.

Tanner took out his gun and looked down at it as if he didn't know what it was. He had not drawn his weapon in over twenty years, except on the range. But he wasn't about to become an observer when so many problems were staring him in the face.

He saw Fatima, dressed in a disheveled angel's costume, looking less angelic than wicked. Her halo slipped and fell to the ground. She held one arm tightly across Jessica's throat and pressed a knife at it, standing at the side of the path leading to the van.

Kincaid froze for only a second. He turned toward the van—engine idling—then looked back at Jessica's vulnerable panic. The triumphant look on Fatima's face immediately sickened him.

Fatima grinned. Kincaid thought she couldn't have looked more like the devil himself if blood were oozing from her mouth. Fatima prodded the knife tip at the woman's throat, making her stifle another scream.

Tanner watched from his position as Parker and Kincaid both drew their guns. They approached the hostage and perpetrator from different angles. Tanner remained where he was, watching the scene unfold in front of him. He realized he would have to submit a report on whatever happened next, so he wanted to watch it firsthand.

*****

Fatima slowly removed the knife from the girl's throat as if she was giving up. Then she shoved it hard into her back, puncturing her right side, and glaring at Kincaid as she did so. This time, the girl didn't scream. She just moaned and dropped to the ground. Fatima let her fall and ducked among the many nearby racks of costumes. Throwing off the shimmering white gown, she rapidly crept under the hanging costumes, away from her pursuers. She needed to make her way to her brother for their escape.

*****

Kincaid holstered his gun as he rushed to Jessica's side. He grabbed a white costume from the rack closest to him, balled it up, and clasped it to the bleeding wound. The blood was dark and thick and was coming out in a steady flow.

"Don't worry," Kincaid told Jessica. "You'll get through this all right."

Director Tanner appeared at Kincaid's side. "Will she be all right?" he asked as he stooped down to talk with them.

"She will be if you'll call the ambulance and have them get over here, *now*. The knife might have punctured her kidney," he replied.

"They're behind the VIP platform."

"Then call them, now. Hurry!" Kincaid said as he sat on the ground and cradled Jessica's head in his lap. He held the makeshift bandage and pressed over her bleeding wound to stench the flow. They had only met once before this celebration, but she had been nice to him and he needed to save her life.

*****

Special Agent Haley Parker, gun drawn, quietly searched among the costume racks for Fatima. She stepped over several fallen costumes, watched, and listened for any hint of Fatima's location or movement. She got to the end of one rack, stopped, then silently turned to go down the next row of costumes.

Without warning, Fatima threw a brown Nephite robe over Parker's head, held it tight at the base of her neck, and pulled, jerking the unsuspecting FBI agent backward and down to the ground. Parker's head slammed against a nearby tree root, when she landed, dazing her.

Fatima pulled a zip-tie from her pocket, roughly flipped Parker onto her stomach, and secured her wrists together behind her back. She picked up her captive and dragged her toward the van where her brother waited for her. This interference had gone on long enough and Fatima vowed to get rid of this infidel woman and her partner, so she and her brother could get back to their mission.

****

Director Tanner ended the phone connection after calling the on-site ambulance, when he saw a woman dragging Parker toward the idling van. "Mohammad has Special Agent Parker," Tanner yelled over the noise of the crowd. He pointed Kincaid in their direction.

Kincaid turned and glared at the sight. "No! That's his sister. You take care of Jessica," he said, leveling his handgun at Fatima's head. Several people ran for cover, screaming. Tanner kept the pressure on Jessica's wound.

Focused on saving this girl's life, he couldn't *do* anything to help Parker or Kincaid. He didn't like leaving them on their own, but he was needed here until the ambulance showed up.

Fatima backed up against the back door of the van, opened it with one hand, and tried to toss Parker inside. Parker resisted and Fatima slapped her in the jaw. She then hurled her into the back of the van before the woman's senses cleared from the bump to the head and slap to the face.

Suddenly, the crowd thinned enough to give Kincaid confidence in his shot. He took it—one shot with his SIG—purposely striking Fatima in the calf as she tried to jump into the back of the now moving van.

She stumbled, grabbed the sides of the van doors, and heaved herself inside. Half a breath later, she flew out the same door, landing on her back on the dirt road, after Special Agent Parker kicked her in the chest with both feet.

Kincaid heard sirens and saw the ambulance negotiating the crowd, trying to get to Jessica Brock. He looked back at Jessica, then at Fatima and the departing van, gritting his teeth in anguish. *Choices*, he anguished.

Tanner kept pressing the cloth on Jessica's wound. "I'll take care of Jessica until the ambulance arrives. You go get Parker," he yelled as Kincaid raced toward him.

*****

Parker struggled to get loose from the zip-tie on her wrists. Looking around the inside of the van for anything to help her, she saw boxes of what must have been hundreds of pounds of plastic explosives.

Mohammad stopped the van, turned around and grabbed a short piece of lead pipe lying beside the driver's seat. He slammed it against the base of the struggling Parker's head, knocking her unconscious. She silently collapsed to the floor of the van, among the many boxes of plastic explosives.

Mohammad put another zip-tie around Parker's ankles and looked for his sister. He saw Fatima lying on the ground, on her stomach, behind the van and made the snap decision to drive away—mission before family. He saw the man standing over his sister, with one knee against her back, holding her to the ground. Her blue jean leg had a growing blossom of red on it. The man must have shot her. Speeding up, he drove out the back service gate of the property. He still had a lot of work to do before the sun set.

*****

As soon as the paramedics had taken over the care of Jessica, Director Tanner ran over to Kincaid. The younger man's weapon was still in his hand and pointed toward the ground. Tanner's face was red, his heart raced, and he was out of breath.

Kincaid knelt on top of the wounded Fatima with one knee in the center of her back, holding her on the ground while she struggled. She screamed and threatened him in English and Arabic with language unbecoming any kind of lady in any culture.

He bent down and whispered into her ear. "As soon as you settle down, I'll take the pressure off your back. Until then, just *shut up*." Kincaid checked his pockets for a zip-tie and came up empty. He looked up and saw Tanner, still jogging toward him. "Why are you here? Where's Jessica?" he demanded.

Tanner pointed toward the ambulance. "The paramedics have her now. They said she needs emergency surgery. The kidney *was* punctured." He pulled a zip-tie from his pocket and handed it to Kincaid, who tightened it around Fatima's wrists, behind her back.

Tanner knelt near Kincaid. Their eyes met. They both held Fatima down while she screamed and struggled, more to throw a tantrum than to get free. They had no arrest authority, so they waited for the local police to arrive and take custody of her.

"I have to go after Mohammad," Kincaid declared. "I can't let him kill her, too."

"No, you don't, Orson. Let the police get him."

"He's got Parker—my *partner*! I've already lost one partner too many, in this life. I won't lose another one."

Fatima turned her head to one side and shrieked. "He will kill *both* of you if you find him. You are *nothing* to him!" Spittle ran down onto one cheek as she screamed.

She groaned as Kincaid put more weight on her back to shut her up.

"Orson, wait. We don't have jurisdiction here. The Church is not a law enforcement agency. We can't speed off after a suspect just because we want to."

"Director, I *know* we work for a religious organization. I *know* God will help us, but at this moment, what if I have been chosen by God to make this right? What if he has trained, protected, and hired me, so I can do this job—right *now*? Here? Today?" Kincaid took a slow breath to gather his thoughts. "This is *not* the time for fasting and prayer. It's the time for action. If we don't hurry, we might never see Parker alive again," he said, pointing at the van as it turned onto the nearby highway, and sped away.

Director Tanner hesitated, looking at the younger man in front of him.

"I need your car," Kincaid said, holding out his hand for the keys.

"Where's yours?"

"Parker has the keys. C'mon, give it to me," he demanded. He held out his hand, palm up.

Without another word, Tanner fished out his rental car key and dropped it into Kincaid's beckoning hand.

"When I find the van, I'll hold him at bay and call the police to arrest him. I won't go in guns blazing," Kincaid promised.

"When you find the van," Fatima spat, "He will *kill* you and the other Mormon infidels anywhere *near* him."

Kincaid put a hand on the bullet wound in her calf and pushed his thumb into the hole to support himself, while he stood. "Oops. My bad."

Fatima shrieked again, this time in pain. Kincaid left her in Director Tanner's care until the police arrived to take over. He mentally blocked out her screaming and her threats and epithets. It hurt him more than anything to think he should have done more to keep his partner safe. But he *knew* it was true. Now, he had to make up for that deficiency.

~Chapter Twenty-Three~

Kincaid drove in circles. He'd lost sight of the van and had no idea where it might have gone. His cell phone vibrated. Kincaid didn't recognize the number, except that it was local. "Yeah?"

"I see I have lost you. Is that right?" a familiar and evil voice taunted.

"I'll find you. Don't worry."

"Why don't I give you time to think about it, while you search for me—and for your lovely partner?"

"Yeah, do tell."

"I left a bomb on the temple grounds. It is big enough to blow up the temple and kill hundreds of the people there—both performers and visitors. That is what's nice about bombs. They don't discriminate. I am setting the timer device on the bomb for sixty minutes from... now."

Kincaid reached out and turned on the count-down feature on his phone. One hour.

"But I'm afraid you will only have time to either find the bomb or rescue your partner. You won't have time to do *both*. My guess is that you will be in between the two bombs when they simultaneously detonate." Mohammad severed the connection.

Kincaid started to sweat. What should he do? What *could* he do? He pulled his car to the side of the road and dialed Director Tanner's number. "I just spoke with Mohammad," he said without prelude.

"Good. What does he want?"

"No, it's *not* good. It's not what he *wants*. It's what he's *done*. There's a bomb on the temple grounds. It's set to explode in… fifty-eight minutes. He said it's big enough to blow up the temple and kill hundreds of people in and around the building. You need to evacuate the temple grounds *now* and get everyone as far away from it as possible."

"I'll notify the Prophet's six-foot-perimeter bodyguard and see what he wants to do. He's the one with the final say in matters such as this. You get Special Agent Parker. I'll take care of the temple and the people. Don't worry about them."

*****

Kincaid got back on the road, trying to think while driving. Where could Mohammad have gone? Where could he hold Parker without being seen?

His cell phone vibrated again. "Hello?"

"I spoke to the six-foot-perimeter man, and he spoke with the Prophet. The message he gave was *all will be well.*"

"Are you *kidding* me?" Kincaid ranted and beat on the steering wheel with both fists.

"Orson, you're new to this. But when the Prophet *speaks*, it's up to us to have the *faith* to listen and obey."

"Yeah … okay. But you're still looking for the bomb, right?"

"You bet. I've got six other deputies helping us search for it. I'll get back to the search as soon as you hang up."

Without a word, Kincaid pushed the quit button on his phone. Inside, his guts churned like he'd eaten rotten food. He remembered the missionaries in Mexico had quoted a scripture that said, *'if a person needed an answer to a problem, they could ask God, and he'll tell them the answer.'* He knew those weren't the exact words the missionary had used, but he hoped he remembered those words close enough to have the right idea.

So, Kincaid offered a silent prayer, with his eyes open, as he drove down the road, searching for Mohammad. He knew he could save a lot of lives by finding and stopping that mad man. He might also be able to save his own partner. But he needed to know *where* Mohammad had gone, so he could stop him.

A thought instantly came to Kincaid. Mrs. Droggan said she hadn't spoken with either of her children. But both children knew where she lives in Camden because they were raised there. The large metal building in back of the house would also be a great place to hide a hostage. He hoped it was not too late to save Parker and Mrs. Droggan, if she was also being held as a hostage.

Kincaid set his GPS to the address Parker and he had visited the day before and drove as fast as he dared.

*****

Director Tanner rallied six off-duty police officers at the TOC. They all had years of police experience. As Melchizedek Priesthood bearers, they were all worthy to enter the temple, themselves. He pulled them all inside the TOC trailer, where no one else could hear them, and gave them their instructions.

The Tabernacle Choir sang a hymn that fit in with the theme of the ceremony, forcing Director Tanner to speak loudly to his search team.

"We have a credible bomb threat right *here*, right *now*. They have notified the Prophet, and he is relying on us to find it before it detonates. We don't see how it could be inside the temple, so we need to concentrate our search on the grounds and vehicles parked near the temple or near the people. We have...fifty-one minutes before it's set to detonate. Questions?"

"Has county EOD been notified?"

"Yes, but they're on another call now and can't get here in time."

"What do you want us to do if we find any suspicious

packages?"

"Everyone get your phones out. I'll give you my number. I want you to call me first, if you find anything that looks dangerous. It's *my* stewardship—my *responsibility*. I'll decide."

Everyone nodded in understanding.

After he gave them his cell number, he stepped over to a large white board. On it was a sketch of the area. He took a red marker and divided the temple grounds into assigned sectors for everyone to search. As soon as they were issued their assignments, they went on their way.

As they dispersed, Tanner stopped and thought about what he had told them. It was *his* stewardship. He alone would take the responsibility for making the call of what to do when they found the bomb. He shook his head and said a short prayer before heading out, himself.

When he raised his head, he walked around to the front of the building and stood with his back to the temple's main entrance. In front of him were the Tabernacle Choir and the dignitary seating where the Prophet, his counselors, several other general authorities, and local political leaders sat. At least seven-hundred members and guests alike were enjoying the performance and the spirit of the moment.

The choir finished and the scene changed. As the music blared, all the performers rushed onto the stage at the same time. They sang; they danced. They were oblivious to what was about to happen if he didn't do his job perfectly.

Director Tanner was a bundle of nerves. He knew his blood pressure must be off the charts, and his wife would kill him if she knew how physically active he was, today. But she would be even more upset if he didn't come home at all because he had allowed the bomb to detonate.

After almost forty-five minutes of searching for a bomb, he had only one more place to check. As he approached the back of the VIP seating stage, he noticed a lot of electric cables on the ground. Surely, they went to the sound system and the microphone at the pulpit from which the Prophet would soon give his final address. But there seemed to be far too many cables.

Tanner bent down to look under the stage. He wiped a stream of sweat away from his eyes. Part of it trailed down one eyeglass lens, making it difficult for him to see in the dark. He wiped it away. Reaching into his breast pocket, he pulled out his cell phone and activated the LED flashlight. He turned the light on and pointed the beam under the stage. Other than the cables, there was only a footlocker-sized wooden box. He figured it held the sound system, but he needed to check it out, to make sure.

The Director crawled under the stage, lifted the top of the wooden box, and froze. The box was filled with brick-sized blocks of plastic explosives, with a smartphone on top of the blocks. Wires extending from the phone, led to several detonators stuck into the blocks. Tanner wanted to scream. He wanted to run. He wanted to faint, hoping it would all be a bad dream when he awoke. He stared at the face of the smartphone. There were eight minutes before the detonator would activate.

Suddenly, the music and singing ended. Tanner froze, wondering what was going on above him. A thunderous applause. The show must be over. The Prophet would speak, now. He heard the applause diminish and steps on the creaking stage above him.

"Brothers and sisters, guests and friends. We are so glad you came to join us as we celebrate the opening of this new temple," the Prophet said. "Temples bring a large measure of safety and security to us, because they are placing the Lord where he can give revelation and refuge to those inside, who have prepared themselves to feel the Holy Spirit."

'That's easy for the Prophet to say,' Tanner thought. *He didn't know there were only seven minutes before detonation.* Tanner remembered the words he had said to comfort Kincaid: *The Prophet knew best and would protect us.* But at this moment, his faith in that statement was waning.

Tanner had been a military police officer in the Special Forces Unit at Fort Bragg, North Carolina. Although he had honorably earned his long tab at Camp Darby, he had not been tested in combat like his new employee, Orson Kincaid. He was somewhat jealous of the kid for having combat time when he, himself, had none.

After six years in the Army, Tanner left and took a job with the CIA as a Ground Operations Specialist. Their training had been rough, but he had completed the training well and was ready for overseas work in the elite ground branch teams of the CIA. But he'd had an accident and was forced to choose to take a support role or to go to the Farm to teach.

Now, Tanner realized he didn't know enough about bombs to defuse one. But he reached forward and turned off the smartphone, hoping that would be enough to stop this one. The screen went dark. Ten seconds went by; twenty seconds, then... nothing happened. Tanner put his face in his hands and cried in relief. He would be sure to tell the EOD Squad what he had done so they could look at it again before they dismantled the stage.

Director Tanner crawled out from beneath the stage and sat in the shade between the choir and dignitary stage. His breaths came with difficulty. He pulled out his handkerchief to wipe his face. Then suddenly, he felt a terrible, stabbing pain in his left arm. Remembering he still had his cell phone in his hand, he looked down at the screen. Smiled. Using the last of his strength, he typed three short words, hit Send. Then everything went black.

*****

Kincaid finally turned onto the Droggan's street and slowed his vehicle, stopping it two houses away from the Droggan's house. He texted Tanner with the address, asking for police backup. He waited for a response, but after two minutes without any, he went in on his own. Time was running out.

He exited the vehicle, felt for his backup gun at the small of his back, and pulled his primary weapon from his shoulder holster as he approached the house. No telling exactly what he should expect inside. But he wanted to be ready for anything.

Crunching over the gravel driveway, he peered around the corner of the house, toward the backyard, and saw the large metal building. The van was parked near the door to the shed. At least he was in the right place.

As he climbed the steps of their front porch, his smartphone vibrated. When he pulled it out, the text message said, "All is well." He smiled. Tanner *had* come through. Now it was *his* turn.

He pocketed the phone and approached the front door. Someone had shut it but left it unlocked. He slowly opened the door, listening for any sounds and watching for movement.

Nothing.

As he cleared each room in the house, he wondered if Mohammad might use his own mother as bait or even as a hostage to help himself get away. If she wasn't at home, where else could she be? With each of the rooms clear of people and activity, Kincaid headed out the back door, toward the metal building.

He saw one window in the side of the building. It must be in the wall of an office. The window was closed, and an old wool blanket covered the window like a curtain. Watching the window for anyone looking out, he raced toward the van.

Putting his hand to the van's hood, he felt it was still warm. He looked inside the window of the driver's door and saw stacks of plastic explosives in the back. Kincaid shook his head. *This was not going to end well for everyone*, he thought to himself.

The building had one door that was wide and high enough for heavy vehicles and one door for pedestrians, beside it. Both doors were shut. He didn't know if there were any other entrances or exits, but he didn't feel he had time to check. He had to take the chance there were no other doors.

Kincaid glanced at his phone. Director Tanner might have stopped the bomb at the temple, but there was still six minutes left before Haley Parker would die. Kincaid gritted his teeth and rushed inside the building.

*****

FBI Special Agent Haley Parker was tied to a wooden chair with her hands secured to each of the arm rests by plastic zip-ties. Her captor had also secured her feet with zip-ties to the front legs of the chair. A piece of gray duct tape covered her mouth. Her chair sat atop a large, plastic tarpaulin, like those used by interior painters, over a hard-pressed dirt floor.

Parker looked around for any avenue of escape and any weapons she might use when she got loose. Hand tools and power tools laid on benches and tables where they had last been used, years ago. It looked like the building had once been an automotive repair shop, and then a furniture construction and repair shop. It was now abandoned and had been for a long time. The dirt floor of the office was mixed with saw dust, metal filings and old, dirty automotive oil. She continued flexing and relaxing her arms and feet, trying to loosen the ties.

*****

Mohammad finished putting the final touches on the scenery of his video studio. He attached a large piece of green cloth to the wall behind Parker, so he could include a more dramatic scenery when he opened his live feed via the internet for this distinctive execution of a Special Agent of the Federal Bureau of Investigation.

He had donned his black clothing, minus the ski mask, and made the final touches on his lighting angles. Being meticulous, he reached down and straightened the tarp where it had been kicked up on itself; tightened the green screen more and reached for another alligator clip to hold it in place.

His knife lay on a table, off screen, like a prop, so he could get to it when necessary, without the inconvenience of a sheath on his hip.

Parker constantly shifted and jerked in her seat, testing the zip-ties and searching for any advantage to escape.

Mohammad walked over to Parker and stood behind her with her ear to his mouth. He caressed her hair with one hand, then grabbed a fistful of her hair, bent down, and whispered in her ear. "Don't worry. This is only a rehearsal." The temptation to laugh at his joke nearly escaped his lips.

With that, Parker, quickly leaned forward and snapped back again, slamming the back of her skull squarely against his face. His nose erupted, blood spraying on Parker's head and back. It ran down Mohammad's chin and the front of his fresh black shirt.

"Stop the countdown on the bomb," he ordered his technical assistant. "There is no hurry on that. We can start it again, later."

Mohammad cursed the infidel woman, reached for a nearby rag, and pressed it against his nose. After a minute, he checked the bleeding. It had stopped enough for him to continue. He glared at Parker with unsheathed hatred. "I will deal with you in good time," he growled.

Parker kept her eye on the nearby knife and watched his movements each time he picked it up. She desperately searched to find a weapon nearby that she could use in case she could break free and get to it.

Mohammad cleaned himself off, forgetting to give the order to resume the countdown, again. He returned and stood behind Parker's chair. This time, he picked up the long bladed, dull knife in his right hand—the hand that was minus the first two fingers due to an unfortunate incident in Syria, almost one year ago.

"Start the recording for the final rehearsal," Mohammad said to his assistant—the only remaining witness to the upcoming killing. The footage would keep a permanent record of the live-feed execution that all his fans and followers around the world would be watching. The meter read almost three-quarters of a million viewers. He snarled. There should be more than that. There should be nearly two million.

When the tech assistant gave the signal, Mohammad began by squaring his shoulders and staring into the video camera lens. "Welcome, my friends. Today we have a special execution of an infidel who deserves to die for several counts of breaking the law of Allah. Not only is she a woman who is dressed immodestly, drives a car and smokes cigarettes, which are all crimes under Allah's law. She also works for an infidel organization that has caused the death of many valiant Muslim fighters—the FBI." Mohammad held up her badge for the viewers to clearly see it.

Parker struggled more fiercely to free her hands or even her feet. She did not want to become a propaganda ploy for a fake Muslim assassin. Not today, not ever. She was incensed at him even more for saying she was a smoker. She had never touched tobacco in any form. When her strength was almost spent, she felt a slight give in the zip-tie holding her left hand to the chair's arm.

~Chapter Twenty-Four~

Kincaid crept among the tools, broken down vehicles, piles of lumber, and shelves of old automotive parts that filled the metal building. One row of shelves that was at least eight feet high and twenty feet long, was full of backyard barbeque-type propane tanks. He estimated there were about one hundred of them and hoped they were all empty, realizing they could cause quite a mess if someone connected them to an explosive device.

When he looked closer, Kincaid noticed small blocks of plastic explosive attached to each one, with detonators and wires connecting all of them together. Seeing no sign of a timer, he swore under his breath. He instantly felt the urge to run for his own safety. His experience with explosives was limited to recognizing that a bomb might go *Boom*!

First, he had to find out if Parker was a hostage in this building. He had to get her out of there, quickly, if either of them was to survive. This would not be a small explosion limited to a contained area which they could outrun. This was going to be the mother of explosions.

As he got to the center of the shed, Kincaid looked around and noticed one end of the building was closed off by a two-by-four wooden frame, about twelve by twenty-four feet in size. It was covered with drywall on the inside, maybe for an office or secure storage area. He slowly made his way toward the room. There was only one door, no windows, and the walls had extra padding, like a sanitarium might have on the inside, to protect the patients. Or like—*soundproofing*.

Whack!

A sudden sound, like flesh hitting bone, drew his attention. Kincaid ducked and trained his weapon on the direction of the sound—the small room toward which he was walking.

Kincaid heard muffled curses from inside the same room. He walked toward the door, his SIG Sauer at the ready, safety off.

He tried the doorknob. It was not locked. Worried that the hinges might squeak, he didn't crack it to peek inside. Bright lights shown from under the door. If he were still in his military unit, he would have access to miniaturized video equipment that would let him see what was inside before he entered, guns blazing, he knew. But no such luck, today.

With a flurry, he kicked in the door. As he rushed into the room, the bright lights in the recording studio blinded him and darkened the rest of the room. He soon found Mohammad standing behind Parker, with his knife at her throat. He blinked twice, then fired his gun, hitting Mohammad in the left shoulder. It wouldn't leave as big of a hole as he left last time with his .308 caliber, high-powered rifle round, but it would slow the man down, now.

Mohammad fell against the wall behind him. He dropped his knife and grabbed his wounded shoulder. "Aayeii! I just got that shoulder *fixed*," he yelled between clenched teeth, grabbing at the new wound, and falling to the floor.

"Yeah, I know. I'm the one who put the *first* chunk of lead in it. And quit bellyachin'," Kincaid ordered. "I just grazed your shoulder." He stepped over electric cables and video equipment to get to his target, holding his gun on Mohammad, continually. "Now, stay away from my partner," he said as Mohammad made a move toward Parker.

Parker struggled in her seat, violently trying to get loose. She mumbled, fiercely, but Kincaid couldn't understand what she said through the tape over her mouth. She tried to point across the room with her eyes, but Kincaid did not catch the warning.

Mohammad sat on the floor, slumped against the corner of the room. "You? In Mexico? That was you? You must've been special ops. And *now* what are you?" He shot a glance at his knife, still lying on the floor, but he didn't make a move to retrieve it. He looked up at Kincaid with cold eyes. "You wouldn't be so cocksure of yourself without your gun, *cowboy*," Mohammad said, accusing Kincaid in a New Jersey accent.

"What happened to your Middle East accent, Kenny?" Kincaid mocked. "Did you lose it when I shot you? Or when you fell to the floor?"

"Put down your gun, and my Middle Eastern accent will be the *last* accent you ever hear," Mohammad threatened.

Amused at the unexpected burst of bravado from the wounded terrorist, Kincaid holstered his gun, unsnapped the shoulder holster, shrugged out of it, and placed it on the worktable, near Parker.

Kincaid realized this was probably not the smartest decision he had ever made, but he had waited too long for this moment. The irony was, he had chased this guy around the world, and found him right here, in the USA. A single bullet was too easy for this murderer. The phony Muslim needed to suffer for all the people he had assassinated over the past two years.

Parker bounced in her chair and shook her head at Kincaid. She screamed and hollered, but her message went unheard because of the tape still over her mouth.

From the selection of bladed tools on the table, Kincaid picked up a large Philips head screwdriver and a six-inch leather awl with a length of heavy-duty thread still in it. He jammed the awl in the top of the table, moved to the center of the room, never taking his eyes off Mohammad.

Parker kept up her violent swaying in her chair, grunting while trying to shoot tractor beam eyes at her thick partner. She thought she could almost smell the testosterone in the room and realized her partner had been hypnotized by its power.

Mohammad got to his feet, retrieving his long-blade knife from the floor as he rose. "You might be good with a gun, but I am master with the blade." He twirled the knife handle in one hand, tossed it to his other hand, and felt the pain and weakness from his wounded shoulder. He twirled it back to his uninjured side again while circling his prey.

"You know, *Kenny*...," Kincaid began.

"My name is Mohammad Sayf al Din," Mohammad spat, his rage flushing his face.

"Okay, *Moh*. It doesn't have to end this way."

"So, now you don't *want* to fight? You put two bullets in my shoulder, and now you worry about dying?"

"Oh, yeah, I'm also the one who took your fingers," Kincaid confessed with a feigned, grin of contrition.

Mohammad glared at Kincaid, enraged. "That, too, was you? In Syria?"

"Yeah, I'm afraid so. I've been whittling on you for quite a while." By now, Kincaid could not hide his glee at the way their history had intertwined.

"I will take great pride in *whittling* on you, too, as you put it."

"But you don't *have* to do this. You don't *have* to do any of it. I'm guessing your mother is behind your turn to terrorism. Am I right?"

"She has *always* supported my sister and me."

"Hmm. Is she also behind your hatred for the Mormon Church?"

"You don't know what you're talking about!" Mohammad spat.

"Really? Don't you remember your whole family was Mormon once upon a time?"

"Never!"

"Oh, yeah. It's true. If you want, I'll go with you to your

living room and show you the photograph of your family posing in front of the Los Angeles Temple. You, your sister, and *both* your parents. By the way, why *did* your daddy leave mommy with the kiddies?"

"He did *not*. We left him because he got drunk and beat her every night. Then, when he started striking me and Kathryn, Mom took us away."

"And why do you think he started drinking? Could she have been too controlling?"

"That is a *lie*!" Mohammad shrieked. The gleam in his eye changed from anger to deathly rage.

"Okay, I *gave* you a chance," Kincaid said as Mohammad lunged at him.

Kincaid blocked the initial attack and pushed Mohammad back several steps. He rapped the back of Mohammad's hand, where the two missing fingers must still be sensitive to pain.

Mohammad shrieked.

They both circled each other, one with a snarl and the other with a strong yet sedate smile of confidence. Mohammad lunged forward again, flicking his blade upward. As Kincaid jumped backward, the tip of the blade caught him in the chin, missing his throat but splitting the chin open.

Kincaid wiped the blood from his chin with his sleeve. He parried several of Mohammad's aggressive attacks. The man lunged toward Kincaid again. Leaning toward Mohammad, he grabbed the wrist and slammed his opponent's right hand, palm down, on the nearby worktable. The knife clattered to the floor. Kincaid swung downward with the screwdriver, thrusting it through the flesh of the hand. The point of the tool cut straight through the half-inch plywood table beneath it.

Mohammad screamed again. The more he tried to jerk his hand free, the more it tore tendon and muscle, bleeding profusely and causing further pain.

Kincaid grabbed Mohammad's free hand, twisted the wrist,

and held him in an arm bar. The more Mohammad tried to bend his elbow, the more pain the arm bar caused. Slowly, Kincaid planted Mohammad's left hand against the wall behind the table, palm away from the wall. He grabbed the awl again and shunted it through his hand and into the drywall.

Mohammad screamed like a little schoolgirl. With both hands immobilized, the more he struggled, the more pain he felt. Realizing his dilemma, he stopped moving, and struggled to catch his breath.

Kincaid pulled the awl out, quickly put it through the hand yet again and again, placing two stitches into the hand, securing it to the drywall. The palm-up position of the hand held the armbar so Mohammad couldn't move. "Sorry. I ran out of zip-ties," Kincaid said. He took a strip of duct tape off the same roll Mohammad had used on Parker. He slapped it over Mohammad's mouth. "I don't want to listen to your whining, until the police get here," he said. "Stay there while I free my partner," he said, gesturing toward Parker.

Kincaid turned his attention to Parker. He tore the tape from her mouth, expecting to hear platitudes of gratitude from her while he freed her hands and feet.

"Behind you!" she yelled.

Kincaid spun. He reached for his gun, before he realized it was still in its holster, on the table where he had left it. In the spin, he fell to the floor in front of Parker, landing with his back against her knees. He tried to look through the bright studio lights toward the camera but saw nothing.

"Maybe this will help," said a raspy, smoke cankered voice from the darkness.

The studio lights turned off, leaving only the fluorescent lights in the ceiling to illuminate the room.

Kincaid peered into the sudden darkness, feeling vulnerable while his eyes got used to the dim lighting.

An elderly lady stood from her seat at the computer and

walked a few paces closer. She puffed on an unfiltered cigarette and blew the smoke toward Kincaid as she lazily pointed a revolver at him. She held the gun at waist height with one hand. Her finger was two knuckles deep over the trigger.

"Mrs. Droggan?" Kincaid asked, in astonishment.

"Yes, and you expected...?"

"I thought your children had taken you hostage to get to us," Kincaid said. He stood to his feet, directly between his partner and the elderly lady. He held his hands at shoulder height as soon as he got his balance. Hoping his partner was still thinking clearly, he needed her to take advantage of their situation.

Parker noticed the gun in the holster at the small of her partner's back. Her hands were still secured to the chair arms, but the zip-tie securing her left hand was looser than the right hand.

"Why didn't you help your son when we were scuffling, just now? You could have saved him all this pain," he said, jerking his head toward the bleeding young man pinned to the table and wall, like a fly in a spider's web.

Mohammad tried to look up at them. The act of stretching to look up over-extended his wrists and caused him lightning bolts of pain. Between the whining of pain and the growling of rage, his eyes seemed to glow red.

"It was entertaining watching the two of you struggle," she said with a sneer. "And I wanted to get everything on video. I am, after all, his technician."

"What about Fatima?" Kincaid asked.

"Her name is Kathryn, and she has been another pawn in my plan to get back at you Mormons," Hillary Droggan spat.

"Get *back* at us? What did the Mormons ever do to you?" Kincaid asked, incredulously.

"Do to me? They destroyed my family!" she shrieked. The aim of her gun wavered as she screamed. She slowed her breathing, took one deep breath, and took one confident step forward. "You know, I used to *be* a Mormon," Hillary said, conversationally, as if they were in her living room, sipping tea. "My husband and I joined the Mormon Church when we got married. Life was good until we discovered we couldn't have our own children. My husband saw no reason to keep attending a church so oriented toward families if we couldn't have our own. I got the idea that adopting children might turn him into a better man and save our marriage, so we adopted Kenneth and Kathryn. I loved them as if they had come from my own womb," she said in a dreamy voice.

Mohammad stopped struggling and stared at his mother in total disbelief.

"But it didn't help, did it?" Kincaid softly stated more than asked. He needed to give Parker more time.

"No, it didn't. That was when my husband started drinking. He lost his job because of drunkenness. After a few weeks without a job, he blamed *me* for everything wrong in the world, and beat me when he was drunk. I turned to my bishop and told him how my husband treated us. I asked for his help," she said. The tone of her voice sounded like she had been waiting a long time to tell her story to someone who could appreciate it. "I showed him my cuts and bruises and *begged* him for help."

Parker finally pulled her left arm out of the zip-tie. She slowly reached for Kincaid's backup weapon at the small of his back. She was careful to make sure Hillary did not notice her movement behind her partner.

"And do you know what the bishop—the *'judge in Zion,'* the shepherd of his flock—told me?" she asked, with dramatic sarcasm.

Kincaid shook his head but remained mute. He felt Parker tug the gun from his backup holster. He didn't know what she would do next.

"He told me to be a better wife and homemaker. To support my husband better, and to pray for him to see the error of his ways." She snarled as she spat out the words.

Kincaid realized she must have been holding in this bitterness for far too many years. They must have cankered her soul. "So, what happened?" he asked. He needed to keep the old woman talking and give Parker time to do whatever she planned to do with his gun.

The FBI agent slowly slipped the handgun from its holster and flicked the safety off. She knew Kincaid always kept a round chambered, so she knew it was ready for action.

"One night, my husband caught me on my knees, praying for him, and accused me of trying to undermine his authority in his own home—with *his* family. He beat me again. So, I finally took the children and left while he was in a drunken stupor. The children and I moved to New Jersey, where he would never think to look for us. Thank goodness, he never even tried. But I swore, way back then, I would make the Mormon Church *pay* for not supporting me in my time of greatest need."

Tears flowed down Mohammad's cheeks and over the duct tape at his mouth. He seemed to be hearing his mother's story for the first time.

"When my Syrian-born children were old enough to ask questions about their heritage, I directed them to a local Mullah, and he taught them all about Islam. As a teenager, Kenneth committed a crime and was sentenced to juvenile detention. He ran into the more extremist forms of Islam in *juvi*." She cooed the word juvi as if it tasted exquisite in her mouth.

"When he got out, he expressed a desire to go to Syria, to fight for his people. Of course, I encouraged him. Kathryn went a year later, which gave me time to develop a specific plan. You see, I had tried to create strong bonds between myself and my children. When they needed anything, I was there for them. So, it was rather amusing when I told them our problems *stemmed* from the Mormon Church. They came up with the plan themselves to do damage to the church. When you Mormons built a temple not too far from here, they took that on as their primary target—and a sign from Allah. I just sat back and praised them as each part of their plan developed and came to fruition."

She laughed, bitterly, taking her eyes off Kincaid for a moment.

Parker watched vigilantly from behind Kincaid, waiting for her moment. She hoped Kincaid would dive to the floor so she could get a clear shot. But the dufus just stood there! Finally, when Hillary looked away, Parker vigorously shoved the gun between Kincaid's legs and pulled the trigger repeatedly.

The SIG discharged once, hitting Hillary Droggan above the knee. She screamed and dropped her own gun to the floor.

After the first shot, Kincaid's gun jammed, catching on the material of his trousers—now singed and torn. The gun dangled from his crotch, hanging on by the material that was jammed in the gun's slide.

"What did you do? Are you crazy?" Kincaid shouted at Parker, as he hobbled around with the hot gun hanging on the crotch of his trousers. He rubbed the singed material with one hand and methodically checked to make sure he still had all his parts. "You could have—I could have lost—you almost...!" He stopped screaming and gently pulled back on the slide to remove the gun from his pants. He burnt one hand when it touched the hot slide. Tearing his gun free, he lunged forward and snatched up Hillary's gun from the floor.

"Yes, but I didn't," Parker yelled back at Kincaid. "And you got her gun away from her. Right?"

Kincaid grabbed the old lady by both shoulders and sat her down in the chair at the computer. He needed to stop her bleeding and dress the injury. While he pressed one hand to her bullet wound, Hillary leaned over to the laptop computer connected to the video camera. Mohammad connected the video camera to the internet for the now-aborted execution. She pressed a couple of buttons and shot to her feet.

Kincaid fell backward onto the floor from the sudden

movement.

"It doesn't matter now," Hillary growled, sounding more predator than wounded prey. She spun the laptop around so they could see the screen. "I changed the timing of the bomb. You now have only *two minutes* before this whole city block goes up in flames."

With that, she shambled out the door and through the corrugated steel shed, toward the exit, giggling and moaning as she hobbled.

Mohammad also moaned and groaned, trying again to free himself from his bindings.

Kincaid pulled a knife from his boot and cut Parker free from her remaining ties.

As he and Parker rushed over to the computer, Mohammad worked his hand free from the drywall, through gritted teeth and blinding agony. Wiggling the screwdriver until it came loose, he freed his other hand from the table. He ran out, after his mother… either to stop her now irrational plan or to help her execute the plan effectively.

Kincaid and Parker stared at the computer with wide open eyes.

"We've got to stop Mohammad, er, Kenneth," said Parker.

"We've got a ticking bomb right *here* to fix, first," Kincaid emphasized.

"There's only one minute and a few seconds left. I have no idea how to turn it off," she yelled.

"Stop yelling. Let's leave the bomb to itself and go after Mohammad before he returns to the temple." Kincaid retrieved and holstered both of his weapons as he spoke.

Parker nodded. Together, they raced out of the shed, and around to the front of the house toward Kincaid's vehicle.

*****

Kincaid raced past the wounded Hillary Droggan and drove a shoulder into her back as she hobbled toward her house, knocking her to the ground. She hurled infidel epithets at each of them. Parker ran close behind her partner, stepping away when Hillary tried to grab her leg. Both partners raced after Mohammad, who hurried toward his van.

Kincaid saw Mohammad jump into the van and start the engine before he even shut the door. He watched as Mohammad took off down the driveway, throwing dirt and gravel behind him. The van left a cloud of dust and debris in the air for Kincaid and Parker to inhale.

In response to a neighbor's 9-1-1 call for shots fired, a fleet of police cars had just assembled out front of the house. The lead detective was getting his team ready to storm the house when the van came screaming down the driveway.

Mohammad rammed several police vehicles as he drove his bludgeoned van between them and sped away.

"Hold your fire!" the lead detective yelled to his men. Not knowing whether the driver was theirs or an innocent neighbor, several officers dove out of the way of the reckless driver, without returning fire.

Kincaid and Parker sprinted toward their car, parked on the street, two houses away. Parker held her badge up in one hand, and repeatedly yelled, "FBI!" so the police wouldn't shoot them.

Kincaid started up the engine. Parker rolled down her window.

"I saw stacks of plastic explosives in the back of the van," Kincaid said.

"I know. Stop here a minute!" Parker said, sticking her head out the open window.

Kincaid slammed on the brakes as he came close to the broken police barricade. He looked over his right shoulder and saw Hillary staggering to a stop on the front lawn.

"Get everybody down!" Parker yelled to the nearest responders. "There's a bomb inside the metal building in back!"

The echoed cry of *Bomb! Bomb!* raced through the police ranks in the street.

With that, Kincaid did a reverse J-turn and sped after the van.

"Mohammad has at least half a ton of plastic explosives in that van," Parker told Kincaid.

Kincaid nodded his head. "He might make a last-ditch effort to ram the van into the temple. We can't allow that to happen."

*****

Dozens of experienced police officers raced to take shelter behind their vehicles. Weapons drawn, they ducked down, anticipating an explosion at any moment.

When it came, the blast blew away the entire three-thousand square foot shed. It ignited another larger explosive charge hidden inside the house's basement. Debris and shrapnel were hurled fifty meters in all directions.

Hillary Droggan was roasted as she spread her arms wide and looked into heaven with an eerie smile accentuating her wrinkled face. Paint on the nearest sides of the police vehicles bubbled and peeled off the vehicles in the heat of the detonation.

The force of the discharge shoved the nearest police cars several inches backward, across the pavement, before they stopped. The police officers themselves, although shaken, cautiously arose from their places of shelter and looked around at the singed results of the multiple detonations. The metal shed and three homes were blazing infernos.

The few fire trucks that were on the scene immediately sounded their sirens, bringing the police officers out of their stunned silence. The fire fighters needed to make a path so they could drive through the mess to do their job, now. Hearing the sirens, the police raced to their vehicles and moved them out of the way as best they could.

*****

The sound had been loud enough to hear from inside Kincaid's vehicle, already a quarter mile away and still speeding after the van.

Parker tapped 9-1-1 into her cell phone. "This is Haley Parker, FBI Special Agent badge number 3878. Multiple bombs have exploded at 14511 Ardmore, Camden, New Jersey. Police are already on the scene but may have been wounded in the blast. Send fire trucks, EMTs, and Explosive Ordnance personnel to take care of the fire, the wounded, and to search for more explosives at the scene."

She listened for a few seconds, then continued. "We are in pursuit of an old model Ford Econoline van, medium brown color, with no other distinguishing marks. We suspect it's also loaded with approximately one thousand pounds of plastic explosives. It is speeding east on Lansdowne Street and may be heading for the new Mormon Temple on Highway 150. Request all law enforcement vehicles remain out of sight to avoid detonations in residential areas. We will continue to pursue this vehicle ourselves."

~Chapter Twenty-Five~

Friday afternoon in New Jersey was warm, and the sun shone through the clouds. The light breeze tickled the leaves at the stems. For some reason, the traffic was thin and running *normal*—if *normal* was a word one could use to describe traffic in New Jersey. The new temple grounds were clear of all dignitaries, spectators, technicians, and performers. Only several full dumpsters in the back were evidence of any kind of festival earlier in the day.

Kincaid could have caught up with the van, but he didn't want to risk an explosion in the residential and commercial areas where the van sped. He didn't shoot at the van for the same reason and stayed back a reasonable distance.

Kincaid glanced at Parker and saw her fussing over her hair, but then she winced. When she pulled her hand away, there was blood on it.

"What kind of wound you got there?"

"Huh? Oh, this? In the van, he used some kind of pipe on me. Knocked me clean out. I woke up tied to that chair."

"If it's still bleeding, keep pressure on it." He took a clean handkerchief from his pocket and passed it to her. "Here. Use this."

Parker pressed the white handkerchief to the side of her head and held it there.

"I've got to know," said Parker once they were on a level straightway. "What's up with you and guns? You'd think a special ops sniper would actually enjoy his work."

Kincaid glanced sideways at his partner. "Now? You want to talk about this now?" he demanded.

Parker gave him a stubborn stare. "If you don't plan to catch up with Mohammad soon, you can at least talk while we're driving," she scolded. "So, give."

With the exception of Kincaid's family, Ted Pineda had been the only one to know the answer to that question. Kincaid had full confidence Ted had told no one else. Kincaid hadn't told a soul, either... until now.

"When I was four, my older brother and I snuck into our parents' bedroom. I found what I thought was a toy gun and shot and killed my seven-year-old brother." He turned a corner, still following the van, and took a moment to get his composure before continuing.

"For weeks afterward, I had nightmares of my brother exploding or disappearing. In every dream, I had his blood on my hands. Every morning, when I awoke, I laid in a puddle of piss and puke."

"When I was five, my father had enough of the nightmares and took care of it his own way. He took me out to the desert, near the Dragoon Mountains, and taught me how to handle a handgun. Every weekend, we drove to the desert to shoot for five years. I started with a .22 caliber revolver. Over the next two years, I worked up to a .45 caliber semi-automatic handgun. At first, whenever I began to cry or refuse, he would tell me to *wipe my chin and load another magazine.*

"When I was ten, and my father felt I was ready, he introduced me to rifles and shotguns. So, every other weekend, we shot at various distances and caliber rifles—usually at bottles and cans, occasionally at clay pigeons. My father seemed impressed with my natural ability for marksmanship. At fourteen, he bought me my first hunting rifle and scope. I was even better with the rifle than the handgun."

"So, why did you join the Army and become a sniper?" Parker asked, her curiosity peaked.

Kincaid thought about it for a moment. He had not considered that question for several years. "I guess I wanted to prove to myself I had a skill that would get me away from home. It was a way to get out of Saint David. To get away from the memories of killing my brother."

"But why join the Army? Didn't you know you would probably kill more people in combat?" Parker asked.

"Yeah, I knew. I was a good shot and loved the outdoors. So, I thought it was an even trade. The Army gave me a vocation I can't use in civilian life—without going to jail if caught."

"So, you ended up here, in a job you didn't *actually* want, doing what the Army *trained* you to do. Right?"

"That about sums it up," Kincaid agreed. He took a right turn, staying about one hundred meters behind the van on roads that became more rural as they drove. "Except now, I'm not enjoying it as much as I used to." ops sniper would actually enjoy his work

"It sounds like you were groomed for this job. No one else in the Service would know what to do or even have the drive to do it like you have."

"Yep. By the Grace of God, here I am," Kincaid said, remembering the words of the Prophet and already having resolved himself to that reality.

*****

Inside the van, Mohammad quickly reached behind him and grabbed a heavy vest. While driving as fast as his old and damaged van would go, with the weight of the explosives, he put one arm at a time through the arm holes of the vest and adjusted it to fit better. He screamed with the pain of both injured hands and his wounded shoulder. The van veered over a curb momentarily, but he kept driving. The vest was already loaded with six blocks of plastic explosive. He shoved four more blocks in the pockets for good measure.

"When this blows," he said to himself, "both the truck and the vest should put a hole in New Jersey, big enough to see from the space station. If they think I'm a mama's boy, I'll show them how I can think for myself. I *hate* the Mormons because of their high and mighty attitudes. That is what will seal their fates and send them straight to hell." He snarled and looked in his rear-view mirror. Seeing a car following him and guessing it was Kincaid, he increased his speed as fast as the clunker of a van could go. Mohammad suddenly turned off the road into a freshly tilled field, driving cross-country straight toward the temple. The field was bare and only a half mile from his objective.

Kincaid and Parker followed the van mere seconds behind. Kincaid knew his rental car would not make it through the soft soil. He stopped at the field's edge to see how well the van fared in the loose dirt.

Mohammad bumped and banged the van through the dirt, slowing his progress as the dirt quickly became too deep for the old van. Finally, Mohammad's van mired down and stopped a mere three hundred meters from the temple grounds. He could see the fence surrounding the property and cursed his bad luck. "Allah, do not forsake me, now," he yelled from inside the stalled van.

Kincaid jumped out of his car and raced toward his target. He pulled his 9mm SIG from his shoulder-holster as he ran. Parker also pulled out her weapon, running a few strides behind him.

*****

As soon as his van bogged down in the furrowed soil, Mohammad turned around and saw a man and a woman racing toward him with their weapons drawn. There was no way he would let them capture him. He connected the two electric switches to his vest, reached over his shoulder, and blindly flipped on the dead man's switch on his back. He cursed at his wounds and asked Allah to make him strong. Then he ran and stumbled through the loose dirt and high furrows toward the temple. His wounded hands were bleeding again. The rags he had found in the van, wrapped around each one, were soaked and dripping with his blood. He realized the next thirty minutes would show his mastery over his pains.

When Kincaid got to the van, he took a quick look inside its back window. Inside the back of the dark van, he saw a red-light blinking, and quickly turned back toward his partner. "The bomb inside the van has been activated," he yelled. "Stay here and call for EOD to come take care of it. Make sure no one else gets close to it."

"What do you plan to do?" she asked him.

"I'll make sure he gets nowhere *near* the temple."

Parker nodded her understanding and grabbed her phone. Kincaid drew his secondary SIG from the small of his back and took off again, running toward Mohammad.

Two police cars, with their lights flashing, pulled to a stop at the edge of the road. Parker jogged back to them. She pulled out her badge as she ran to inform them of the situation.

Although the dirt was soft and deep, Kincaid was making progress. He saw Mohammad getting closer and closer to the temple as he ran. He considered shooting at Mohammad to stop him, but a 9mm bullet at this range wouldn't even knock him down. Then there was also the possibility the round would set off the explosives in the vest. He quickly decided not to take that chance.

Along the way, Kincaid ran past a stack of shovels and hoes that the farmers must have used to weed the loose dirt. He slowed and grabbed a spade-head shovel, taking it with him.

When Kincaid was a mere ten meters from the madman, he saw a small red light blinking below Mohammad's neck. He realized Mohammad wore a suicide vest and had already armed it. Despite his better judgment, Kincaid stopped, dropped to one knee, took a steady aim, and shot once, low.

Mohammad fell and struggled to get back to his feet. He gripped the calf injury with both hands, where Kincaid had just put his bullet. Again, he rose and continued hobbling toward the temple, unwilling to give up his goal—his personal jihad.

Kincaid holstered his handgun as he ran. Not wanting to risk setting off the explosive vest with another bullet, he took his shovel and whirled it around him like an Olympic hammer thrower. After two spins, he released the shovel, hurling it in an arc, toward Mohammad. The shovel flew true and struck the terrorist in the back of the other thigh, splitting the skin and muscle with the spade tip from a distance of twenty-five feet.

Mohammad fell to the furrowed dirt on his face. He reached around and pulled the shovel blade from his leg, screaming as he removed it. Cursing and breathing hard, he turned and sat down in the dirt, facing Kincaid. He held out both wounded hands, gingerly grabbing hold of a dead man's switch in each one. "I don't see your partner. I guess she stayed with the van," he shouted to Kincaid, who was less than ten meters away.

Kincaid turned to look back at the van. It was too far to yell a warning. He faced Mohammad again.

"One switch detonates my vest, and the other detonates the bomb inside the van," he said, showing the switches to Kincaid. "I wear at least twenty pounds of plastic explosives. It would *kill* you at this distance." Mohammad winced and adjusted his position, trying to decide which leg wound hurt more—a bullet wound, or shovel blade wound. He knew they were both probably bleeding badly, and he didn't have much time left. "So, which one do you want me to blow first?" he challenged Kincaid.

In a heartbeat, Kincaid realized he could shoot this terrorist in the head without even flinching. But if there was a chance he might repent and live to serve the living God, Kincaid didn't want to be the one to take that opportunity away from him. He quickly decided he was finished playing this lunatic's games.

"I don't care which one you blow, first. In fact, let me help." Kincaid took aim and shot the switch out of Mohammad's left hand, shattering Mohammad's hand along with the switch. The spent bullet cascaded into the dirt, missing the vest. Kincaid fell to the ground, hoping to avoid flying shrapnel from the exploding vest.

Instead, the bomb in the van, several hundred meters behind him, exploded in a ball of fire. With the unexpected blast, Kincaid's heart flew into his throat. He could only hope Parker had moved away from the van, or at least was not so close as to have been killed by it. Kneeling between furrows, he slammed his forehead into the dirt in agony at the thought. With anticipation, he raised his eyes back to his target.

"So, you killed your partner," Mohammad declared in a haughty voice. "How *interesting*. An American soldier who loves himself more than his colleagues. You surprise me." He sneered, the edges of his mouth drooped, betraying his bravado.

Kincaid stood to his feet, wiping the looser dirt from his clothes. "You won't destroy God's temple *or* His church," he said. Anger and hatred dripped from each syllable. He walked closer to the wounded man, who was still sitting in the dirt. "In fact, you won't get any of your forty-two virgins or any other empty promises that Allah might have made to you, because you won't kill any American infidels today. I know you no longer work for any Muslim extremist groups. I know you are only carrying out the vengeful wishes of your hateful mother. What a twisted piece of work *she* was. And how unimaginably pathetic it was of her to manipulate her own children to do her bitter will. Face it, *Moh*, she played you like a tightly strung infidel, fiddle."

Mohammad squirmed as Kincaid kept stepping closer. *How*

could he have learned that? He himself had just learned about his mother's hate for the Mormon Church in the past several weeks. "Your church abandoned her when my father beat her and started beating my sister and me."

"So, go after *one* man," said Kincaid, now just a few steps away. "Why blame an entire culture for the mistakes of one man?" It was a risk, but he had to distract and stop the misguided Muslim sitting in the dirt before him now.

The look in Mohammad's eyes suddenly sharpened. "What? And miss all this bloodletting? Ever since my first knife kill, I have always looked forward to the next one. I want nothing *more* than to kill my next victim. In fact, if I live through tonight, I will find *another* victim and *another* excuse to kill them and another way to show it to my fans over the internet." A twinge of pain caused a twitch in his lower-left eyelid. He was losing the battle to control his pain.

Kincaid was barely close enough to see the single eyelid twitch.

Mohammad readjusted the switch in his right hand. He felt his sweat dripping onto the switch, making it slippery. If this enemy took two more steps, he would take at least one arrogant infidel with him.

In one swift movement, Kincaid grabbed the switch in Mohammad's hand and clamped his hand over the top of it, so Mohammad couldn't let go. He then reached behind Mohammad's neck and flipped off the control to the dead man's switch. Kincaid suddenly realized this maniac had been planning to run into the temple and detonate his vest inside, with as many people around him as he could get. What a shame the temple was closed and the workers had all returned to their homes.

Mohammad pushed and released the button atop the dead man switch in his hand and screamed in anguish as he realized he had overplayed his hand.

"No-o!" Mohammad cried in the anguish of his soul,

repeatedly thumping his wounded fist into the loose dirt around him. He turned over to crawl toward his ultimate goal—to destroy the Mormon temple. As soon as he did, Kincaid reached down and quickly flipped the switch back on. The red light behind Mohammad's head gave off a ghostly glow again—without Mohammad's knowledge.

Kincaid stood back and marveled at the amount of rage in this man.

Mohammad growled and snarled in pain and anguish as he crawled closer to his goal. He purposefully dug his elbows into each furrow and dragged his injured knees behind him as he crawled. Now, he refused to take his eyes off the building before him.

Kincaid let Mohammad crawl in the dirt for a few seconds as he trudged back toward the burning van. Then he turned and cupped his hands around his mouth. "Hey, Moh," he called. "Try that switch again. I didn't turn it off." With that, Kincaid turned and jogged back to the blaze that had been the van. A fire truck had pulled up to the road's shoulder and was hosing down remnants of the burning vehicle. Several police cars and two ambulances sat nearby. The police-controlled traffic as the last of the day's light fell below the horizon.

Mohammad stopped crawling, rested on one hip, and reached for his switch. Without checking the power light at the back of his neck, he pushed the button, hesitated a few seconds, and lifted his finger to see if—

Boom!.....The concussion hurled Kincaid to the dirt. The explosion sent a dusty breeze past him at fifty meters distance. A gust of dirt and debris fell on him from above before it was over.

He smiled and gave one arm a single pump as he got back to his feet. "Yeah! That's one less fanatic the world has to worry about." As much as Kincaid hated this Executioner, he didn't want to be the one to kill him. He had no problem allowing the man to kill himself. Kincaid considered the world a safer place with Mohammad dead. But in the back of his mind, he mourned that the man had to die before repenting of all the evil he had done during his life.

As he strode through the loose soil, Kincaid saw the burning van and started a quicker gallop, remembering Parker and hoping she was safe. When he got closer to the blaze, he looked around in relief as Parker stepped out from a nearby wooded area.

"You all right?" Kincaid called, gasping for breath.

"Yes, I looked inside the van window and saw when the mechanism switch activated, so I jumped into the trees before it blew. The Sheriff's deputies took over the scene from there. What happened to Mohammad?"

"He blew his own switch, so the field will be well fertilized when the farmer sows the seeds."

"How did you feel about it this time?" Parker asked, concerned.

Kincaid stopped and thought about it for a moment. He looked up at his partner with a smile. "You know, I didn't enjoy it. I did it because it had to be done. I just thought about what a sad waste of a lifetime before he died."

"It's a shame there's nobody to arrest," Parker mentioned. "In the FBI, we like to arrest perps whenever we have to use our weapons."

"Well, we could go out there with a body bag and pick up the hundred-plus pieces of your perp, if you want."

"I think I'll pass on that one and leave it for the forensics team. Did he leave a big hole in the ground?"

"Yep. You can't miss the pink crater in the middle of the plowed field, about one hundred meters from the fence around the temple. The good news is, he didn't even *splash* the temple grounds."

~Chapter Twenty-Six~

Kincaid entered his apartment and dropped his suitcase at the door. He looked around him and chuckled at the still-empty space. His belongings were to be delivered in two more days, so he still slept in his sleeping bag on a foldup Army cot in the master bedroom. Some things didn't change from the Army to civilian life. Hurry up and wait.

He had been powered by three to four hours of sleep every night since he left home ten days earlier, so his sleeping bag and cot looked great to him, about now. He allowed himself a moment of looking forward to sleeping. But he had some chores to do first.

Walking to the refrigerator, he looked inside. Not because he was hungry but out of habit. His milk had turned to cottage cheese that smelled so bad not even paprika or pineapples would have helped it. His one loaf of bread was now stale, but not to the point of molding, and the bologna sandwich he had left on a plate in the fridge was hard enough to play hockey with.

When he shut the fridge door, he felt something undefined was different. Not a difference that made him want to draw his gun, but the kind that made a person feel happy and fulfilled. Had the apartment changed? Or had he changed in the past week and a half? He couldn't decide, but he had his suspicions.

Kincaid had been unable to attend the actual dedication of the New Jersey Temple. He decided to remain in his rental car in the temple parking lot while Haley Parker, Director Tanner and all the other temple recommend holders who had come for that one event, attended. He didn't feel badly about not going inside. He felt happy that the others still had a temple to do the Lord's work in. Looking forward to the time he could join them made him feel warm and fuzzy inside.

Now, in his apartment, Kincaid didn't eat. He didn't shower—although he needed one. He wanted just to lie down on his cot and sleep until the next day. For perhaps the first time in his life, he knelt and offered a prayer of gratitude and thanksgiving before falling asleep with his electronic scriptures in his hand. Yeah, he knew what had changed since he left.

*****

The next day was Saturday. Kincaid woke up early and felt more alive than he had in several months. He went for a run around the Sugar House Park, then came back, showered, and went down to the laundry room to do ten days' worth of laundry. Kincaid didn't really have clothing for ten days, but he had worn several pieces so many times, he figured it might take a few cycles to get them clean again.

Lauren was there when he stepped through the door, dressed more conservatively, in dark blue tights and an oversized t-shirt, without her mound of hair extensions. She was folding her clothing as she took each piece from the dryer. She turned and looked at Kincaid with an eye of recognition. Then she smiled and said, "Well, well. Aren't you that new guy who abused Bishop Brock a couple weeks ago?"

Kincaid blushed. "Hi, Lauren. So, it was you I saw at church that week. I didn't think you were a church member." He stepped to one empty washer and jammed all the clothing from his OD green laundry bag into the washer—whites, colors, and darks.

"Think how confused I was *not* to see you there the last two weeks, until I watched the news story on the terrorist attack in

New Jersey—and saw you there in a video clip."

"Wait! What? That was on the news?"

"Ah-hah! It was you," she yelled, jabbing a finger in his direction. "I wasn't sure it was you until just now. I thought you just had a pencil-pushing desk job at Church Headquarters."

Kincaid's cheeks reddened. He sighed deeply as he dumped in his detergent. "I actually thought that, too, when I *took* the job. But, if *you're* active in church, why did you dress like a non-Mormon when we met? And why did you almost come on to me the first time we met?"

Lauren wrinkled her nose. "I guess it's just my way of separating the wheat from the chaff, if you know what I mean."

"Then, which one am I? Wheat or chaff?"

Lauren bent at the knees and picked her final piece of clothing from the dryer before answering his question. She folded it and laid it on top of the stack in her laundry basket. She looked at him with a smile and cocked her head. "I haven't decided yet. But since it's too forward of a girl to ask a strange man out for a date, if you were to ask me out, we could talk about it."

Kincaid smiled as he put the quarters into the washer and started his machine. "Lady Lauren," he quipped, "that would be *my* pleasure."

*****

It was Sunday morning. When Kincaid walked through the chapel doors, he felt like it had been months since he had last worshipped here. Bishop Brock met him at the door and embraced him; not as a returned prodigal, but more like a son who was struggling to fulfill his calling in the Kingdom.

As Kincaid stood at the door, he searched for a seat among the other members. He noticed every head turned toward him. He didn't know what to make of it, but he thought he saw fear in some of their eyes. Could they be frightened of him? Others seemed lost for words. But when he took his seat, he felt isolated among the congregation and wondered if he should even be there.

When the sacrament was administered to the congregation, Kincaid sat quietly with his head bowed in prayer, not even worrying about anything that had happened in the past ten days. He just offered a prayer of thanks for the richness of his life—and let the bread and water pass him by. The spirit of the meeting still left him filled.

*****

The next day, Orson Kincaid walked through the doors of the COB. He walked up to the metal detector through which all people entering the building had to pass. The supervisor recognized Kincaid and quickly flipped the switch that made it look like he passed through as normal. In reality, the guard had turned the machine off so Kincaid's weapon would not set off the alarm.

"Good morning, Brother Kincaid," said the supervisor and two other security guards.

"Good morning, Brother Kincaid," said a young lady who had never spoken with Kincaid before.

Kincaid smiled, nodded to each of them, and kept on walking. He stepped onto the elevator. Two people getting off the elevator, also church employees, cordially greeted him. Again, he nodded and smiled, even though he didn't recognize them. He wondered how they knew him when he had only been working in this building for several weeks and had spent most of that time away on business trips.

He stepped into his office and dropped his backpack on the desk.

"Morning, hero," said Parker, with a natural smile, before Kincaid could even sit down at his desk.

"Hero?"

"You bet. Haven't you heard the talk around the building?"

"I just got here. What's going on? When I came in, several people greeted me who usually wouldn't have given me the time of day. Is *that* what you're talking about?"

"Well, you're a superhero now, and we don't often get your kind of hero around here. So, get used to the popularity, and *don't* let it go to your head."

"Yeah, right," Kincaid replied as if that would ever happen. "How's your lump?" He saw the bandage on the right side of her head where the doctors had shaved her hair before putting in seventeen stitches.

Parker blushed as she reached a hand up to the bandage. "Oh, this? The doctor said I suffered a minor concussion, so he limited my work with you for the next two weeks."

"Wait. What?"

Parker laughed in the most delightful way Kincaid had ever heard her laugh. It was sweet, almost innocent.

"Have you heard anything about Jessica Brock's condition? I've been thinking about her and want to make sure she's okay."

Parker leaned forward and squinted at him. "Are you getting soft on her?" she asked with a grin.

"No. But I thought I'd send her a get-well card, so she would know I've been thinking about her."

"She's fine. She went through surgery in New Jersey without a hitch, and should be home in a few days. Her parents stayed in New Jersey with her."

Parker walked over to the fax machine at the window and inserted a thin packet into the FBI computer at her desk.

Kincaid saw her working with the papers. He chuckled. "Are you applying for another undercover assignment with the Bureau?"

Parker stepped away from the machine as it did its job. Then she turned to face her partner. "No way. You've cured me of *that* bug. I've had my fill of excitement for a while. These papers are to cancel all my previous requests. I want to make sure I can stay here as *long* as the FBI and the Church will allow me."

"Don't worry. I have no plans for anything else like the last two weeks in my future. So, you're safe with me. But I retired my second SIG."

"Really? Why?"

Kincaid winced. "Every time I pick up the gun, the memory of where it was shot last is too much for me." He cringed at the memory of the gun hanging onto the crotch of his trousers and the smell of burning fabric along with the cordite when Parker had shot Hillary Droggan.

Parker laughed out loud, seeing the visceral reaction Kincaid had shown. "At the time, I *thought* it was best," she said. "You were in my way, my hands were secured to the chair, and you didn't give me many other options."

"I know, right?" Kincaid found her mischievous joy contagious and smiled himself. "All the same, it's going into my safe until I feel like I can shoot it again." He walked toward the door.

"Whatever you say, Hero. Oh, Director Tanner wants to see you," Parker said. "He called a few minutes before you arrived. And… thanks for coming back for me," she added, showering him with her puppy dog eyes.

"Director Tanner is already back to work? I thought he was still in the hospital after having that heart attack in New Jersey."

"Well, it must be a *guy* thing because he refused to stay home on your first day back at the office."

Kincaid stood at the door, nodded once, then left for the Director's office. He worried about the Director. He didn't know whether coming back to work so soon was the act of a hard-core old soldier or if his ego had been damaged and he wanted to earn back the dignity he thought he deserved.

*****

On the way to the Director's office, three other people greeted Kincaid in passing. None of them stopped to talk with him, or to shake his hand. They seemed to have wanted him to know they knew what he had done, without saying anything as if it were a big secret.

"The Director is waiting for you," said Sister Christian with a warm smile as Kincaid turned the corner and entered the outer office.

Kincaid softly knocked and opened the door to the Director's office. Seeing Director Tanner at his desk, he stepped inside.

Tanner looked up from the papers he had been pouring over. "Come in, Orson," he said. "Please, have a seat." Once again, the Director only had one thin pile of papers in the middle of his desk. He came around from behind the old oak desk, shook Kincaid's hand in greeting, and waved him to the only easy chair in the small office.

Tanner grabbed his chair and rolled it around from behind his desk, so he and Kincaid could talk more casually. The wheels on the tile floor squealed unmercifully. He sat, leaning forward, and took a deep breath before starting. The lines on his face seemed to have broadened in the past two weeks.

"You're scaring me, boss. Do I still have a job here?" Kincaid asked.

"It's just that we have had nothing like this happen in the church in the past 170 years, so no one knows the best way to treat you. Did you notice anything different in the hallways this morning?"

Kincaid shrugged. "Oh, I don't know," he lied. "Yeah, okay. Several people in the hallway might have wanted to pat me on the back, and others didn't want to be infected by touching me. They must know someone had to do what I did, or we'd all be out of jobs."

"Well, your hard-earned celebrity status puts us in a difficult position because the church doesn't want that kind of tough-guy image, as a rule."

Kincaid got quiet. "I... *think* I understand," he said, hesitantly.

"On behalf of the entire church, thank you for your work with Special Agent Parker and for all the risks you took to keep the people at the Camden Cultural Festival safe and the event itself as incident-free as possible," Tanner said.

"You're welcome, I guess," Kincaid said, not sure of where this was going. "But I only did my job. You're the one who found the bomb and turned it off."

"Yes, I'm lucky that was *all* it took. If it had been a more complicated bomb, we would all be dead now. But I remember saying what you just said, in my younger days, after every successful mission," Tanner agreed. "I mean it. If the Church was ever on the *soft target* list of any terrorist groups, I'd bet they're rethinking that decision now—because of you."

"Director, to tell you the truth, I don't have many other skills I can use to serve the Lord or His church. I'm grateful for the opportunity to use what I have to help protect the kingdom," Kincaid's mind flipped a switch as a thought leaped to the forefront of his brain. "Hey, what happened to Fatima?"

"The local authorities arrested her for the attempted murder of Jessica Brock," Director Tanner said. "Jessica will make a full recovery, by the way. But the police detectives couldn't find any other evidence of Fatima's complicity in terrorism or murdering innocents because her home and all of her belongings were destroyed in the explosion, along with her mother. We got great video from your cameras of her holding onto Jessica and shoving the knife into her back. She'll go away for several years for trying to kill her," Tanner announced. He paused a moment and cocked his head toward the packet on his desk. "You see those papers on my desk?"

Kincaid turned to look at the desk and glanced at the thin stack. The desk was in its usual neat and orderly condition, except for that single stack of papers. "Yes. I've been wondering about them, too."

"Those are my retirement papers. If I've learned anything in the past two weeks and a short stay in the hospital, it's that I don't belong in the business of security anymore. Especially if it will be as physically demanding as the last two weeks have been." He looked down at his hands, gnarled and riddled with arthritis. "I've done my best over the years, but now it's time to submit my papers and step down."

"Don't be so hard on yourself, boss. You were my spotter when we had to stop that sniper, and I would not have been able to get him without you."

Tanner nodded, took a deep breath, and quickly blew it out, changing his topic of discussion. "Orson, how did you feel about having to kill a few people to save many others?" the Director asked, searching Kincaid's soul for an answer.

This time, Kincaid didn't feel like the Director's attempt to read him was awkward at all. It seemed sincere, compassionate, and loving—even patriarchal. But the question almost knocked him from his chair. "It saddened me that Mohammad died before he could repent of his sins." He stopped to think. "Oh, there was also that guy in the alley in Detroit. But he tried to kill me... And that sniper in the tower, but you already know about him. To tell you the truth, I'm *tired* of killing. I hope I never have to do it again."

"And yet there will always be wicked people trying to take advantage of others and hurt them just because they are weak or because they are Christians."

"So, do I have to be the one who defends the righteous?" Kincaid allowed the sarcasm to leak out of his heart. Then he said, "When do I get to see the Prophet?"

Tanner looked up at Kincaid again. He sat forward in his

chair and the hinges squeaked loudly. "The Prophet was unable to see you. He wanted me to speak with you on his behalf."

Just then, there were three gentle taps on the frosted glass of Director Tanner's office door. Both men turned to look as the door opened, and Elder Hollister poked his head inside.

Relieved at the interruption, Tanner jumped to his feet. Kincaid did the same, recognizing the Prophet's secretary and thinking the Prophet must be close behind.

Elder Hollister's eyes flitted between the two men. Then he focused on Director Tanner and stepped into the small office. "Excuse me, Director. I just wanted to shake Orson's hand and thank him personally for all he has done." He extended his arm toward Kincaid.

As they shook hands, Elder Hollister did not look the younger man in the eye. "I-I guess you have not yet told him, then?" He stammered.

"No, not yet."

"Told me? Told me what?"

Elder Hollister quickly backed out the door again, again apologizing for the interruption.

"Told me what?" Kincaid repeated.

Tanner slowly sat again and gestured for Kincaid to do the same.

"The Prophet believes it is not in the best interest for you and him to be seen together, now."

The announcement was like a smack across the face to Kincaid. "What? Why not?"

"Remember I told you about that tough-guy image? Well, it goes deeper than that. If you are seen with the Prophet, it could be interpreted that he condones the killing, and he does not want to make you, him, or the church any more of a target than it already is?"

"A target?"

"Yes, like the fastest gun in the west that every young tough man wants to beat in a shootout, to make a name for himself." Tanner realized the words came across as crass and unfeeling, especially after all Orson had done for him, the Prophet, and the church, overall.

"You never answered my first question when I came in the door," Orson said through the haze of understanding beginning to cloud his eyes.

Tanner was caught off balance. "What?"

"I asked you if I still had my job."

As Tanner sat back in his chair, it squeaked again. "We want you to go back to Arizona. Go to school. Strengthen your relationship with your family. Get a part-time job or maybe start a business of your own. We need to give this some time for the dust to settle before we decide exactly what to do."

That was not the way the Prophet had counseled Tanner to break the news, but Tanner thought it was close enough.

Kincaid felt some anger rising inside him. "I suppose that means my baptism has also been canceled?" It was more of a question, but it came out more like a challenge.

"No, no, … no. Not at all," Tanner said, stalling for time to think and form his words. "When you get established in your new ward or student branch, ask your bishop to call me. I will explain the situation and ask him to continue with plans for your baptism. You have done nothing that should demand the postponement of the ordinance, at all. Will that work for you?"

As Kincaid sat in the easy chair with his head bowed in contrition, confusion, and a cacophony of sweet spirit reassurances and outrage battling for his attention, a warm feeling seemed to immerse him, as if someone he loved was holding him close.

Then he looked up at his director and mentor in the Gospel. "It's true, isn't it?"

Tanner knew immediately to what the younger man was referring. He stood and held his arms out to the Latter-day hero. "Yes. It is true."

They embraced, and the warm feeling intensified, covering both men.

"Please keep in touch with me," Tanner said as they stepped back from each other. "Call me at my personal cell number if there is anything I can do to help you. This may actually be a blessing in disguise."

Orson nodded and smiled thoughtfully. "Yeah, like someone once said to me, *It's by the grace of God that we end up where we can best serve.*"

Tanner mused at that for a moment, then got a twinkle in his eye. "Do you really believe that?"

"Absolutely!"

As Kincaid walked out of the small office and stood waiting for the elevator to take him down, he was already thinking of schools he could attend with his G.I. Bill money, places he could go in Arizona to set down new roots, and ways he might approach his family about his next visit.

Then, out of nowhere, he realized exactly what he could do. He was going to start his own private investigation company. He would root out any people who might be planning or preparing to destroy America. He could draw on his military contacts to help him. Yes! That was what he was going to do. It just felt right.

When he strutted out the front entrance of the COB—for the final time—he had already mentally begun structuring his own business. The possibilities were endless, and he was excited about where such an enterprise would take him.

~THE END~

William Staub

Resides in St. Augustine, Florida
Married with 4 children

Attended Brigham Young University -
Studied Special Education to teach emotionally
challenged students.

Retired Army Officer, teacher, and actor

Novelist - Narrator of Audiobooks (Voice-Overs).

Retired from Department of Defense developing interactive multi-media instruction to help cut DOD spending on travel, per diem and instructor costs.

Worked with a brain trust to standardize all of the instruction given by HT-JCOE at Fort Huachuca, Arizona.

Services provided:
Research · Program Management · Strategic Planning · Data Reporting · Editing · Writing · Ghostwriting

As an author.....
Writing my books includes a lot of my own experiences and helped me shed a lot of anger and some of my nightmares. My hope is that I can show my readers how to engage in wartime activities and still be a God-fearing man worthy to have God direct me and protect me. It has been difficult, but with a loving wife who never gave up on me and the Holy Spirit, I survived and can write my books as a way of expressing myself while entertaining the readers.

Other Books Written
on Amazon

CPSIA information can be obtained
at www.ICGtesting.com
Printed in the USA
BVHW020846240323
661078BV00006B/648